CELESTIAL STORM

THE CELESTIAL MARKED SERIES: BOOK FIVE

EMMA L. ADAMS

To be notified when Emma L. Adams's next novel is released and get a free prequel short story, *Celestial Hunted,* sign up to her author newsletter.

The air always seemed to smell like brimstone these days. Black fragments of demonic residue drifted on the breeze, leaving dark stains on the whitewashed plaster of the nearby houses. The humans were going to have to deal with their new decor, because it wasn't going away. Not with the war between heaven and hell moving closer to Earth by the day.

And now, here I was, faced with Faye Carruthers, creator of the website that specialised in stalking the crap out of me and my fellow celestial soldiers, and all I could think of to say was, "Why did you have to let those vampires photoshop a picture of me into a coffin with the caption 'I'm undying to meet you, Devi'?"

Fiona grinned. "That one was pretty funny."

My best friend's expression said, 'OMG, I'm meeting my hero.' If I wasn't so bloody tired, I'd have had more to say to DivinityWatch's creator, especially since Faye was supposed to be a fugitive, on the run from the celestials for summoning a demon and attacking the guild four years ago. I'd long suspected Faye was innocent, but the sight of her in Haven City, wearing ripped jeans and a battered jacket and leaning against a motorcycle, hammered home how batshit the last week had been. She still wore her guild-issued wristbands, stripped of the celestial guild's emblem, which covered the arrowhead mark on her left wrist. I had an identical mark on mine, but on my right wrist, I bore a demon mark, the same as the celestial mark in reverse. Both were given to me by the same Divinity who'd marked me, then fell from grace to become an arch-demon.

The arch-demon I'd killed today.

A nearby car tilted onto its side, and a hulking creature shambled out of its shadow. *Demon.* Looked like the battle had left a straggler behind.

"Stand back," I warned automatically, though Faye was still technically a celestial, expelled or not. Drawing my celestial blade, I leapt onto the car. The demon collapsed beneath it with a high-pitched scream. *Child's play.*

With a lunge, I stabbed downwards. My blade passed through fabric and three terrified-looking vampires rolled out from the rapidly deflating scorpion demon costume.

"You have got to be kidding me."

The three vampires yelped and tried to hide under the car. I lifted my blade and it disappeared, and there came the distinct sound of a phone camera clicking.

"Look, a battle with hell literally ended five minutes ago," I said. "You couldn't wait a little longer to prank me?"

Actually, there was never a good time to dress up in a demon costume to play a practical joke on someone trained to kill demons, but for immortals, vampires could be alarmingly lacking in common sense.

Now Faye's awed expression mirrored Fiona's, except it was directed at me. I scowled back. "Do you have people from your site following me?"

"It's me they're following," she said, not cowed by my irritation. "You can't blame them for wanting a glimpse of the famous Devi Lawson."

More like infamous. I turned back to the vampires. "You're lucky I didn't scorch your brains out. If you're going to hang around a battlefield, at least make yourselves useful and help clean up."

The vampires scrambled out from under the car and fled. Another camera snapped from somewhere behind me, and I gave Faye an exasperated look. "Last week there was a poll on whether or not I'm hiding a forked tail. You'd think they'd have better things to do with their time, considering we just stopped the apocalypse. Why now?"

"You want to ask why I came back?" Faye said. "I'll level with you, Devi: I've no intention of going to the guild, and if you turn me in, I'll make you regret it. But Fiona tells me you're trustworthy."

"The celestials don't like me much, either," I said. "You can ask for a list of my accomplishments. Having a forked tail isn't one of them, though. Sorry to disappoint you."

Despite having both demon and celestial magic, I remained human. Just call me Devi Lawson, minor internet celebrity and scourge of rogue demons. *And now, slayer of arch-demons.*

Lythocrax, the arch-demon who'd attacked Haven City, lay dead a few streets away—or he had, before he'd turned to ashes. I'd only managed to kill him because another arch-demon had given me her power with her dying breath, which had enabled me to transform into the arch-demon himself and pull the information on his weakness from his own mind. Death was too final a punishment for someone who'd tried to destroy everything I cared about, and killing him would have repercussions I didn't care to think about right now. My head pounded, my body ached from the beating I'd taken during the fight, and the last thing I needed was to be hounded by vampires.

"Look, Faye, not to be rude, but what do you want?" I asked.

"To talk," she said. "I have information I think you want to hear."

"She does," said Fiona.

"I don't want to know the four best positions to have sex with a vampire in, or the size of the Wingless Warlock's—"

"Not that kind of information," said Faye, with an eye-roll. "Look, the site's a cover, you know that, right? I have real intel. Like who that arch-demon you just killed was working with, for instance."

Well, shit. Talk about dangling bait right in front of me. Lythocrax had claimed to be the first arch-demon to fall from the heavens with his divine magic intact, courtesy of some rebel angels called the Divine Agents. If Faye had the faintest clue who they might be, I might find out who was truly responsible for killing my former partner.

"You'd better be right," I said. "But I'm not discussing anything confidential in front of the vampires."

"I thought not," she said. "I have somewhere safe to talk. Fiona can vouch for me."

"She's safe," Fiona whispered in my ear.

Considering she still wore an expression of hero-worship, I wasn't completely convinced. But I was tired enough that a meeting in a gutter would be appealing as long as I got to rest my legs. "All right, but I'm bringing my car."

"I'll be waiting here." Faye put her helmet back on and turned to the motorcycle she'd left parked at the roadside. She must have driven right through a nest of demons, if the brimstone and demon blood all over the exterior was any indication, but she didn't seem bothered about leaving a trail all over the road. The roads were already a mess of blood and bits of shattered demonglass, after all. Someone who lived in *this* realm had thrown demonglass around, drawing the enemy right into the streets, but it burned out fast, so there shouldn't be any danger of a second attack via the same route. I should know, since demonglass was my own power source.

Fiona followed me back to where I'd parked my car.

"You can trust her," she murmured. "The guild set her up. Same as you."

"Why did she pick now to show up?" I asked, skirting around abandoned cars. "Does she think I'll bail her out of prison if the guild arrests her?"

Faye might be innocent, but I had enough crimes of my own to answer for without adding someone else's on top of it. Faye and I had initially come from different branches of the guild and had literally been on opposite sides of the planet when she'd been framed, so it made no sense that she'd risked coming here to find me. Unless... *unless she knows about them.*

I'd had to dive into an arch-demon's slimy thoughts to learn who the real enemy was. Faye was a fugitive who shouldn't know a thing, but it was the only explanation for her choosing to show up now. She had a price on her head worth more than half the celestial guild.

I found my car, unlocked it, and got in. Fiona climbed into the passenger seat, her hands clenching on her lap. Her own demon mark—from the fire demon who'd nearly taken her life—gleamed on her wrist, a reminder that I wasn't the only one whose fate was tied to the demons.

"Just hear her out," said Fiona, as I started the engine. "She spoke to me because she figured from my demon mark that I'm not with the celestials, but she seems to know a *lot* about what's going on behind the scenes."

"Might not be a good thing, Fi." I wove through the street, occasionally beeping at curious humans to get out of the way. "The last thing I need is more publicity. I swear, if she wants an interview involving entertaining awestruck vampires again... wait, that was her idea, wasn't it?"

"Nope," said Fiona. "Anyway, it's a private chat, not an interview."

"If you say so." Fiona would probably want the private chat more than I did. She'd admired Faye from afar for years, but until today, nobody had actually known the name of DivinityWatch's elusive creator. Even before I'd unwittingly dragged Fiona into my particular realm of crazy, she'd been obsessed with the idea of getting a glimpse of an angel. DivinityWatch masqueraded as a harmless celestial fansite run by humans, but carried an undercurrent of communication between preternaturals and humans alike.

I slowed the car when I caught up to where Faye waited beside her motorcycle, dark brown hair streaming out from underneath her helmet. With a nod to me, she climbed onto the bike.

I'd never ridden a motorcycle, but I found myself envying the way she could easily weave in and out of the abandoned vehicles, the cool breeze washing away the taint of brimstone. Or maybe I was remembering the feeling of having wings a little too fondly. I might have loathed taking on the form of the arch-demon who'd marked me, but the wings… they'd definitely been a perk. The smell of brimstone pursued me even through the open window, and the sticky heat made me even more aware of the grime and blood all over my skin. Lythocrax's blood. I needed to clean up, but all I'd been able to do was apply wet wipes to my hands so I wouldn't get demon blood all over the wheel.

I hadn't exactly woken up this morning expecting to witness two arch-demons die right in front of me. Never mind that I hadn't been the one to kill Abyss, though she'd ended her life by giving me what was left of her magic. Lythocrax… he'd been arrogant enough to assume his weapon wouldn't turn against him, and he'd paid for it. Had a human ever slain an arch-demon before? I didn't know, but the other arch-demons might all be plotting my demise this very instant.

"Relax," said Fiona, seeing my hands clench on the wheel. "She's not leading us into a trap."

"That's not it." An arch-demon. Mother of all seven

hells, I'd killed an *arch-demon*. Apparently I'd been in shock about the whole thing up until this moment. My chest tightened and I took a few steadying breaths, my hands trembling.

Fiona rested a hand uncertainly on my shoulder. "Breathe, Devi. I swear it won't take long. I wouldn't have asked you to do this now, but the celestials are too busy to notice…"

"That the number one most notorious criminal in the city is back?" My panic receded as I wondered how in the seven hells Faye had managed to evade the celestial guild for four years. Not that they were the most competent of people, but still.

Faye drew to a halt outside a familiar tower block. It belonged to Nikolas, my warlock partner, though he'd never lived there. And the entire place was surrounded by vampires.

"Don't worry," said Fiona. "They know she's safe."

"Ah." I stopped the car. "I'm not walking through that."

"Devi, they're on your side."

I turned to Fiona with an exasperated sigh. "Look at the state of me. My clothes are a wreck. My hair looks like I'm cosplaying Medusa. And I'm covered in so much blood that I'll be a pincushion of fangs by the time I get through that crowd. Who even knows what effect this arch-demon blood will have on the idiots?"

"They won't bite you," she said, though she didn't sound certain. "Do you have spare clothes in the boot?"

"Yes. I'm not stripping off here, either." I pulled out my phone instead and sent Nikolas a message explaining where I was. He'd be helping the warlocks deal with the aftermath of the battle—since they'd lost their leader shortly before it started—which left the rest up to me.

I reached under the seat for my bag, and then leapt out of the vehicle to applause and vampires' cameras snapping. Maybe I should have used Abyss's power to transform into someone else in order to sneak into the building without being tailed. It'd be a waste of good magic, but god, vampires were *annoying*.

"This way," said Faye, then called across the road to the vampires, "Guys—Devi is exhausted and needs to come in before she gets mobbed by the press. Can you hold onto your curiosity for an hour or so?"

An hour? Considering how bone-tired I was, she'd be lucky if I stuck around for ten minutes.

"You know the vampires?" I asked. "They know who *you* are?"

She grimaced. "I had to tell them, otherwise they wouldn't have let me in, and I needed a safe place to stay while I'm in the city."

"And you risked showing up here because…?"

Instead of answering, she made her way towards the crowd, forcing me to follow. The vampires were sensible enough to step aside, and I managed to get inside the building without dripping demon blood on anyone.

The building she'd picked to stay in was a shelter for vampires who'd ended up on the fringes of the law after contracting a demonic virus. The celestials at the time had marked them for dead, so Nikolas and I had helped relocate them somewhere safe. It figured that most of them worshipped DivinityWatch and Faye by extension, but they must be incredibly devoted to allow her to stay here when her presence meant any of them might be arrested for harbouring a criminal. Innocent or not.

Faye unlocked the door to one of the ground-floor apartments and led Fiona and me inside. Darkness filled the space, dispelled when she hit the light switch.

"Okay," said Faye. "So I guess you have questions."

Yes. I did. Too many to count. I followed her into the dimly lit living room and sat down in an armchair, fighting the urge to curl up and sleep.

A mass of darkness shifted beside me and I jumped when I realised someone else was sitting there next to me. Fiona let out a yelp and sprang backwards.

The master of surprises, Clover, looked calmly at the pair of us as though we'd run into her at the park. Clover was scarred, terrifying, and possibly the person I'd least expected to find in the home of a fugitive celestial. Actually, since I'd learned she was an angel reborn as a human, finding her anywhere was weird enough.

"What the hell?" I said. "Clover, is this where you've been hanging out?" We'd spoken on the phone once recently when I'd been desperate for her expertise, and she hadn't been any help whatsoever. Admittedly, despite her angelic origins, she had no memory of her former life, but I'd come to rely on her advice. "Wait, is *she* your source? You're not getting your info from heaven, but from… DivinityWatch? Or Faye?"

"She's good at finding things out," responded Clover. "Better than the guild, even. I suppose she did learn directly from them."

I realised my mouth was hanging open and closed it. Nothing should surprise me where Clover was concerned, and yet. "So—you're spying on heaven? Or hell?"

"Both," said Faye, taking a seat in a free armchair. "I don't post everything I find out on the site, obviously. I deliberately encourage rumours that are close to the truth but won't put any lives in danger. Like when that demon virus was affecting vampires. There was a lot of false information going around."

"Wait, that was you, too?"

She nodded. "Yeah. We used to have links with someone on Purgatory, before they blew the place up."

"So it's true?" I asked quietly. "Purgatory—the freaking *inspector* was there before it blew up. The celestials weren't happy at all, last I heard."

"That's nothing new," Faye said.

"Yes. You were framed for summoning a demon, weren't you?"

"I set up the site before then," she said. "It was a hobby of mine when I was a guild employee. Maybe that's why the enemy framed me, maybe not, but they needed a scapegoat."

"So they made it look like you opened a portal to hell on top of the guild." It wasn't until the former Inspector Angler, who was supposed to have died in the attack, showed up working for Lythocrax that I'd known for certain there was more to the incident than it'd seemed. He might be dead, but who knew how many others had been marked and paid with their lives?

Faye nodded. "Yeah. I was temporarily at the guild between missions at the time. It wasn't until later that I figured out the attack was an inside job, but I—"

"Stopped it," I finished. "You stopped it, and got framed in the process."

Her jaw clenched, and so did her fists. "Yes, I did. I never saw *who* opened the portal, but I can guess."

There was a long pause. I looked between her and Clover. "Rebel angels," I said softly. "Rebel angels and their spies inside the guild itself. You know about them."

"Right." Clover dipped her head. "The Divine Agents are mobilising."

2

Fiona leaned forward, frowning. "Is nobody going to tell me who the Divine Agents are?"

"Nobody knows exactly who they are," said Faye. "I only heard the name when one of their spies let it slip after I caught him."

"You *caught* a spy?" I asked. "In the guild?"

"No, on a demon realm," she said. "I spend half my time in the nether realms these days, and let's just say Earth isn't the only realm the rebels are interested in. But we never knew the identities of any of the Divinities who betrayed their brethren. It wouldn't have occurred to me that one or more of them might have already fallen."

"Lythocrax," I said, turning to Clover. "You knew?"

She shook her head. "Not exactly. I only had your report to go by, and until today, nobody else I know had ever heard his name. Did he tell you he was a spy when you confronted him?"

"I ripped the information out of his head when I used Abyss's ability to transform into him." My skin prickled again, and the echo of his anger passed through me. "It would have been nice if someone had told me it was the Divine Agents who pushed him out of heaven and sent him after me."

"You're saying the Divine Agents are—angels?" asked Fiona.

"Aside from Lythocrax? Yes," said Faye. "Clover and I have been trying to intercept their spies for years. They're as active in the nether realms as they are in this one, so we should have figured out Lythocrax was one of them sooner, but he must have gone by a different name when he was divine. What did he tell you, Devi?"

"A bunch of lies, mostly," I said, not wanting to tell her about the fallen—children of the Divinities, now safely hidden on Lythocrax's old realm. "The real info, I dragged out of his mind. He fell from heaven into hell on purpose, which is how I got this." I held up my right wrist and its arrowhead mark.

"Let me see that." Faye approached me, leaning in to look at the mark. "It really is the inverse of your divine mark."

"I know," I muttered, not at all in the mood to discuss what'd led it to manifest. "It's all mine, and so is my soul, since he's dead."

"But you weren't the only one who might have developed a similar mark," Faye said, taking her seat again. "This has been going on for at least four years. The incidents never seem to be linked, but there have been a lot more. A lot of the deaths in the field over the last decade could be traced back to him if any witnesses had survived."

A chill raced down my back. "How do you know?" *You*

shouldn't know. I'd thought I was alone, when the guild had let me walk away after my partner had died on that mission. Faye shouldn't know that—but she shouldn't know about the Divine Agents, either.

"Clover and I have spent years searching for discrepancies in the guild's mission records," she said. "Unexplained deaths on missions, generally with no witnesses. I assume that because the blatant attack on the guild four years ago got a little too much publicity, they decided to use a subtler approach."

"The demon eggs." My demon mark had first awakened—though it'd been invisible at the time—during a routine mission in which my partner Rory had died after handling saphor demon eggs had caused him to take in a rare and little-known magical parasite. Everyone knew about the virus now, but what they didn't know was that Lythocrax had set both of us up with the help of an insider within the guild itself.

"There could only be one champion of heaven, Devi. Your friend failed the test. One had to die so that the other could live... such are the rules of divine magic. It was nothing personal, Devi."

I shivered, raw hate curdling inside me. It wasn't just me they'd tricked, but damn, did I wish I'd drawn out Lythocrax's death.

"I don't get it," Fiona said. "So Lythocrax activated your demon mark on purpose, but never showed his face? How were you supposed to know what to do with it?"

"I wasn't," I said. "The whole point was that I was never meant to find him, or know he existed. No one was."

"Exactly," said Faye. "Until you confronted Lythocrax,

we didn't know any of the Divine Agents' identities. Since he slaughtered everyone on Purgatory, we're having to redo our whole strategy."

I frowned. "How the hell does Purgatory fit into this?"

"Purgatory lies between this realm and heaven," Faye said. "By killing heaven's gate's guards, the Divine Agents can slip in and out of heaven undetected."

"Fuck," I said. "I thought you had spies there. How did you not guess the Divine Agents might try that?"

"Devi, our attention was on the shadow realm at the time," said Clover. "Until mere days ago, I assumed Lythocrax's aim was to take the nether realms, not Earth."

"He wanted revenge more than anything." My skin crawled at the memory of his twisted thoughts intertwining with mine. "I humiliated him badly when I sneaked up on him and forced him to hand me my magic back." *And I found out his true name.* Not that it mattered. I'd killed him, and now his allies might show up on the doorstep any day now in the guise of angels. "He—he did all of it, though. The vampires' king. Damian Greenwood —I bet *he* was the spy who set you up, Faye, if he was at the guild at the time. He's dead, though. Might the guild still be compromised?"

"Perhaps," she said. "But my spies outnumber theirs, I guarantee it. Why do you think so many guild members jumped at the chance to help the vampires a few months ago? They took direction from me, as planned, via DivinityWatch."

"But do you have insiders in heaven?"

"No. We get our info on heaven through Purgatory, and the guild. Now Purgatory is lost, though—we're going to have to find a new strategy."

"I don't get what you want *me* to do," I said. "I've pretty much established I'm a free agent and don't take direction from anyone. So you want, what, an alliance?"

I was done making deals with demons, and I had enough on my hands with Nikolas wanting to take leadership of the warlocks. And then there were the fallen, who I'd saved from the shadow arch-demon, with the help of—

I swore loudly and jumped to my feet. "Oh, *damnation.*"

"What?" said Fiona.

"The rogue Grade Four celestials." I pointed at Faye. "You knew—you knew about them, too, right? They were upgraded on Purgatory…"

"Yes," she said, her mouth pinching. "They were."

"They're following the Divine Agents," I said. "That's the real reason you asked to see me, isn't it? You're the only one—aside from Clover and whoever else you're working with—who knows who upgraded the rogues' celestial powers and sent them back to Earth."

"They don't know a thing," Faye said. "To my knowledge. They thought they were dealing with real angels. I think it's possible to bring them back over to our side."

"They're batshit insane," I said. "Their leader is, anyway. You have way too much faith in me, considering you've never met me before."

"I told her you can do it," said Clover.

I tugged a hand through my tangled hair. "I'm one person. And every demon in the nether realms will be gunning for me when they find out what I did to Lythocrax."

"They won't," said Faye. "Lythocrax had few allies and even fewer friends—on the demons' side at least. He spent most of the last few years isolated on his own realm, and the other demons never met him."

Maybe she was right. The celestial rogues, though… they were fanatics, too dangerous to allow to run around unsupervised. "You really think I can convince them? If the Divine Agents already have them, they're lost."

"They aren't lost," she insisted. "Don't forget you were meant to be the Divine Agents' tool, too."

"They *killed Rory.*" Oops. I probably shouldn't have shouted that part. Quieter, I said, "I wouldn't go near the Divine Agents if they offered me a million pounds. They killed my best friend."

"I'm sorry, Devi."

I swallowed hard. My anger about Rory's death had mostly been directed at the celestial guild, who'd dismissed my mission report, but I'd known rationally that the guild couldn't have prevented his death. We hunted demons, people died. But now I knew the celestials had been partly responsible after all? Someone had to pay.

I turned to Faye. "I'm going home. I'll think about your offer, but I'm not making any promises. Are you in contact with the celestial rogues yourself?"

"No," said Faye. "But I hoped you might be able to introduce me."

Only if you take them off my hands.

"First thing tomorrow," I found myself saying. "I have zero confidence that they'll listen to a word I say. I just want to clean this demon crap out of my hair and sleep. Deal?"

The following morning, I cracked my eyes open to see Nikolas Castor lounging on the bed beside me. His dark red-tinted hair was damp as though he'd recently washed it, and he was fully clothed. "I was beginning to think you'd sleep the day away."

"Mmf," I said into the pillow, and he smiled and tucked my hair over my shoulder, kissing the spot between my neck and my ear. I squirmed and rolled onto my back. "Divinities. How long was I out for?"

"Fourteen hours at last count. You were dead to the world."

"Fiona's probably sent a squad of vampires to check up on me." I groaned when I remembered what I'd promised Faye yesterday, flinging an arm over my head to block out the sunlight streaming through the curtains.

"Relax, I told everyone to leave you alone," he said.

"Good." I ran a hand through my tangled curls, relieved that I'd at least washed off the demon blood before I'd crashed. Yesterday had exhausted me to my very bones, and I wasn't in the mood to talk to a bunch of fanatics, even if they *had* helped me steal the fallen out from under the shadow arch-demon's nose. "Any fatalities, declarations of war, or other demon shenanigans?"

"Not to my knowledge," he said holding out a glass of clear liquid. "I think you need to recharge, though. You pushed yourself to your limits yesterday."

I sipped the foul-tasting demonic power restorative. "Can't have people thinking slaying arch-demons is easy."

"No." He paused for a moment. "You were—"

"Lucky? Yeah, I got that," I said. "It's Lythocrax's own damn fault for getting cocky and choosing my weapon of choice as his weakness." Most demons didn't choose their weakness. That included Nikolas himself, since he was a demigod—half human, half arch-demon. I didn't actually know his weakness, though he'd confided his true name to me as a show of trust. "I just don't want the other arch-demons to think I'm issuing a challenge. Has Casthus said anything since we stole the fallen?"

"No," said Nikolas. "It wouldn't surprise me if he was more preoccupied with Zadok."

"That's not good news either." Nikolas's younger brother had pretty much been responsible for Abyss's death when he'd thrown her out of her own palace. Since her weakness was sunlight, she was as good as dead even before she'd fled to Lythocrax's dimension and died right in front of me. *I swear I don't ask for these things to happen.*

"No, but Zadok brought this on himself." He got to his feet. "As for what you told me about the Divine Agents— I'm fairly confident my father has no idea who they are. Or Zadok, for that matter."

"No, but they're being spied on. Maybe right now." Worry squirmed inside me. I'd known for a while that the Divinities had wanted to set the demons against one another for their own entertainment, but Lythocrax's actions had been designed to bring Earth to the forefront of the war. And now I'd made it into even more of a target.

"Yes, I'm not sure meeting with the celestial rogues is the best idea," he said. "They're lucky I managed to stop Javos's people from attacking them."

"I have *no* idea what I'm going to say to them," I admitted. "Faye seems convinced I might be able to sway them back onto our side, but *they're* convinced it's the real angels giving them orders. What are you doing today?"

"Meeting with Javos."

I winced. "Yeah, I'll take the fanatics, thanks. Are you taking leadership of the warlocks? For sure?"

"I'll need to get voted in first, and the warlocks are still recovering from the battle. That the arch-demon died here, on Earth, will cause issues, too."

"Shit, really?" I said. "Should I have killed him in his own realm instead?" I hadn't considered that the location where I'd dealt the killing blow might be an issue. After all, I'd never have believed I could do it until I was pushed into a corner. I was just so freaking *tired* of the demons trying to destroy everyone I cared about.

Earth would not fall to the demons. I wouldn't let it.

"I think most of the demons care little that he died," said Nikolas. "Especially if they learn he was a spy for heaven's rebels."

"Maybe, but I didn't do it for the demons. I did it to stop him from killing my friends. And what about Abyss? She was an actual arch-demon, not a rebel or spy. Hell's army is one short however you look at it."

"She was also on the run, without a real army of her own," Nikolas said. "And she worked with Lythocrax willingly. The others would say she deserved what she got."

"Because she thought he could help her overcome her weakness," I said. "And Lythocrax picked his own weakness and still managed to get himself killed. Idiot. Did he not think one of his own people might turn against him?"

A slither of doubt remained. He was dead, and yet... dealing the killing blow had almost been too simple.

Had the Divinities *wanted* me to kill him? Surely not. Now I knew there was a rebel faction behind this and not the major players, the fact that the Divinities had seemed to get some perverse entertainment from watching Earth fall made more sense. But how would I ever know for sure if I made decisions of my own free will, and not because some divine being wanted to watch me struggle like a fish caught in a net?

I laid the glass back on the bedside table and put my head in my hands. "We never catch a break, do we?"

Nikolas drew his arms around me. "No, we don't, but we're made to survive."

"Think that applies to you more than me." He might look human—mostly—but as a demigod, he was a force of nature incarnate. And yet, for all that, I loved him. Every day that passed made it harder to deny it. "I wish we could run away from all this."

"Someday." He lifted my chin and brushed his lips against mine.

My phone buzzed. I sighed and drew away from Nikolas, finding a new number calling me.

"Hello?" I said warily.

"I had an inkling you might be having cold feet," Faye said.

"I can't imagine why I'd think meeting with a bunch of cultists sent here to cause the end of the world would be a bad idea," I said dryly. "When do you want me to pick you up?"

"Give me an hour," she said.

"Sure." I hung up and climbed to my feet. "I might as well go ahead and meet with the rogues. Deranged or not, they're working for the Divine Agents. They also have a bunch of their own resources."

Including mission reports from the guild itself. Maybe even the ones I'd never found. Not that I had any real reason to hunt them down except for closure on what'd happened on that last fatal mission with Rory.

Not closure. Revenge.

I pushed the thought away and headed for the shower. The celestial rogues might have listened to me when I'd asked them to help rescue the fallen, but that was because the fallen were the offspring of the Divinities, and rescuing them didn't contradict whatever mission they'd been given. Now the Divine Agents had lost one of their spies at my hands, though? Armageddon might be next on the menu after all.

After I'd showered, I scraped together a meal from the leftovers on the table and went outside, where I found Rachel and Fiona facing off in the yard. Fiona's hands blazed with flames, devouring every tennis ball Rachel threw at her.

"Might want to practise with something less flamma-ble," I called to them.

"What would be the fun in that?" Rachel leapt up, threw a tennis ball, and Fiona jumped up to meet it.

Fiona had been an even more ordinary human than me before she'd been bitten by a vampire carrying a demonic virus. The virus in question took the form of a magical parasite in the form of a fire demigod who'd left some interesting side effects behind when Clover had removed his soul from Fiona's. She bore a mark shaped like a pyramid on her pale wrist, and our theory was that demon magic levelled up in a similar way to celestial powers. My demon mark had manifested over two years after the mission with Rory, but maybe her use of magic in the battle had caused her powers to upgrade. The level of her flames suggested Grade Two, at least. Powerful enough to be an asset in a fight.

Rachel jumped, higher than a human could, her hand-made boots cushioning her fall. Her bubblegum-pink hair stuck up at all angles, and her tan had darkened in the unusual summer heatwave. Rachel was a chameleon, with the ability to mimic almost anyone's appearance, but she spent most of her time in her human-like disguise to avoid scaring people by getting her three sets of teeth out at the supermarket.

"Nice," Rachel said to Fiona. "You'll be joining the rest of us in no time."

"Joining you in doing what, exactly?" asked Fiona, pausing with her hands flaming. "Not sneaking into demon realms?"

"No," said Rachel. "Believe it or not, I never did that before Devi showed up. She's a bad influence."

"Hey," I said indignantly. "I'm not that bad, am I?"

"I used to be a respectable person before I met her," said Fiona, with a grin to show she was joking. She did have a point. We'd once been next door neighbours and I'd kept my past as distant from her as possible until she'd been kidnapped by a demon as bait to lure me into Pande-monium. "Is Faye meeting us soon?"

"Uh." I paused. "Don't take this the wrong way, but the celestials are fanatics. They'll take one look at your demon mark and freak out."

"But—"

"We'll stay behind," Rachel said firmly. "As backup. Are you taking Nikolas?"

"He's busy with the warlocks. Besides, it won't take long. I'm not going to say anything that might provoke them. As far as they know, I'm just on my way to thank them for their help with liberating the fallen."

Fiona frowned, and when I walked back to the house to grab my props, she and Rachel followed.

"I can't promise this will go well, but they don't know where we live." I still technically had my old flat, though I pretty much lived at Nikolas's place now. So did Rachel, since she'd stopped working for Javos after he'd nearly strangled me to death.

Fiona looked so crestfallen, I added, "You'll have plenty more opportunities to speak to your hero, don't worry."

"Yeah." She brightened. "I can't believe she showed up at all. She knew me from the photos of the two of us. It's not a bad thing that she's going with you to talk to the celestials, right?"

"No," I admitted. "To be honest, it's a relief that someone else knows about the Divine Agents. It'd have been nice if Clover had decided to tell me earlier, but I guess nobody would have worked out Lythocrax was heaven's spy. Least of all the guild."

"Yeah," said Fiona. "Faye doesn't know if there are any spies in there, or if they left."

"That's their problem, not mine." I couldn't deal with everyone at once. Even the celestial rogues, I wished I'd just left them behind on Babylon after we'd saved the fallen. I wasn't to know that shit would hit the fan immediately after, but Casthus had acted oddly when he'd let me reclaim the fallen—almost as though he *wanted* me to. Which made no sense, but it wasn't like anyone else would know where to find Lythocrax's realm.

I picked up a handful of demonglass, which gleamed,

reflecting fragmented shards of the room back at me. When Faye showed up, the two of us would use the demonglass to hop directly to the rogues' hideout. With a little luck, there wouldn't be a Divine Agent waiting on the other side.

3

The universe said otherwise. When I opened Nikolas's front door to let Faye in, it was to find Clover standing behind her, looking more like a creepy serial killer than a former angel.

"Clover," I said. "Hi. You know we're going to deal with a bunch of fanatics, don't you?"

"I wouldn't miss it."

Wonderful. Transporting three people through my demonglass was theoretically possible, but if we got split up, it'd be harder to make it back. And who knew how the rogues would react to Clover's presence?

"Right. All aboard the Devi demonglass express." I held up a handful of demonglass shards, calling to mind the image of the rogues' hideout on Bolt Street.

The shards remained stubbornly blank.

"Is something meant to be happening?" Faye enquired.

"Uh." I stared harder at the shards. "I mean, the rogues might have moved the demonglass I put there. Or destroyed it."

All of us looked at the shards. Nothing happened.

Faye cleared her throat. "I brought my bike, but I can't take all three of us."

"Great." I hadn't been keen on the idea of bringing Faye with me via demonglass, but travelling on foot had its own set of downsides, not least of which was that it was impossible bring backup.

When I mentioned this, Clover said, "Naturally, I'll come with you as backup if you drive."

Figures. "In that case, you two are paying for the damages if they wreck my paint job again."

I'd never been on a more awkward drive. Faye sat fidgeting in the passenger seat, looking like she wished she'd ridden her bike instead, while Clover maintained such a silence that I kept forgetting she was in the back and startling when I spotted her scarred reflection in the wing mirror.

"The outcasts said they wanted to go into the guild and replace them directly," I said to Faye, in an attempt to fill the silence. "Does that sound like the Divine Agents' handiwork?"

She nodded. "Yes. Out with the old, in with the new. They must have been upgraded close together. From what Lydia told me—"

"Lydia is still alive?"

"She's on the run, like me," Faye said. "But the way the Divine Agents work is that nobody's supposed to know they're pulling the strings. Abyss thought she decided to work with Lythocrax of her own free will. The celestial rogues genuinely think they were picked to be upgraded on their own merits."

"And I thought Rory and I volunteered to go on that

mission out of choice," I said sourly. "Got it. The Divine Agents couldn't have been watching that closely, considering the rogues ran off to help me rescue the fallen. I doubt that was on their plan."

"Actually, they would," responded Faye. "The fallen… from what Clover tells me, Casthus's plan to sacrifice them in order to unite the seven hells would have been catastrophic for the Divine Agents' cause. It might even have destroyed everything they worked for."

"So… they pushed the rogues into helping me?" I asked, my hands gripping the wheel tightly. "No wonder they didn't ask questions."

Even my victories were fabricated. Both sides, pushing and pulling at me until I snapped. That I owed my rescue of the fallen to the bastards who'd engineered Rory's death didn't bear thinking about.

"They did," Clover said, "but that doesn't mean your actions were in vain. You saved the fallen from a terrible fate."

"Why'd *you* come?" I snapped. It was probably some celestial sin to yell at a former angel, but she looked at me calmly, her scarred face not betraying her divine nature.

"Why else? They answer only to the angels."

"Then you don't need me to come," I said. "I can't believe you've been sneaking around behind the guild's back all this time. It's not much of an angelic thing to do."

Faye gave me a glance. "From what she tells me, you've been getting consulting advice on explosives from the same angel for years."

I jerked the car around a corner. "I didn't know she was an angel, did I? When did she tell you? *How* did you two meet?"

"At the guild, of course," said Clover. "I knew of Faye's innocence and sought her out to protect her against the guild's hunting patrols."

"So that's how you escaped?" I said. "Seven hells. I didn't actually come back to the city until over a month after the attack and all I heard at the guild were these stories about how you used demonic magic to avoid being caught. It makes more sense that it was Clover, to be honest."

"I tricked her into telling me she was an angel," Faye added. "She revealed herself when a demon nearly killed me. But she doesn't have much of her power left."

"I know," I said, thinking of how she'd helped Fiona get rid of the demonic parasite. "The angels have a hierarchy a bit like the demons, don't they?"

I'd studied their system at the guild, but it'd been a long time since I'd had need of that information. Knowing our enemies were in the Divinities' ranks changed the playing field.

"I doubt I was a high ranked angel," said Clover. "Their grading system is rather similar to the celestials' and the demons', and considering I was reborn on a demon realm, it's safe to say I was probably a Grade One or Two foot-soldier."

"You're a stronger celestial than that."

"A Grade One angel outranks a Grade Four celestial," she said.

I rolled my eyes. "Right, they only gave us a fraction of their power. Got it."

We were out of the city by now, growing closer to Bolt Street by the second, and I didn't have the faintest clue how to introduce my companions to the rogue celestials.

Especially Faye, since they might not believe her innocence. I hoped they didn't know that Javos had nearly sent an army after them and it'd only stopped because of Nikolas's intervention and Lythocrax's attack distracting everyone. *Maybe this was a bad move.*

I expected the security spells and slowed my car down accordingly, but Faye and I still jumped when flames leapt into the air on either side of us.

"Don't worry," I said. "It's just an illusion. Not a good one, either." I no longer feared the fire, but having it used against me set my teeth on edge.

The flames died down, revealing several people in dusty clothes surrounding our car. Their blond leader, Harvey, tapped on the window. He was a broad-shouldered fair-haired man with a forgettable face. So forgettable that it'd taken me forever to remember that I'd known him before he'd upgraded to Grade Four.

"Hold it," I said, undoing my seatbelt and pushing at the door until he obligingly moved to let me climb out of the car. "This is Faye. An ally. She—well, we—need to talk to you about the celestials."

"Devi, killer of arch-demons," said Harvey.

"That's me," I said, as though I decorated my flat with the corpses of arch-demons every day. "So, how are things here? Great job with the fallen, by the way—"

Smoke tickled my throat, making me cough, and I turned to the bland brick house that had once served as their headquarters. Flames licked at the inside of the windows, and judging by the acrid taste of the smoke, they were no illusion.

"Why are you burning the place down?"

"We don't need it anymore," he said calmly. "We have fulfilled our purpose."

"What, rescuing the fallen?" Damn it all, maybe Faye had it right and the Divine Agents had *wanted* me to save the fallen. *I can't even have one small victory.*

Harvey's hands lit up, and his celestial blade appeared, gleaming in the sunlight. His eyes were on Faye, who'd just got out of the passenger seat. "You dare to bring the traitor here?"

"Traitor?" I said. "You're working against the guild yourselves. Faye was framed. She never destroyed the old guild headquarters, not at all. She's a celestial, like you."

He lowered his weapon. "If she is an outcast, then she may want to join our cause."

"Yeah, I don't think so," said Faye. "You're clearly unhinged."

I shot her a warning look, and stepped in front of her as Harvey walked forwards with his blade gleaming.

"Watch it," I said. "I gave you the benefit of the doubt because you weren't responsible for murdering the warlocks. If you break the law for real, then I'm your enemy."

"We're on the same side," he said. "And our purpose in Haven City is momentarily on hold until we complete the next stage of our plan."

"And it involves burning your headquarters to the ground? Look, don't you have important intel in there?"

"It is of no importance."

To me, it is. The files might have told me which Divine Agent insider had engineered Rory's death. Now the guild alone had that information.

"I hope none of your people were inside." Five of them

surrounded the car, their hands blazing with celestial light. Like a—

"Stop!" I yelled, but it was too late. Their blazing hands brightened, connecting like the points of a pentagram.

A flash engulfed us, and the tarmac became cracked and empty bare ground. A red sky stretched across the blank horizon. The five celestials lowered their hands, the lights dying down. Behind them, more celestial outcasts appeared, staring at us—in particular, at my car.

My *car* had landed on Purgatory. Everything contained within the pentagram had been brought over here.

"You complete numbskulls," I said. "How am I supposed to get home now?"

Ground-level fog masked our surroundings. There was no way to tell how many other celestials were out there—and more to the point, Purgatory was no longer heaven's territory. Not since Lythocrax had killed all the angels.

A growl sounded, and a biter demon lunged out of the shadows, right at me.

My left hand ignited, the light burning the demon's head from its shoulders. The other celestials snapped into action, drawing celestial blades to take on the sudden swarm of demons. My right hand lit up along with my left one, shadowy magic spilling out. Zadok's magic, which he'd given to me to save my life. The demons screamed, swallowed up in the shadows, and the celestials' blades finished them off.

A celestial's sword swung at my head. I jumped backwards, raising my own weapon. "Watch it."

Harvey pointed his blade at me, dripping with demon blood. "Demon."

"Yes, I do have demon magic," I said. "You wanted me to join you for that very reason, if you've forgotten. Stop this madness and come back to Earth."

Purgatory wasn't a neutral zone. With the angels dead, it was wide open for the Divine Agents to take, and it looked like demons had already begun to swarm the place.

"We are here for divine purposes," Harvey said self-importantly.

"Sure you are," I said. "Totally divine, in a place infested with demons. Who gave you the orders?"

Go on. Tell me who's pulling the strings.

Clover picked that moment to get out of the car. "Hmm," she said. "This place has changed."

Everyone stared at her, even Harvey. "Who are you?" he demanded.

"You remember me, don't you?" she said, treading towards him. "I'm Clover. Retired celestial. I am, or was, an angel."

"You lie," Harvey whispered.

"No." Light bloomed from her body, achingly bright, and the outline of heavenly wings appeared behind her shoulders.

Whoa. She'd never shown that trick to me before. Maybe it wasn't possible on Earth.

As one, the celestials all dropped to their knees.

"Emissary of heaven," they murmured.

Really.

Harvey rose to his feet, pointing his blade at me. "Why would an angel ally with traitors?"

"With Devi?" said Clover. "Because she's our only hope, fools."

"Uh, no," I said. "I didn't sign up for this. Clover—"

"If the angels say so," said Harvey. "She will lead us into the light, if she embraces what she truly is."

"I know who I am," I informed him. "It's everyone else who seems to have a problem with it."

"Choose darkness and fall," he said. "Or align with the light and with us."

"Yeah, no thanks," I said. "Do you not think it odd that there aren't any other angels here? Just nasty, monstrous demons?"

I wished I could show them the dead body of the freakish Devi clone Lythocrax had sent after me, but it'd probably disintegrated by now.

"The angels are here," said one of the others. "They speak to us, and they'll lead us to salvation."

There were more celestials than before. They must have added to their ranks. I scanned them, seeing vaguely recognisable faces… and one familiar one.

Lydia.

Last time I'd seen her, she'd been jailed as a suspect for murdering several warlocks. She'd also been the person who'd originally told me about the outcast celestials and claimed to have been kidnapped by them. Either she was working for the enemy or they'd found her again. It was hard to read her expression. All of them wore the same slightly distant look, as though listening to a voice nobody else could hear.

"Are you still planning to take the guild?" I asked Harvey pointedly.

"We have moved on to bigger and better things," he said. "When our master rises, our plan will be ready."

"Master… who exactly?"

"The Divine One, of course."

I groaned. "You're being brainwashed. Try following Clover—she's the real deal. And by the way—have any of you seen the inspector?"

No response. Let's face it, Inspector Deacon was a goner. He'd been doomed the instant he'd stepped into this world.

"If you wish to join us, Devina, then I will pay the celestial guild a visit in one week's time. By then, our plan will be in motion."

"And if I say no?"

He raised his blade again. Faye shifted behind me. As a Grade Three celestial, she didn't have a chance of fighting her way out of this one.

"My assistant will be there to keep an eye on you, Devi," he said. "I strongly suggest you say yes."

Damn. So there *was* an insider.

"I'll consider it, but only if you let us leave this place. All of us."

Clover moved in front of Faye and me. "If you need an angel to help your cause, I will be glad to assist."

"What?" I said, alarmed. "Clover, you can't stay here. You're…"

Clover raised a hand and light blazed towards me, wiping out my vision.

4

The light faded, and I found myself on my knees, in the middle of Nikolas's living room.

"Where the hell is my car?" I exploded. "Oh—shit, sorry, Nikolas."

Nikolas looked from me to Faye with a bemused expression. He, Fiona and Rachel had fallen back to the room's edges out of range of the burst of light as Faye and I had crash-landed.

Faye scrambled upright. "This isn't exactly how I hoped to meet you," she said. "Er. I'm Faye. Former celestial."

Nikolas stepped forwards to shake her hand. "Nikolas Castor. Warlock."

"Shadow warlock." Awe crossed her face. "I knew you existed, but you're too elusive. We never managed to get a picture of you for the Warlock of the Week feature."

"Yes, cameras seem to break around him for some reason," said Rachel.

That, and he used his mild psychic ability to send

potential photographers running in the opposite direction.

"And you are?" asked Faye warily.

Rachel tossed her bubblegum-pink hair over her shoulder. "Rachel. Warlock. You've met Fiona, I assume."

"Is there any reason you landed in my house?" Nikolas enquired.

"Clover," I said, like that explained anything. "The rogues took a holiday and Clover just kind of—threw us here. Is my car around?"

Rachel bounded to the window. "Your car's outside."

Good. I'd half expected to find it wedged in a wall. "Clover hasn't lost her edge," I said. "She stayed on Purgatory. I can only assume being an angel grants her immunity to their evil divine overlords, but she wasted a bunch of power pushing two people and a car onto Earth and then *stayed* there."

"Did you say Purgatory?" said Nikolas, with a look at Faye as though debating whether or not to kick her out.

"Yes," I said. "By the way, Faye is the person the celestials think was responsible for the demon attack that destroyed their old headquarters. She knows about pretty much everything, up to and including the fallen, Casthus, the celestial rogues… anything Clover knew, basically. She's an ally, for what it's worth."

I believed that, but it didn't mean I *liked* that the person behind the site which had allowed vampires to invade my privacy was in on every single one of my secrets.

"I'm sure Clover has her reasons for staying behind with the rogues," Faye said.

"I bloody hope so," I said. "She's seventy and has a bad

leg and no resources. Purgatory was a wasteland *before* they killed all the angels. She barely has any power left, while they have a shit-ton and the Divine Agents yanking their strings like puppets. And now I have to tell the guild the inspector is dead or imprisoned, and the rogues are going to come and 'pay a visit' in a week."

Apparently, it was my destiny to keep dragging the guild out of trouble for all eternity.

"Are you two going to the guild now, then?" Rachel asked.

Faye shifted her weight as though ready to leave. "No," she said. "I'll have to show myself to the guild eventually, but I'd rather do that in my own time."

"I thought you and Clover had a plan," I said. "Now she's gone. Did you expect her to do that?"

"I've learned to expect the unexpected as far as Clover's concerned," she said. "And I'm planning on staying in the city for now, provided nobody blows my cover. I should head home and check the vamps didn't break anything while I was gone."

"Oh, I can go with you," Fiona said.

Not to deprive her of the chance to fangirl over her hero, I said, "Sure. I don't know how long I'll be at the guild for, but it's probably best that I go alone. Would have been nice to have Clover with me for moral support, but apparently she'd rather go sightseeing on Purgatory."

"I'm sure she has a plan," said Faye. "Half the time she doesn't even tell me what she's doing, and we've been trading information for four years. I'll see you around, Devi."

She and Fiona left, while I turned to a frowning Nikolas. "If anything, I should thank the Grade Fours for doing a runner. Now Javos can't send his warlocks to hunt them down."

"He's more concerned with challenging me over leadership of the warlocks," Nikolas said.

"Seriously?" I said. "That's not much of a choice for them. They can choose someone who effectively led armies on Babylon, or a temperamental prick who nearly strangled a human to death."

"Most of them don't know that, Devi," said Nikolas. "They want stability, especially now. If I took leadership, some of that would disappear."

"Javos accidentally destroyed their own headquarters," I pointed out. "I wouldn't call that stable in the slightest. Where are they based now, anyway?"

"A temporary headquarters has been put together at the home of another warlock," he said. "I'd prefer to avoid offering up my house."

"In case we end up sheltering Zadok, a bunch of wayward vampires or the fallen again?" I said. "Or the entire celestial guild, at this rate, assuming they listen to me."

Rachel snorted. "I think Niko should just declare himself leader and be done with it."

"It's not that simple," he said. "The battle left a lot of damage, not least to the humans. There are an awful lot of complaints and lawsuits facing the next leader."

"Argh," I said. "Sorry. I'm probably responsible for at least some of that, since Lythocrax and I pummelled each other half to death in the middle of a public street."

"It looks like the guild's stepping in to pay for some of the damages," Nikolas said. "But the warlocks have to deal with the rest, and for now, Javos is still in charge of funds.

If I wanted to take over, he could offload all the city's problems onto me and make my life difficult."

"The good news is that the warlocks can't find the rogues now they're gone," said Rachel. "Right? Unless they're still on Earth?"

"No, they set their old headquarters on fire," I said. "So you can tell Javos there's no point in sending anyone to hunt them down. As for me, I guess I have to tell the guild a cult of maniacs is coming to take them over in a week."

Rachel caught my arm on the way out of the door. "That's not the only reason you want to go back to the guild, is it?"

I hesitated. She knew me too well. Unlike Fiona, she didn't see through rose-tinted glasses, or believe the best of me.

"No," I admitted. "I wanted to sneak into their files, since the rogues destroyed their backups. There's an insider there, too."

"What, from the Divine Agents?" asked Rachel.

"Yeah," I said. "This has been going on for a while. Damian Greenwood was one, but they as good as said they have spies there now. I need to stop the Agents from getting to anyone else."

"Hmm." Rachel's mouth pressed together. "If you say so. Just—remember the real enemies are outside this world."

Using the celestials as puppets. Anyone might be an enemy. Lythocrax's death wasn't even the end of it.

I left Nikolas's house to check up on my car, finding that it had only a few scratches. Thank the Divinities for small mercies. "Good," I muttered. "They don't design these things for inter-dimensional travel."

"What the—?" Rachel exclaimed, pointing at a flashing light in the sky.

My heart plummeted. *Another attack?*

A second flash followed, closer. Like lightning unaccompanied by a storm. Then, screaming.

"Seven hells." I stood on tip-toe, trying to see over the houses. "What now?"

The screams grew louder. I sprinted to the road's end, Rachel on my heels, and around the corner, expecting to see demons exploding out the sky like when Lythocrax's army had attacked. Instead, a human stood there, fire pouring from his hands, and two celestials faced him down. One had her blade out, burning white-gold.

"What's going on?" I demanded.

"This man is using demon magic," said the celestial.

So he was. His hands flamed with infernal light, while lightning kept flashing further down the street. The guy was maybe my age, mid-twenties, with dark skin and dreadlocks. He looked utterly terrified. And his aura was grey.

"Put the blade down," I told the female celestial. "He's human. Grey aura."

"Devi?" said the female celestial, recognition flashing across her face. I knew her. She was Sandra Yun, former partner of one of the demon virus's first victims a few months ago. "How do you know he's human?"

"Aura vision doesn't lie."

Another flash came from ahead, and a little blond girl sprinted around the corner, pursued by a woman I assumed was her mother. "Help her!" she said.

The girl yelled, and lightning sparked over her hands, like a paler version of the shadowy lightning Nikolas used. But her aura was as grey as the man with the flaming hands.

Speaking of—the flames had gone out. The man stood rigid, turning his hands over, and jumped when one of the celestials grabbed his hand.

I took a step closer to look. No marks covered his hands or wrists. No indication of any demon marks like mine... but mine only existed because my Divinity had fallen. Ordinary humans shouldn't be able to develop demon powers.

But Fiona did. And she wasn't marked at first. Is Azurial back? No—Clover had ripped out the part of him that was possessing Fiona. This was different.

"Help her," repeated the girl's mother.

The two celestials exchanged helpless glances.

"Call the guild," I told them. "Tell them *not* to overreact, for everyone's sake. I don't think these incidents are isolated." The ongoing screaming carrying over the rooftops was proof of that, at least.

But who was responsible: the Divine Agents or the demons?

Lightning flashed over the girl's head again, and the celestials' attention turned to her. At the same time, the screaming grew louder, closer.

"Don't hurt them!" I warned the celestials, and took off in the direction of the screams.

Around the corner, a large number of people had gathered in the street, facing a house which had a pair of devil horns balanced on the fence. This must be the warlocks' new headquarters. I hadn't known it was so close to Nikolas's house.

"I'm not in charge," said a swarthy warlock with a forked tail. "You'll have to ask—"

"Me," Nikolas said calmly, walking up as though he'd been behind me the whole time. Warlocks moved damned fast when they wanted to. "What exactly is going on here?"

Voices rose, drowning one another out, but I got the gist: the humans had all, spontaneously, developed what appeared to be demon magic. Flaming hands. Lightning strikes. Invisibility. None of them had any demon marks. Nikolas moved from one to the next, taking questions, and finally stopped beside me and said, "We can talk inside the headquarters. I'm the warlocks' leader, so you can ask me anything."

"I think you'll find *I'm* the leader of the warlocks." Javos approached from the opposite end of the road, scowling.

He'd always struck me as a living, walking statue of a Greek god. Huge, muscular, with arms big enough to snap my neck. He'd lifted my entire body off the ground one-handed when he'd strangled me. And that wasn't even getting into his telekinetic powers, which he'd used to accidentally destroy the old warlock headquarters. His gaze passed over the confused-looking humans to Rachel, who didn't meet his gaze. She'd stopped speaking to him after the strangling incident. Since she was the only person he actually liked—possibly because she'd developed an attachment to him after she'd been rescued from Pandemonium's tunnels as a kid—he wasn't happy, to say the least.

Nikolas moved closer to Javos, and I heard him whisper beneath the humans' worried muttering, "Don't be absurd. You rescinded the position when you broke the law. These humans need someone to speak to who doesn't try to terrorise everyone he meets."

Javos's eyes narrowed. "Fine, take your *humans,*" he spat.

He turned on his heel and marched off, back the way he'd come. The humans huddled closer together, looking warily at the warlock's retreating back.

I moved to Nikolas's side. "Are you sure you want to deal with this yourself?"

"It needs to be sorted out, before..." He looked at the celestials, who'd reappeared behind Rachel and me as though they didn't have a clue what to do with themselves.

"Before the guild takes their usual inept approach and makes a mess of things?"

My phone rang. Right on cue, the guild was calling me.

"Is that them?" asked Rachel. "Niko, I'll help. Devi... you should probably get rid of your celestial friends."

"That's the plan." *Shit. Maybe this is the Divine Agents' new move.* I was supposed to warn the celestials about the rogues' oncoming visit, not warn them off attacking innocent humans.

I put my phone to my ear. "Yes?"

Mrs Barrow, the celestial's newest leader, said, "Devi, where are you?"

"With the warlocks. Why?"

"I need you to come to the guild."

Uh, yeah, I was kind of on my way there before shit hit the fan.

"Is it to do with the humans spinning fire from their hands?" I asked. "Because they're not demons and it's not their fault. I have no idea what's going on, but if you're thinking of arresting anyone—"

"We're being absolutely overrun with complaints," she interrupted. "My colleagues are demanding action and the council will be here any day now, in the aftermath of the former inspector's disappearance. They know something is terribly wrong."

"You're telling me," I muttered, thinking of Purgatory. I needed to tell her in person, as unlikely as it was that she'd believe me. Nobody had last time, since the Grade Fours were listed as dead and my word counted for nothing in their eyes.

I looked back at the humans crowding around Rachel and Nikolas. More innocents, taking the fall for something that wasn't their fault.

"Look," I said. "If warlocks can coexist with humans and celestials in peace, and they have demon magic, there's no reason why humans can't. Just let it all blow over and it'll be fine. Hell won't get a war from this. Don't play into their hands—again."

"Warlocks have been part of our community for as long as the city has existed. These... humans might have dealt with hell for all we know."

"Oh, you know that's absurd," I snapped. "You buy all your supplies from the warlocks, remember? The guild is dependent on their resources, so you have to keep them in your good books while shoving your prejudice under the carpet. But as soon as humans develop demon powers through no fault of their own, it's a crisis. Tell your people not to do anything stupid."

And I hung up, belatedly noticing everyone was staring at me. Oops. The humans had heard.

"Don't worry," I said to them. "The guild's not spectacular at dealing with change. If it's any consolation, people who are cool with warlocks and vampires will be fine with you, too."

Not that that would be much of a reassurance. If their demonic powers turned out to be permanent, there was one possible reason: a demon's mark. But which demon?

"I doubt the guild will listen to you after you just yelled at them, Devi," said Rachel.

"No," I admitted. "But maybe I just want to punch someone in the face, and Bad Haircut Sammy is usually a willing candidate."

5

———

ad Haircut Sammy did indeed greet me at the entrance to the academy which now served as Haven City's main celestial guild's headquarters. After losing two bases in as many years, I didn't blame them for just sticking everything in one place.

"You're back, traitor?" said Sammy. How he'd managed to survive when so many good, decent celestials had lost their lives was a prime example of natural selection fucking up big time. I could only assume that the Divinity who'd marked him had been high, and not in a heavenly sense. Big and hulking with hair that looked like a flying saucer, he was possibly the least motivated celestial soldier ever, except when it came to annoying the crap out of me.

"Lovely to see you," I said. "Mrs Barrow invited me here, so get out of the way."

I'd also been incredibly rude to her on the phone, but it wasn't like I was a registered celestial any longer. She had no power over me. Neither did Sammy, come to that.

The resident bully had pretty much lost his reputation after accidentally helping a demon he thought was the former inspector, and he'd spent all his time since then trying to get the guild to blame me instead.

I'd never had the best relationship with the celestials. They swept up everyone unfortunate enough to be marked as a celestial soldier and drilled us with propaganda. I'd spent the entirety of my celestial training at the academy engaged in petty rebellion and driving my tutors out of their minds. Aside from Rory and Clover, Gav had been my only real friend. I'd long suspected Lythocrax might have had a role in his death, too.

Mrs Barrow strode into the reception area. Tall, with her dark hair pulled into a bun and her glasses perched low on her nose, she wore the celestials' usual pale grey uniform, embossed with a silver arrowhead badge and another marking her as the guild's new leader. A blond celestial soldier wearing the same uniform stepped out beside her. Lydia.

Huh? I'd thought she'd permanently joined up with the outcasts on Purgatory. I'd also thought there was no way out. She wasn't even Grade Four. Unless…

She's the insider. That, or she was playing both sides as a spy. Maybe not all the rogues were the Divine Agents' tools after all.

I addressed Mrs Barrow. "I came here, like you asked."

Mrs Barrow lowered her spectacles to give me an impressive glare. "I think you made your views quite clear over the phone, Devi."

"Just wanted to make sure you didn't already arrest anyone," I said. "The warlocks are already handling the matter, anyway. The guild isn't qualified to—"

"The guild is certainly qualified to handle demons, Devi."

"Is that why you let them take you over?"

She scanned my face. "I'm not your enemy, Devi."

"Yet."

Let's face it, Divine Agents or none, I'd end up on the wrong side of the guild in the end. It was inevitable. They wanted to do everything by the book, while the demons were on another page and the Divine Agents wanted to burn the whole system down.

Mrs Barrow sighed. "We have issued an invitation to all the affected humans to come here to the guild for testing. They won't be harmed."

"The last time people were brought to the guild for *testing,* they were turned into a monstrous demon-infected army." Bile rose in my throat at the memory, and my nails bit into my palms. Admittedly, Mrs Barrow herself hadn't even been in the city, but the guild as a whole had let it happen. "Besides, these humans have no training, no knowledge—anything. The warlocks are in a better position to offer them guidance."

"Last I heard, the warlocks were having leadership issues of their own," she said.

Dammit. I'd suspect the guild of spying on the warlocks, but Javos was such a loudmouth anyway, he'd probably yelled at anyone who came near that he was the warlocks' true leader. The last thing Nikolas needed was a bunch of terrified humans to handle, but if he didn't, who knew what the guild would do to them?

"That's none of your business," I said to her. "And it has no effect on the warlocks' ability to help the affected humans. If anything, the warlocks are more used to dealing with demon magic. They'll be able to identify the type and work out whether it's a permanent issue."

"Devi, you seem to have forgotten that we did the exact same for you and the other novices when you first developed your celestial powers."

"Yeah, with one slight difference: you believe demons are evil," I said. "You wouldn't treat them like people. And even if you did, some of the other guild branches wouldn't. Is it affecting people outside the city?"

"To my knowledge, it seems to be restricted to Haven City alone. However, the battle has caused numerous side effects across the globe."

So it's just in this city? Maybe it was an aftereffect of the battle. But while I wore a demon mark of my own, I was far from an expert on their magic.

"The victims' auras are grey," I told her. "They're unmistakably human. You'd never be able to legally allow them to register as demons. Or celestials."

Her brows rose. "You have aura vision."

"Yes, I *am* Grade Four, under this." I waved my demon marked hand.

"Because you tricked your way to heaven's gate, according to what I've heard."

I glanced at Lydia, who shifted guiltily. *Thanks a bunch.* Whose side was she really on? Admittedly, I *had* manipulated an angel into upgrading my celestial powers, but it was in order to stop the end of the world. It wasn't like I'd been blindly following the orders of the Divine Agents like a certain group of rogues.

"I assume you mean Purgatory," I said. "I'm not the one who locked you out. For the record, the inspector's disappearance isn't my fault either. He chose to work with demons—don't deny it, you know he wasn't working in the guild's favour. If he left, maybe he was running away."

Mrs Barrow gave me a long look. "None of us can figure out why he went there, but the realm has entirely locked us out."

Except the person standing next to you. Lydia must be able to hop back and forth between the worlds whenever she liked. She was also likely working under a cover story, but I wasn't about to wait for an explanation when the Divine Agents might arrive on the doorstep any day now.

"Look, fine," I said. "The rogue celestials you didn't believe me about? Purgatory is their new hideout. Lythocrax killed all the angels and tried to set that realm up as his base, but now he's dead, they're planning to come here. Harvey, their leader, told me they'll be paying you a visit in exactly one week. I'll remind you that their long-term goal is to take your place. So you might want to focus on them, not the humans."

Her eyes searched my expression for any evidence of a lie. "You must know that I can't take your word for it without proof, Devi. Unless you'd like to open the way into Purgatory yourself?"

"I don't think that's a good idea. This building is full of novices. The rogues are all Grade Four. They skipped to the top level."

She was sceptical, but she'd given me a chance—and more to the point, I'd successfully diverted her attention from the humans and their demon magic. For now. Besides, I'd had a stroke of inspiration.

"I don't care what you think is hiding there, Devi," said Mrs Barrow. "One of our own is missing. If you're capable of opening a way through, then I'd advise you to do so."

"Right, right." I felt Lydia's gaze burning a hole in me, but I ignored it. "Where did the inspector cross over? It'll be easier for me to follow him that way."

"In his office, of course," she said, moving aside to beckon me through into the hallway.

Lydia tried to catch my arm, but I shook my head imperceptibly and walked on, past staring novices and seniors alike. Despite the academy's layout being unfamiliar to me—I'd completed my training at the old academy-turned-headquarters which had burned down a few months ago—I knew the way to the former inspector's office. If he'd left any secrets behind, they'd be hidden in that room. Since he'd been replaced by a demon a few months ago while the real him rotted in a prison on Pandemonium, I'd been having trouble telling the difference between his own decisions and those he'd made while under hell's influence. Let's face it, there wasn't a huge gap there. He was evil through and through, celestial mark or none.

The door to his office opened when I pushed it inwards. Burn marks covered the walls of the small office, and the points of a pentagram were etched into the floor. This must be the spot where he'd vanished, pulled into Purgatory.

Mrs Barrow halted behind me in the doorway. "None of us knew he was gone until we saw the light of the pentagram from the window."

I stepped around the desk, which was mildly singed. "If you really want me to do this here, I'll need to set up a boundary. The people on the other side aren't demons. They could just stride right in." And had done so, if Lydia was any indication. I could take down one Grade Four, but not all twenty-odd of them at once. Mrs Barrow ought to know that, but she still didn't believe me.

I'd have to put on a convincing show, then.

Mrs Barrow wisely stood back as I burned five points of a pentagram into the floor. She knew the words to gain entry, so I wouldn't be able to fake them, but I wasn't out of tricks yet.

I turned up the light and said, "I, Devi Lawson, request passage to—"

At the last second, I tapped into my demon mark, allowing shadowy magic to spill out into the pentagram.

Darkness sizzled up the walls, and every alarm in the building came to life in a high-pitched wail. I let the lights die out, and as chaos erupted in the corridors, I threw more shadows to the room's edges to block Mrs Barrow from sight, hoping she'd think it was a side effect of the pentagram exploding.

I dove under the inspector's abandoned desk, opening drawers, searching for anything incriminating. His laptop was gone, so I assumed it'd been removed from the office along with all other potential evidence. *Worth a try.*

I gripped the demonglass in my right pocket, then vanished. The shadowy magic would hide my absence, and if Mrs Barrow noticed I'd gone, she'd think I was on Purgatory. Not ideal, but there *were* no ideal conditions for robbing the guild.

I landed in the bushes outside the main building, where I'd hidden some demonglass the last time I'd been here. Using Nikolas's attention-diverting ability on a few of the passing novices, I slipped into the building through the side entrance. Then I made for the place where the guild stored all their records. To my immense disappointment, I didn't run into anyone on the way. They might have at least made it a challenge. Throw in some booby traps, maybe an alarm or tripwire or two. Instead they were running around like headless chickens while their former best demon hunter robbed the place.

The guild had lost some of their records when their old headquarters burned down, but from the sheer number of folders spilling from the shelves of the record room, they must have moved a lot of them here a while ago. The old mission reports were arranged chronologically, and it was easy enough to find the ones from two years ago. I paced down the row of shelves, then stopped, frowning at the dusty files. What was I thinking? Any regular demon mission might have been the work of the Divine Agents. The whole point was that it was impossible to tell. Wasting hours poring over poorly-written mission reports cobbled together by barely-literate novices like Sammy would not satisfy my drive for revenge.

The wail of the demon-proof alarms continued to echo through the building. It really didn't take much to send the guild into a panic, and while Mrs Barrow might be a halfway decent leader compared to the inspector, even she'd have trouble handling twenty highly motivated rogues who believed it was their divine mission to wipe the place out.

Damn. I don't have time for this.

I grabbed a whole wad of files and shoved them into the inside of my jacket. Might as well have something to show for my efforts. After grabbing every likely mission report for the last four years, I approached the dustier shelves at the back of the room. There were extensive records of trade with other realms, another thing I'd wanted to look into. The celestial rogues had traded with the warlocks behind the guild's back, so there wouldn't be any evidence of *that* here, but maybe…

Footsteps sounded from behind the shelf. I stiffened, then saw a familiar blond head pop up.

"Devi," Lydia murmured, her voice barely audible beneath the echoing alarms. "Don't worry. I'm not with—them. Or the guild."

"You'd better not be lying," I said, shoving another wad of folders into my jacket. "I take it you're not going to let them walk in here in a week's time?"

"Clover has helped me set up defences around the whole building," she said in a low voice. "It should keep them out. Trust me, I'm not one of their lackeys. Faye asked me to spy on the rogues because I've spent time with them before."

And you have a better reputation than I do. She'd been the model celestial before all this had gone horribly wrong.

"All right, I'll hold you to that," I said, lowering my voice as the wailing alarms finally quietened down. "Time to make my dramatic reappearance."

Her forehead scrunched up. "You know, you could have just used that hypnosis ability of yours to rob the place. You didn't need to set the alarms off, too."

"It's a deterrent. To stop Mrs Barrow getting any ideas about going after the inspector."

I stuck my right hand in my pocket and used the demonglass to transport myself back into the inspector's office. Then I pulled the shadowy magic back into my demon mark and let it fade out.

Mrs Barrow jumped when the shadows cleared,

revealing me standing in the middle of the room like I'd never left. "I thought the demons had taken you!"

"It'd have been your fault if they had!" I yelled, mostly to draw her attention away from my bulging jacket. "Look at the state of the place. It's bloody pandemonium."

I couldn't resist the pun, but the normally unflappable boss was on the verge of panic. I nearly felt bad for her, but she wouldn't have listened to me if I hadn't scared her out of attempting a rescue mission. Let's face it, the inspector wasn't coming back. And if Lydia was telling the truth, neither were the rogues.

"You've made your point, Devi," she said wearily. "You can go, but if you learn anything new about those humans with demon magic, I must ask you to tell me. When the other guild branches find out, they might take action themselves."

"Tell them not to do anything rash. And if I were you, I'd retest your demon detectors."

I strode out with as much dignity as I could muster with half the guild's files stuffed into my coat.

Nikolas waited outside the academy's gates, unobtrusive and casual. He raised an eyebrow at my jacket, which had several papers sticking out of the top. "Thought you might need a hand."

"I had it covered. Don't worry, the guild will leave the humans alone, and Lydia's helping set defences against the rogues. Are the humans okay?"

"I sent them all home with a copy of the manual given to new warlocks when their powers manifest."

"When *do* they manifest?"

"At the age of ten or so."

"Wonderful. Humans reading 'Demon Magic for

Dummies' and the celestials thinking I brought hell on Earth into their guild. It's the inspector's fault, though. The other celestials will have to live without Purgatory for a bit." Which meant no new Grade Fours. Since the last lot I'd dealt with had ended up dead, maybe it was for the best. And after all that, I did understand Mrs Barrow's concern. It wasn't just that the inspector had disappeared and the rogues planned to invade the place, assuming she believed me. The guild's reliance on Purgatory had only become apparent to me after I'd found out it was where celestials at Grade Four or higher completed their training. Without it, heaven's army would be severely hampered.

Maybe this is the end of the guild as we know it.

The guild had ended for me a long time ago, and yet without them… who would keep the Divine Agents off Earth? Maybe Clover had a plan, maybe not. As for Lydia, she was the least rebellious person I knew, and I wasn't a hundred percent certain she wasn't just trying to stay alive at any cost.

The streets were quiet as I drove us home. Nikolas appeared lost in thought, and I felt bad that he had to handle the humans on top of the tantrum-throwing warlocks.

"Fiona offered to help teach the humans," he said. "She'd likely do a better job of it than I would."

"You taught *me* magic."

"You were at an advanced level from the start," he said. "Besides, I need to start amassing my resources among the warlocks if I want to make a serious bid for leadership. The others might not trust Javos's judgement after the incident at the old headquarters, but it's too soon after the battle for them to accept a major change. The presence of those humans with demon magic isn't helping."

"Ah, shit," I said. "I told the guild to leave them alone. I didn't want to dump the problem on you, but—you know how things ended up the last time the guild decided to try experimenting on people with new magic."

His mouth tightened. "I know. The humans are more of a danger to themselves than anyone, but if the nether-world tries to claim them, I'm unlikely to be able to stop it."

"I wish I knew how it happened." I shook my head. "It's okay. We can only do so much. The warlocks will come around, anyway. You led the warlocks on Babylon for ages."

"That didn't have the outcome I hoped for," he said. "Besides, they were trained as Babylon's army from birth. Warlocks who grew up in this realm have more freedom and are harder to win over as a result. After all, they aren't dependent on me for their survival."

I turned this over in my mind. "What did Zadok do to win them to his side, then? Bribe them?"

His hands clenched at the mention of his brother's name. "More or less. He had his own army, which I didn't keep in check as much as I should have. I've always lived in two worlds, and now... now it looks like I have to choose one."

My heart sank. Both of us had hoped Casthus would bugger off back to his own realm, but what had started as a quick visit had gone on for too long now. I hoped *he* didn't find out about the humans.

We pulled up outside Nikolas's house. Rachel had made several plates of sandwiches, so we had a sort of picnic in the living room while I sifted through the files I'd swiped from the guild.

Ten minutes into scanning old mission reports and my eyes glazed over. "Bloody paperwork," I muttered. "*Why* the inspector decided to open a door to Purgatory in his office—you know, I shouldn't be surprised, he and the council haven't half a brain cell between them, but maybe he ran to heaven's gates to get away from all this bullshit." I tossed the wad of papers aside.

Rachel raised an eyebrow. "What are you even looking for in there?"

"Evidence that the Divine Agents interfered in guild missions. Let's face it, the inspector might have known, but he'd sooner do the can-can on the roof than admit to making any kind of mistake."

"Let me see that." Nikolas picked up the files. "What sort of discrepancies are you looking for?"

"Faye said any mission where there were fatalities and no witnesses is suspicious. But let's face it, I walked back alive from the mission that killed Rory and nobody believed me anyway." I heaved out a breath. "I think the trading records are more likely to have actual useful information. Let's see which nether realms they got their props from."

The guild had to log every single item they bought from the warlocks, including which realm it'd originally come from. They'd at least have to admit where they'd got their demonglass—not that they had any left, that I knew of.

"They're so pedantic." I moved a new stack of papers from the floor to the sofa arm next to me. "They log everything the warlocks give them. The inspector wouldn't have filled out all these himself—I'm guessing he had some poor novice do it."

"I thought you were looking for evidence of insiders at the guild," said Nikolas. "Trading records would only show the legal transactions, not who might have gone into the demon realms behind the guild's back."

I didn't blame him or Rachel for their confusion. Looking up records from two years ago wouldn't do much except satisfy my own curiosity... but I had to know.

My hands shook as I reached the right date. I wouldn't forget it in a hurry. If the guild had legally procured saphor demon eggs... here was the proof.

Nothing. No records, legal or otherwise. I skimmed through the whole lot and found zero mention of demon eggs. Not that I'd really expected an admission, much less a name to point the blame at, but I found myself annoyed at my own disappointment.

"I don't know about discrepancies," Nikolas said, looking up from the reports. "But the mission numbers doubled the summer of two years ago."

"Really?" I'd wondered if that might be the case. I'd been too numb from Rory's death to notice that an unusual number of members of our guild branch had died in a short space of time. After all, I'd left the guild immediately afterwards. I took the paper he offered me and ran through the dates. Seven dead in a week. For one guild branch, that was a lot. Nikolas was right. The mission numbers had doubled that spring and summer, and so had the deaths. Including...

There it was. My report—the one the guild had

supposedly lost, and the one Damian Greenwood had found.

"He put it back," I said. "Or, someone did."

Report written by Devi Lawson. Mission set by Inspector Deacon.

I looked at the name, numb all over again. My hands trembled, and I put the papers down.

"He knew," I said quietly. "He sent me on the mission himself. It wasn't the council who ordered it."

Which meant there was a very good chance he also knew the demon eggs had been planted at the site of the mission. I didn't know why I'd never considered it before. It'd been the inspector who'd denied my report, after all, and left it lying around on the desk for anyone to find. I'd thought that was an act of carelessness, not maliciousness.

Maybe he'd *let* Damian Greenwood read it.

"What is it?" asked Rachel.

"I think the inspector was an insider," I said. "Maybe he didn't know he was, but he spoke to the angels often enough that one of the Divine Agents might easily have taken their place. The mission he sent me and Rory on—he was the one who received the orders from heaven."

"From who, though?" asked Rachel. "I mean, who in heaven? The angels have names."

"I sure as hell don't know them," I said. "Besides, nobody's going to question the word of an angel, are they?"

"No," said Nikolas, looking up from his own stack of mission reports. "But with no other eyewitness as proof—how did Faye learn of the Divine Agents' existence, exactly?"

"She got the name out of someone in the netherworld,"

I said. "A demon spy must have let it slip. But they're not being as subtle as they used to. Look what they did to Purgatory. The guild might not have a lot of contact with heaven, but if any other celestial in the world tries to upgrade..."

"I don't see what use a years-old report is, then," said Rachel. "Especially when the inspector's as good as dead."

"I know, but..." Damn, there *must* be a clue I'd missed. I turned over the page. I'd reached the end of the year's mission reports. The others were older. Three years... four. The attack on the guild wouldn't be recorded as a mission so there was no use looking for that in here. I'd already seen all the news reports at the time. I had the official story memorised. But someone had opened the portal inside the guild. They couldn't do that without assistance—and props.

I looked at the records open in front of me. Someone had done an awful lot of trading with Pandemonium that year.

"Bugger," I said, eyeing the name on the records. "It was him. Inspector Angler. He bought the props that were used in the attack Faye was framed for—from Pandemonium."

Inspector Angler was the one who'd bought the supplies that the insider had used to open the portal to Lythocrax's realm on top of the guild, sealing his own fate. But maybe he'd unknowingly been talking to a Divine Agent before he'd ever set foot there.

"Seriously?" said Rachel.

I nodded. "I should have known. It's where the saphor demon eggs came from, but the guild doesn't have *that* on record."

But maybe someone there still knew.

Wait a minute. Saphor demon eggs carried demonic parasites, capable of infecting someone and causing side effects. Like, say, humans spontaneously developing demonic powers.

Holy shit.

"I'm going to Pandemonium," I said. "It's time to speak to an old friend."

6

I burned a pentagram into the living room wall, and yelled, "Get out here, Dienes."

"Devi!" said a squeaky voice, in the lower Chthonic demon tongue, and a horned head popped up. Dienes, the little shit, now had a new master, since the appropriately-named city of Pandemonium had changed leaders for the second time this year.

"Don't start fawning," I told him. "I'm coming to see Zadok. Tell him I'd appreciate it if he didn't send assassins after me."

Nikolas's brother had claimed we were allies, but the little horned creature in front of me was a living and breathing example of why trusting demons was a bad idea.

"I'll tell him," said Dienes, and vanished into the pentagram.

"Are you sure this is a good idea?" asked Rachel.

"Since when has that ever factored into my decision-making?" I rolled my eyes. "Maybe Zadok doesn't know if someone's been smuggling demon eggs behind his back, but I think it's something he'd appreciate me telling him."

"I don't think it's saphor demons causing the humans to develop demonic powers," said Nikolas. "I haven't heard a single report of maggot demons showing up during the battle."

"What else can transfer magic by proxy?" I'd thought I'd wiped those damned demon eggs from existence. "Maybe the vamps lost control of their bloodstone stash again."

"I'll check with Madame White," said Nikolas. "Given the state of things on Pandemonium, however, it's entirely possible that something slipped out unnoticed."

"It's been known to happen." Zadok likely didn't know. He'd been the new ruler of Pandemonium for less than two days, after all. I had to admit the idea of Zadok being the new ruler wasn't a terrible one, if just because he had zero interest in conquering Earth.

"I don't think it's a good idea for me to come with you," said Nikolas. "Javos is still demanding a meeting to discuss what to do with the humans, and besides, it's possible that my presence might cause Zadok to keep quiet."

He wasn't wrong. Zadok made no secret of his disdain for his brother, who'd been raised on Earth while Zadok himself had grown up among the warlocks on Babylon. He'd nursed a bitter jealousy towards his older sibling and while none of his attempts to steal Nikolas's army had ever come to fruition, he must have had help when he'd ousted Abyss from her throne. Aside from her weakness, which I'd accidentally told him, not knowing he wasn't already in possession of that information. If anything, he owed me a favour.

"Right," I said, stepping towards the pentagram. "I'll be back in a few minutes."

Hopefully with answers. If demon eggs *had* caused those humans to develop demon magic... maybe I could undo the damage, like I had with the virus that'd infected the vampires. But you'd think at least one person would have spotted a swarm of demonic maggots during the battle.

As the pentagram closed around me, flames filled my vision, a reminder that I was on my way to an infernal realm. Since Zadok's weakness was fire, Pandemonium wasn't exactly an ideal fit, but demigods rarely gained power, and I had no doubt he planned to make the most of his five minutes of fame.

The flames died down, revealing the same hall which had once belonged to Themedes before Abyss had redecorated it with endless corridors of demonglass mirrors. Apparently Zadok hadn't cared for Abyss's taste in decor, because the floor-to-ceiling windows and balconies were back, along with the obsidian floors and the demonglass pillars showing my own reflection—half light, half dark, an aura divided.

Zadok sat on a throne made of a slab of gold, sipping from a goblet. "Devi," he said, in English. "It's delightful to see you."

Like the last time I'd seen him, he wore thick dark armour which covered every inch of him except his head, with gaps for his wide bat-like wings. Dark red hair curled over his tanned forehead, and his aura and wings almost masked the golden chair at his back.

"That looks uncomfortable," I commented, indicating the slab-like throne.

"I've lived in worse conditions." He tipped the goblet to drink the last of the wine, or whatever it was. "You look a little stunned."

"Usually when I come here, demons try to assassinate me."

"Why would I do that?" He rose to his feet, towering over me. "We are allies, after all."

"I wouldn't go that far."

He showed me a wide smile. "Devi, I've missed your company."

"I can't imagine the demons are spectacular conversationalists. Why not redecorate the place?"

"I've taken a liking to sitting on a throne," he said. "Being taken seriously. Smiting the odd dissenter."

I rolled my eyes. "Sure you have. I'm here to call in my favour."

His brows rose. "Favour?"

"You know. For giving you the information that led you to be able to take over this place without being challenged."

Even white teeth showed as he smiled. "Thinking like a demon, Devi. Excellent."

"Don't pull that one on me. I want to talk to Themedes's advisers," I said. "Did you leave anyone alive who used to work in the palace? Or underneath it?"

"Underneath it? I'm told someone scoured the tunnels. The damage was so extensive, I would think a celestial was responsible."

"Yeah, I killed the saphor demons under the palace," I said. "And destroyed their eggs, or I thought I did. I'm looking for the people responsible for trading them to Earth."

"Oh, are you?"

"Yes. Someone sold a huge batch two years ago or so." *Or rather, more recently.* Humans wouldn't die from interacting with them—the fact that using their demonic power hadn't had fatal side effects proved that—but celestials couldn't handle the parasites without dying, burned out by their own fire.

"I'm sure back door trading was more common than your guild knows," Zadok said dismissively. "From what I heard, Themedes even encouraged it."

"You talked to him when he was dying," I said. "And you knew about the saphor demon eggs. Did he tell you that? He shouldn't have known about guild missions." I ought to have asked him the last time I'd been here, but I'd been preoccupied chasing down Lythocrax at the time.

Zadok shrugged. "I got curious. The guild's files aren't secure, and my brother made the mistake of leaving his Earth-made communication device lying around in the castle. He had a large amount of information on you, as well as the guild."

"You knew the saphor demon eggs came from this realm," I said. "Did Themedes tell you?"

"Saphor demons aren't a common species outside of this realm," he said. "Themedes did a great deal of complaining about those foul maggots getting into his palace. If you're looking for the smugglers, however, I strongly suspect that they're dead."

Thought so. "Has there been any illicit trade in the last few weeks?"

He tilted his head. "Trouble at the guild?"

"No more than before," I said, not wanting to mention the humans with demonic magic in case he got ideas about kidnapping them. "I guess you've only been here two days. Never mind."

"Is that all you came here to ask me?" He took a seat on the throne again. "I thought you dearly wished to know how I came to be where I am today."

Oh, boy. I should have figured he'd been impatiently waiting to find someone to brag to about his accomplishment. "No, I figure it involved the usual trickery. Pity you couldn't have applied some of the same to keeping Abyss out of Babylon and stopping Casthus from taking Nikolas's castle."

"It was never his, the fool," said Zadok. "It's his problem that he didn't come up with an exit strategy while he could. When you've been hunted down just for existing, you develop a knack for escaping while you can."

"Some would call that cowardice," I said. "You don't seriously want to stay here, do you? I thought you wanted the castle on Babylon."

"Devi, you must know that my father has no intention of leaving." He cast a look around the hall, his brows pinching together. "My brother ought to have accepted that by now. I admit this place is brighter than I prefer..."

"You did conquer a city in an infernal realm, you know. Fire is kind of their thing. Considering you're terrified of it, you might have picked a different city instead."

He scowled. "Being aware of a potential threat isn't the same as fearing it, Devi."

"Sure looked that way when you ran from Abyss."

"You might run headlong at every potential threat and

hope it doesn't blast you to pieces, but you've never had to survive on a demon realm, Devi," he said. "Not without the weapon built into you that's designed to destroy every demon you encounter. Imagine you weren't a celestial, but human, with limited power. Would you be so reckless with your own safety if you didn't have your celestial blade?"

"If I wasn't a celestial, I wouldn't be in this mess to begin with," I said. "And it wasn't your own safety you risked. You got the other warlocks killed, not to mention jeopardising Earth."

He shrugged. "There isn't a person on Babylon who doesn't deserve to burn along with it when I take back what is mine."

"Was it worth it?" I said, an inexplicable surge of anger taking hold of me. He had all the resources to stop his father and chose to sit on a throne instead. "Making a deal with another arch-demon? Why not ask them to stop Casthus instead of giving you a throne you don't deserve?"

His burgundy eyes blazed to gold. "I have *never* made a contract with an arch-demon, Devi."

"Yeah, right. What about Abyss?"

"Hardly a contract," he said. "I have never signed over my soul to anyone, and I never will."

"Then how did you get here? How'd you kill an arch-demon and escape your father? There's no way you did that by yourself."

"So little faith." A smile curled his lip. "It was you who gave me the idea, Devi."

I blinked. "Excuse me?"

"Demonglass stores power," he said. "Do you recall

how Azurial the demigod leached off his father's power to add to his own? His father was dying, which made the transfer easier, but the means he used to extract that power relied heavily on demonglass. When I heard of your new extraordinary power… that confirmed it for me. If demonglass—active demonglass, connected to a source—can store magic, there seemed no reason why I shouldn't be able to use it to create a weapon."

"What did you do?" I asked, half afraid of the answer.

"Nothing too heinous," he said. "I spent several weeks siphoning off my own demon magic into my demonglass devices. It weakened me significantly, but the presence of those fallen temporarily stopped the other warlocks from trying to kill me. Until *he* showed up." His aura darkened, making his eyes look brighter. "He forced me to put my plan into motion early, which meant letting him think he'd killed me. It was the only way to avoid him hunting me down."

"You brought the demonglass to Earth, then?" He must have, since he'd regained his power so quickly.

"Yes, I did. While I was a prisoner in your house, I took the power back into myself to restore my strength, while using my brother's *kind* attempt to create a connection to Babylon to visit the warlocks who supported me. Oh, don't look so shocked. There are some people on that world who support me, even now… and I convinced them to go along with Casthus's plan to kill Abyss."

"You hijacked his army?"

He grinned. "I know how his mind works. And I knew he wouldn't go to Pandemonium in person. So I entered this realm as part of Casthus's own army. While the others set upon the palace, I took care of that bastard of a fire demon he kept close at his side. Then it was a simple matter of drawing Abyss out of her palace and dealing a fatal wound while she was unable to regenerate. With the sun on her, she had no protection. I confess I didn't know she planned to flee to Lythocrax's realm, but it all worked out in the end, didn't it, Devi?"

I didn't return his sly smile. He thought he was so clever. And he was. He'd sure fooled me, anyway. Not to mention his brother.

"And that's it?" I asked. "No catch? No bargains, or side effects? Where *is* the demonglass you used?"

He held up his arm, lifting the sleeve to show a wristband with demonglass built into it. He must have stolen the idea from my own cuffs.

"The glass does sometimes mask my aura," he said, "but of all possible options, this is the best outcome I could have hoped for. I owe it to you, Devi, for distracting my dear father at the crucial moment. I assume he's plotting your downfall and not mine, but I have every confidence that you can meet the challenge."

"That's it?" I spluttered. "You're just going to leave him to destroy everything—and rule over this place while he rampages around the world I thought you wanted to stay on?"

"It's not me who fears the flames, Devi," he said softly.

I stiffened, remembering the blazing light I'd once been afraid of, for so long. But I'd never run. Never.

"Have you chosen a demon name yet?" he asked.

I blinked at the abrupt subject change. "What? Who even cares? It's not like it'd be of any help, even if I could." Most of the arch-demons gained true demon names after they fell, while demigods were born with them.

"If you take on a demon name, nobody can summon you unless they know that name," said Zadok. "Very useful if you're in the habit of ticking off arch-demons. You have enough magic that anyone can summon you, at any time."

My heart dropped. I hadn't known that. "What?"

"Frankly, I'm surprised my father hasn't already tried. Did anyone follow you here, Devi?"

I shook my head, my skin prickling. "Why?"

Zadok climbed to his feet, peering over my head. "There's someone here who shouldn't be."

I spun on the spot, raising both hands, and the window exploded in a shower of glass. A monstrous demon tore its way through, opening its mouth wide to expose two sets of serrated teeth. Feathery shadow-coloured wings extended from its shoulder blades, while its body resembled a cross between a turkey and a bat.

"What was that about being safe from Casthus's forces?" I said, as a second demon appeared behind it, wings beating.

Zadok flashed me an amused smile. "I was counting on it."

Shadows burst from his skin like an imitation of Nikolas's lightning power, spearing the demons on the spot. My celestial hand lit up along with my demon mark, and I drew a blade that rippled with divine fire.

On cue, the second window shattered, more winged menaces landing on the balcony.

I ran out to meet them, and my blade sliced into the nearest demon's neck. Winged demons that presumably belonged to Zadok fought more of the shadowy creatures in the sky. As they died mid-flight, they disintegrated, vanishing back into whatever foul dimension had spawned them.

Zadok ran past me, taking flight to join them. I remained on the balcony, swiping at anything that dared to get too close.

They're shadow demons. The shadow arch-demon was behind this. I should have figured he wouldn't let his youngest son run around unchecked for long.

Zadok landed on the balcony again, his eyes glowing with golden light. He was in his element. And I was out of here.

"Are you sure you don't want to join my army?" he asked.

"No thanks. I prefer to live in a place where angry shadow demons don't fall out of the sky."

He grinned. "Let me know if you change your mind, Devi."

I didn't dignify that with a reply. Instead, I walked to the nearest demonglass pillar and stepped through, back to Earth.

7

The rest of the week passed quickly, but no more answers came on where the humans' sudden magical powers had come from. While their powers mirrored demonic magic, no matter how many I questioned, nobody reported seeing any demon eggs *or* full-grown saphor demons in the streets. Let's face it, both were distinctive-looking, and the humans would catch on to a maggot infestation pretty quickly. Faye swore up and down that the vampires had kept the bloodstone trade firmly under watch ever since the saphor demons had killed so many of them a few months ago. She was probably right, considering the vamps she lived with couldn't keep a secret if their lives depended on it, but it bothered me that we had no conclusive answers.

It bothered the humans, too. Theories flew wide, on DivinityWatch and outside it, and Nikolas spent longer keeping curious humans off the warlocks' doorstep than actually preparing to lead them. Fiona and I took the more curious ones into the back yard to teach them to control their magic, while Rachel busied herself buying dozens of copies of every basic guide to magic on the market.

"They're going to use the magic anyway," Nikolas had said, when I questioned whether it was a good idea letting that information into so many humans' hands. "It's not a trade secret. Humans just haven't generally been interested enough to learn about us before."

"Except celestials," I'd responded. "You probably bought a year's worth of academy textbooks."

The celestials' academy was technically shut down for summer, with no lessons running, but a fair number of students stayed behind. Most of them were orphans who'd lost everything except the guild, just like I'd been, but I wished Mrs Barrow had taken my warning seriously. At least they hadn't dragged any of the humans in for questioning, since the incident with the exploding pentagram seemed to have put Mrs Barrow off taking matters into her own hands—for now, at least.

The day before the rogues' designated visit, I sneaked into the guild to set up some of my own defences and return some of the papers I'd stolen. I also searched their storeroom again, but I'd combed every corner of the place in search of hidden demon eggs for the last week with no luck whatsoever.

I hopped back through the demonglass from the guild to Nikolas's living room to find Faye and Fiona sitting on the sofa.

"Enjoy your trip to the guild?" asked Faye.

"Everyone knows except them by now, don't they?" I rolled my eyes. "I guess Lydia told you?"

I'd seen her around, but Mrs Barrow seemed to be

keeping a close eye on her. Maybe because she was supposed to have died in battle at least once. I hoped Clover *had* enhanced the guild's defences, but my real worry was that someone would open the doors wide and let those rogues march right in.

"Have you read *every* file in the archives?" asked Faye. "I could have told you which missions were suspect or not, you know."

"That's not what I was looking for," I said. "The demon eggs. Every preternatural store is accounted for, according to Nikolas. That leaves the guild."

"I don't think it's demon eggs you should be looking for," said Faye.

"What else lets a virus spread that quickly?" I asked. "Those humans—they developed their abilities that fast, it can't have happened any other way. Demons can't put their mark on anyone unless that person has contact with something demonic. That's one rule that can't be broken."

Otherwise, demons would have the upper hand. And if they were capable of passing on their mark to random people the way Divinities were, it'd require a near-death experience to trigger the transformation. From what I'd heard from the humans who'd spoken to Nikolas and me, most of them had never had such an experience. Their powers had just shown up out of nowhere.

Faye shook her head. "If they'd all handled the demon eggs, at least one of them would remember."

"It's the only connection I can think of," I said. "Maybe they got bitten by vampires, like when the celestials got infected, but some of them would remember. Vampires can't erase memories. If you can think of anything else, though, I'm all ears."

Faye pressed her mouth together. "I never met Lythocrax like you did. But he… he was a demon of creation. That was his power, right? What if something got triggered when he died?"

"Shit. His realm opened right here." My heart lurched. "Do you think something might have got out when he brought his army to Earth?"

"Who knows," said Fiona. "I talked to the humans all week. They wouldn't know a demonic substance if they walked into it."

I sank into the sofa with a groan of frustration. "You know, you're right. Lythocrax created a demonglass clone of me. I don't know if he made any other monstrosities while he was alive, but the only people who might know wouldn't answer my questions if I threw them into the deepest pit of hell."

"Demonglass clone," said Fiona. "Clone. Uh, do you have any of that other arch-demon's power left?"

"Yes…" I slapped my forehead. "Of course. Yeah, I do. I should have guessed it was Lythocrax behind this. His final parting gift."

And I'd bet his mind contained the answers.

"Okay. Step back," I warned the others, getting up off the sofa.

"What *are* you doing?" asked Faye.

"I borrowed some of Abyss's magic—well, she gave it to me when she died. I don't know how much I have left."

"You became Lythocrax when you fought him." She nodded. "Yeah, I saw some of it from below, but it was kinda hard to make out what was going on up there in the sky."

"I'll try not to break anything this time."

I reached for the power I hadn't touched since I'd left Lythocrax's corpse burning in the road, a familiar sickening sensation gripping me at the close presence of his foul, warped mind.

I felt my body change, wings unfurling behind my shoulders to brush against the ceiling, muscles thickening. I stumbled awkwardly, wishing I'd done this outside. The table containing my lab setup teetered, and I steadied it with a huge demonic hand.

Fiona gaped at me in open horror. "Uhhh. Devi?"

"Relax, I'm still me," I said in my own voice. "Yes, I know he's ugly as sin. That's arch-demons for you."

Unimpeded by an imminent battle, I grabbed the threads of his thoughts, and threw myself in. *Tell me what you did to the humans. Tell me. What did you do when you attacked Earth?*

Flashes of the battle rushed through my mind, viewed through his eyes. I felt his anger, and his triumph as his army continued to climb into the streets, through the portals he created—

I broke free of his thoughts and jerked out of reach of Faye's hand, which blazed with celestial light. "Sorry," she said. "It reacted to you."

"Ow." I let go of the magic, turning into myself again, and staggered against the wall. "It's not demon eggs at all —it's demonglass. I think he booby-trapped the portals."

Faye's mouth fell open. "Demonglass? It was all over the roads—"

"When he brought his army through. People were running around panicking, falling over, fleeing for their lives—that stuff is barely visible when it's burned out. They wouldn't have known what they were picking up."

Faye shook her head. "They wouldn't have. Clever bastard. If it's any consolation, the portals burned out after one use."

"Yeah, but… what if that wasn't the only demonglass he infected?"

My heart sank like a stone, and I turned to face the makeshift lab in the living room's corner. I kept a whole stash of demonglass there.

"He can't do anything, Devi," said Fiona. "He's dead."

"But—there's demonglass all over the city. I left it lying around months ago, in case I need to get somewhere fast."

Faye's eyes widened. "Including—"

"The guild," I finished, feeling sick. "It's well hidden. Nobody's found it yet, but—shit. I should get it out while I can. It'll mean having to walk out the main entrance, but if anyone touched it—"

If a *celestial* touched it, and it really did contain demonic power—they'd die.

I wouldn't be responsible for any more deaths. I had to get it out. But in doing that, I'd lose my ability to transport myself around the city to save anyone who needed help. Lythocrax had left one final trick… no piece of demonglass was safe.

Beyond my own shock and anger, I swore I felt his triumph flicker within me as the last thread of his influence slipped away.

"Wait," said Faye. "Did you see anything unusual at the guild when you were last there?"

"No, but—shit, I can't just leave that stuff inside their headquarters. I should have known Lythocrax wouldn't die without leaving one hell of a mess to clean up."

Nobody questions the Divine Agents. My mind replayed

his thoughts, his anger, but whenever I tried to probe into who the other Divine Agents were, I saw nothing but a blaze of light. Bitter anger stirred in my blood—ancient, deep-seated.

I clutched my forehead. "Ow. Note to self: do not try to understand an arch-demon's mind."

Maybe he'd blocked out his memories of heaven. I'd check later—getting the demonglass away from the guild was more important.

"Are you okay?" asked Fiona.

I nodded. "You two, stay here and keep an eye out for trouble. I'm going to fetch that demonglass." I'd have to hop all around the city to pick it up. The only piece I knew wasn't potentially infected was Javos's, from the old headquarters. Wonderful.

I put my hand in my pocket, unable to stop myself from wondering if that demonglass was damaged, too. Why couldn't Lythocrax have infected something else? It might be I had the situation all wrong, but demonglass stored magic. Lythocrax knew it better than I did. I didn't even know which realm it'd originated in, but it looked like I'd have to check into Pandemonium again sooner than I'd thought.

I squeezed the handful of glass fragments and landed in the guild's storeroom. Then I picked the pieces of discarded glass from the floor. I'd hidden it under a loose piece of carpet and it didn't look like anyone had touched it, but you couldn't be too careful. Next, I hopped to the courtyard—this time, I had to duck behind a bush to avoid a group of novices—and then to the final store of glass on the floor of the inspector's office.

Sorted. I pocketed the glass—then froze at the sound of voices outside the window. So much for sneaking out.

The rumble of voices resolved into familiar ones. Mrs Barrow, and…

Harvey.

8

Swearing under my breath, I pushed the window open, drawing my celestial blade. In a leap, I jumped clear of the window, slamming down between Harvey and Mrs Barrow. The latter blinked at me in surprise, and something hard hit me in the back of the head.

I rotated on the spot. Ow. A stapler. Someone had thrown a stapler at me.

"Get out, demon!" yelled Sammy, throwing a box of staples at me. I dodged, unable to believe he'd seen the scenario in front of him and pegged *me* as the bad guy.

"Harvey's a traitor," I said, more to Mrs Barrow than Sammy. "He plans to take the guild over tomorrow and kill anyone who disagrees."

The dick must have lured Mrs Barrow out to feed her the Divine Agents' lies, paving the way to take the guild. There were so many innocent people inside this building who didn't deserve to get caught up in the crossfire.

Harvey looked between me and the others. "There is a

sickness in this place," he announced. "A demonic taint. I will help you be rid of it. If you wish to accept our help, we'll be back at noon tomorrow." His gaze went to me. "Tomorrow at noon, Devi. Until we meet again."

He strode away down the road. I'd kind of expected him to hop over into Purgatory on the spot, since he'd apparently been taking drama classes from Clover. *It'd be great if she actively did something to stop those nutjobs.*

"Devina," said Mrs Barrow, faintly. "You're trespassing. Why did you just jump out the window?"

"To save you from *him*," I said, jerking my head in the direction of Harvey's retreating back. "I told you, he's coming here tomorrow with an army to take this place over."

Where in hell was Lydia? The only people witnessing this were a bunch of terrified-looking novices, with the exception of the stapler-wielding Sammy.

Mrs Barrow appeared to pull herself together. "Devi, I've tried to ignore your insubordination, but this has gone on for too long. I won't have you poisoning my people against one another. Randy, Groves, take her in."

"You're arresting me." I burst out laughing. "You can't be serious."

They were very much serious.

Apparently, the guild had installed a jail at some point in the last few weeks, inside the old bicycle shed. I sat in a pentagram on the dirty floor, watching rainwater drip through a gap in the ceiling. It hadn't rained in weeks, a sign of the apocalypse if there ever was one. I rubbed the back of my neck, stiff from sitting in a cramped position. Sammy had confiscated my demonglass, not to mention my weapons. The little shit had probably taken them for himself, and it would serve him right if it did turn out to contain an infectious demonic disease. He'd finally stopped taunting me when Mrs Barrow had ordered him to go on patrol. I'd sat through his gloating with more patience than I'd ever thought I possessed, hoping for a private audience with Mrs Barrow, but no luck so far. Hell would freeze over before I discussed the Divine Agents in front of Sammy.

The door to the bike shed clicked open, and Lydia walked in.

"Hey," said Lydia. "Looks like our roles are reversed."

"Thanks for intervening."

She shifted her weight guiltily. "If I'd blown my cover, I'd be dead."

"Uh-huh. I don't know why Harvey didn't attack the guild there and then. But we need to evacuate—"

"No, we don't," she said.

"I'm not sure I trust Clover's word," I said. "Can you speak to her? Today?"

She moved closer to the pentagram keeping me caged. "Why?"

"Demonglass," I said quietly. "It's booby-trapped, Lydia. I picked up every piece I left here, but all the glass in the city has demon magic inside it. Like the vampire virus."

Her face paled. "What?"

"It's true," I said. "When Lythocrax came into this realm, he used portals made out of the stuff, and he infected them with a virus. That's why humans are developing demonic powers—they picked it up in the street, not knowing what it was."

"Damn," she said quietly. I was pretty sure it was the first time I'd heard her curse. "No, I didn't know that. The celestials don't talk to me much. And Harvey… he's losing his mind."

"You only just figured that out?"

"He wanders around Purgatory, talking to people who aren't there." She bit her lip. "If he comes here, he won't be able to get into the guild. But I didn't know—I didn't know about the demonglass."

"We weren't supposed to," I said. "The Divine Agents strike again." For whatever reason, they'd decided to target ordinary humans instead this time around. And the guild would never believe it was real—or worse, they'd blame it on the warlocks, the original source of demonglass in this realm.

"I'll look in the guild's stores," said Lydia, crouching beside the pentagram. "I think they'll know I let you out, but it can't be helped."

The pentagram's lights died, and I rose to my feet, stepping out into the dim shed. "Thank you."

"I got these off Sammy," she added, handing me my coat and weapons.

"Thanks," I said, shrugging the jacket back on. "I appreciate it."

To my relief, the demonglass was in the pocket where I'd left it. Nodding to Lydia, I used the glass to hop back into Nikolas's living room.

"Devi!" said Rachel, leaning forwards on the sofa. "We were about to send out a rescue party."

At her side sat Nikolas, while Fiona and Faye occupied the armchairs.

"Good, you're all here," I said. "Fi, have you told them about the demonglass?"

She nodded. "Yeah, I said you were off to retrieve the pieces you left in the guild. What took so long?"

"Harvey showed up and they kinda jailed me for a bit." I gave a brief rundown of the last couple of hours. "I guess I can retrieve all the other demonglass in the city and harass Javos for more. Or get some from Zadok. He has way more than he needs. But what's already here might be infected, and I don't know what the end result will be for the humans."

"Since Lythocrax is dead, they're free," said Nikolas. "If it's like your mark, or Fiona's, then their souls are still their own."

"It's not like they chose this either way," I said. Why did I still feel like I'd missed something vital? "Lydia spoke to me in the jail. Said she'd search the guild for demonglass. I wish I knew why she and Clover are so convinced they can keep Harvey out of the guild tomorrow without anyone getting hurt. She claimed he's losing his mind and talking to people who aren't there."

"Angels?" asked Fiona uncertainly. "Or ghosts?"

"There's no such thing as ghosts, even on Purgatory," said Faye. "So what did Harvey say at the guild? Did he get in?"

"No, he talked to the staff outside. But they let him lure them out." I heaved a sigh. "Anyway, he said he'll be there at noon tomorrow. With his army. I can't single-handedly keep them out. Lydia seems confident the guild can talk some sense into him, but that's like asking a demon for a birthday present that isn't a one-way trip to hell."

"Shit," Faye said. "Who else can stand up to him?"

"Javos." I gave a short laugh. "He's immune to Grade Four celestial powers. I'm taking a wild guess that isn't a common thing?"

"No," said Nikolas. "He does have a brother, but he's not currently in the city, to my knowledge."

"You might know it." I swore under my breath. Javos would never agree to help the guild. There was nothing I could offer him. He had money, resources, and power despite being deposed as leader of the warlocks. How could I bribe him into helping the guild? He was of the opinion that they should rot in hell. Not that he cared for the rogues either. He'd nearly sent his people to kill them once already. That would have ended badly for the warlocks, if nothing else.

"I think it's worth asking him," said Rachel, fiddling with a strand of hair.

As the only one of us who actually liked Javos, she might be a little biased. But the guild couldn't be trusted to handle Harvey and his band of lunatic outcasts alone.

Nikolas shook his head. "The demonglass at least—he needs to know about that, since he's in charge of the stores. I'll tell him."

"I'll come," I said. "Yes, I know he hates me, but I can handle him."

I hope. I didn't want to send the warlocks into a panic, but odds were, some of them had handled the demon-glass, too. Who knew what other surprises Lythocrax had hidden inside it?

———

To my immense surprise, Javos agreed to meet Nikolas, Rachel and me at the warlocks' new headquarters. When we drove there an hour later, he waited in the hallway when Nikolas unlocked the door, like he owned the place.

"Javos," I said.

"Devi."

We sort of glared at each other for a bit. Then his gaze went to Rachel, and his brows rose in obvious surprise. Maybe he hadn't expected her to ever talk to him again.

"I have something important to report." I led the way into the room Nikolas had picked out as the office for the warlocks' new leader, and launched into my account of where the humans' newfound demon powers had come from.

"What do you expect me to do about that?" Javos asked. "I'm not an expert on demonglass."

"That's not what you said when you pressured me to practise using my powers," I countered. "Any piece of glass in the city might be infected."

"You brought this on us, Devi," he growled.

"Don't you start. This is Lythocrax's doing. He picked demonglass deliberately, since it was his own power source and it stores magic."

"Stores magic," he said. "Like you." There was a look in his eyes I didn't like. Calculating.

"Yeah, if you want to put it that way." Despite his immunity to celestial power, I didn't fear him. I'd faced too many arch-demons to be afraid of an arrogant demigod like him. "It's what caused the virus to spread among humans. I thought it might be the saphor demon eggs again, but it's not like anyone was bitten. Someone would remember."

He drummed his fingers on the desk. "So you asked me here because you wanted me to congratulate you on figuring out why your humans have hijacked our magic?"

Someone was in a mood today. "No, I came here to ask that you check every store of demonglass you have. And the bloodstones, too, while you're at it, in case someone tries that old trick again."

"Nobody has touched my demonglass stores. I made sure of it. As for the bloodstones, they were dealt with. Not a single vampire has been infected since you ridded them of the virus."

Damn. He had no reason to lie, not when the humans with demon powers were as much of a nuisance to him as they were to the guild.

"I'll take that as a thank you," I said. "Also, are there any other warlocks within travelling distance who have immunity to celestial powers?"

"Celestial?" he said. "Why?"

Here we go. "If I tell you this," I said. "You have to promise not to overreact."

In order to get his help, I needed to tell him the truth, and hope that he didn't blow the ceiling off this time.

"What did you do?" he growled.

"Not me. Lythocrax. And the people he's working with."

I gave him a simplified version of the Divine Agents' goals, ending with the rogues' proposed visit to the guild tomorrow.

"So the rogues have gone from their hideout?" he said.

"That explains why my people didn't find them. I admit I wondered if you made them up, Devi."

"You sent your people out there? Javos, the celestial rogues are all Grade Four. They can burn any warlock here to ashes, except for you. And they're coming into this realm again tomorrow. To take down the guild."

"Your point?"

"Javos!" I said. "You know they won't stop there. They tried to ignite tensions between the warlocks and the guild once before and you stepped right into the bait. They'll come for you next, I guarantee it."

He stepped forward, looming over me. "If Nikolas wishes to take the position of leader of the warlocks, then it's his responsibility to face them."

But he's not immune to celestial power.

"The rogues still think you're the warlocks' leader," I said. "Since they left right after the battle. So, what'll it cost me to ask you to come with me as backup when Harvey declares war on the guild?"

"More than you could ever afford, Devina."

"Javos," Nikolas said warningly. "She's right—this is about more than us. These Divine Agents planned to turn the angels themselves against one another. As a fallen angel, Lythocrax infiltrated the demon realms, too. This is very much our problem."

"It most certainly isn't," he snapped. "If the guild is too incompetent to find traitors among their own people—"

"Neither did you," I said. "Look, you won't actually be fighting. You can even wave your hands around and scare the shit out of the novices if you like. Harvey's not that brave, and he doesn't know he's being manipulated. Chances are, he'll take one look at you and run if you show up. Not to mention…" I paused for effect. "The guild will be more likely to want to maintain a working trade relationship with you if you go along instead of Nikolas. They don't know you nearly strangled me or even that you arrested Lydia." Not technically true, but nobody had brought the subject up at any point.

Nikolas gave me a warning look, but he knew the safety of the city might well depend on Javos's cooperation.

"You're the only warlock in the city who's celestial-proof," added Rachel. "Also, if you don't come with Devi, I will never forgive you for what you did."

"I thought you already didn't," he growled, turning to face her.

Rachel stared unblinkingly into his eyes. "I was debating."

"I practically raised you," he said to her.

"Yes, you did," she said. "Then you nearly strangled Devi. And you're a mean dick to everyone who isn't on your short list of people you like."

"You don't like people either," he answered. "Humans."

"I like Devi," she said. "I like not being killed by Divine Agents, which is what'll happen to all of us if we don't send anyone to help keep the Grade Fours out of the guild. Like it or not, Javos, you're the only option. And that's the reason you wanted to become the warlocks' leader to begin with, right? To keep the celestials in line."

Huh. I'd often wondered if that might be the case.

"You owe me," he said, turning back to me. "I'll attend to this ridiculous meeting if you promise never to bother me, or the warlocks, again."

"Deal." Not like I had a choice.

I'd never thought I'd be glad to have Javos at my side to face down the celestials, much less potentially put Nikolas's chances of becoming the warlocks' leader in doubt. I'd probably started another argument between the two of them, but if the guild fell, war would follow.

"I expect you to keep your word," Nikolas said, and led the way out of the office.

Rachel opened the front door and hopped off the doorstep. "He will."

"Damn," I said, in a low voice. "I didn't think he'd say yes."

"Nor me," Rachel admitted.

"I suspected you could do it, Devi," said Nikolas. "But this is going to cause no end of problems. Are you sure the rogues will declare war outright? Won't they give the guild the chance to surrender first?"

"Maybe," I said. "Harvey's already been softening up Mrs Barrow, but he's wildly unpredictable and he'll cut his own head off if he thinks the angels want him to. And I can't count on Clover to show up and help either." Unfortunately.

Rain fell as we walked the short distance to Nikolas's house.

"Is Javos seriously going to go back to being leader again as though nothing happened?" Rachel asked quietly. "Not that we don't need his help, but if the celestials leave without a fuss, we're stuck with him for another few years."

"Oh no, there'll still be a vote," said Nikolas. "He already agreed to it, but he's been sliding out of every attempt I make to set a date for the election. He only showed up today because I said it was you who wanted to see him, Rachel."

"And he didn't believe I'd show up," Rachel added. "If the celestials smite everyone, we won't have to worry about our leadership anyway."

"Glad to hear you're joining the Devi optimism train." I reached the spot where I'd parked my car. And stopped. "What the hell? Who did that?"

Someone—and I had an inkling they had fangs—had painted 'I'm your biggest fan, Devi' on the side of my car. Rainwater had washed half of it away, but if anything, that made it worse.

"Since when did vampires come near here?" asked Rachel.

"I guess they were stalking me." Wonderful. "You can always count on them to show up when it's not necessary."

"Just like the bloody rogues," said Rachel. "I really hope they don't declare war tomorrow. I like having more than two weeks without Armageddon."

"You and me both," I said.

9

At eleven thirty the following day, we gathered down the road from the celestial guild's headquarters, looking out for the Grade Fours. Nikolas, Faye, Javos and I formed a weird group, even more with Fiona and Rachel waiting in reserve.

"It's too dangerous, Rachel," Nikolas said, while I made the same argument to Fiona.

"If the rogues hop into this realm, they need a source," said Rachel. "That means they have someone on this side waiting to let them in. Soon as they do, we'll chase the bastards down."

"Just as long as you stay out of the fighting." I stood on tip-toe to see over the guild's fence. I hoped Mrs Barrow had the place locked against outsiders, in case Clover and Lydia's defences didn't work. Worryingly, neither of them had come out to meet us, but perhaps Lydia had managed to get through to her. Assuming the rogues hadn't figured out she was betraying them. "Faye, is this really the best time to reveal yourself to them? You might get arrested instead. Look what happened to me yesterday."

"I can't step aside and let them get taken over," she said, her jaw set. "They have no idea what's coming."

"That's why it's a bad idea," I said. "The celestials will attack you before they attack Harvey, because in their eyes, you've done worse than he did. And if they're preoccupied with you, his band of rogues will have an opening."

If they brought an army, we were screwed. Only an arch-demon could actually wipe out a group of celestials that size, and the best we'd be able to do was stall them.

Despite my desperate hopes to avoid a conflict, all of us were armed and dressed for battle, including Javos. His dark clothes must be custom-made to fit him, because Javos was too big for any normal human-sized clothes.

"He's late," said Javos, eyeing the guild's gates.

"Maybe he was bluffing," said Rachel.

"I doubt it," I said, though worry prickled down my spine. "Trust me, those rogues don't do false alarms."

"Might they have staged a diversion?" asked Faye.

"From what? Everyone they want to kill off is gathered in one place. It was always the guild they were after." Harvey had said he'd be here at noon, and I'd got the impression the guy was punctual. Maybe not.

"Is there still a source inside the guild?" asked Faye.

"Not to my knowledge," I said. "They can't get inside, believe me. Not directly through Purgatory. And I moved all the other—" I broke off as my side burned suddenly, like my jacket had caught fire. Light blazed out from my pocket, blinding me. "Seven hells, they're using my demonglass."

I dug my hand in my pocket and pulled the glowing

glass free, wincing when it burned my hand. Throwing the glass to the ground, I tapped into my demon mark and unleashed its shadowy magic, but the light kept on growing. I swore, stomping on the glass. The light flared up to the sky, like a beacon to the heavens—and Harvey crash-landed on me, sending both of us sprawling onto the concrete.

"Ow, you *moron.*" I kicked him off me, rolling to my feet. The light's fading glare left red splotches on my vision.

Harvey got up, brushing dust from his clothes. "I expected you to be inside the guild, Devi."

"That was your way in?" My hand throbbed with burning pain. I hadn't wanted to waste any of the regenerative power Nikolas had given me, but I needed my hands to be in working order, so I quickly healed the damage. "Nice job, dickhead."

Clearly, he'd aimed for the nearest source—mine. I was damned lucky he hadn't brought all his friends along for the ride.

Harvey's gaze travelled from me to Faye, Nikolas, and Javos. His hand lit up with celestial power. "You dared to bring your monstrous warlock friends with you, Devi?"

"They're here to make sure you don't do anything stupid," I said, with a glance at the guild headquarters. "Like starting a war."

"There will be no war if I get what I desire," Harvey said. "The guild desperately needs new leadership, and now you've sent these monstrosities to confront me..." His celestial blade appeared in another flash of light, both sides shining silver-white.

Javos and Nikolas immediately moved into attack

mode, their auras darkening and their eyes blazing. *Dammit, Nikolas, you're not immune to his fire.*

"I'll take that as a threat," said Javos, stepping in front.

Harvey yelled as his body rose into the air as though yanked by invisible strings. Javos grinned, raising his hands. Harvey struggled, kicking out, but Javos's telekinetic power held him captive.

"You monstrous demon!" Harvey yelled.

"Yes," said Javos, flipping Harvey upside-down with a quick gesture. "I am." It was pretty clear Javos had been waiting to fuck with a celestial for a while, but where in the seven hells was the rest of his army?

There was the distant sound of breaking glass, followed by screaming.

Nikolas growled from behind Javos, "What did you do?"

Crap. Maybe he is a diversion.

More screams rang over the rooftops. The guild's doors flew wide and a group of celestials ran out, drawing their weapons.

"Where are the demons?" one of them asked.

"Don't come outside!" I shouted. "This prick wants to get into your headquarters."

"You... scum," Harvey hissed, his face reddening as blood rushed to his head. He didn't look like he was in any position to conquer the guild, and yet... *where did that screaming come from?*

"It's a setup." I jerked my head at the still-struggling Harvey. "What did you do? Did you send the rest of your people to start a fight?"

He struggled, his face turning red-purple, but he was unable to resist Javos's magic.

"Tell me what you did," I commanded. "Or I'll kill you. Celestials bleed as much as the rest of us, you know."

His mouth twisted. "The preternatural scum deserve to die. All of them."

Javos's hands made a twisting motion. There was a snapping noise, and Faye gasped aloud. Harvey's body went limp, hanging in mid-air with his limbs dangling. *So much for avoiding a war.*

"Now you've done it," I said.

"Not going to thank me?" The warlock lowered his hands.

Harvey's body dropped out of the air, landing on his feet. A glow spread from his left hand, surrounding his body in a halo of light.

I took a step backwards. "What the—?"

Harvey lifted his head, his eyes glowing as bright as his aura, his expression icy calm.

"You shouldn't be able to stand," Javos said. "You should be dead."

My insides lurched. "What did you do?"

Javos snarled, raised a hand, and Harvey's body lifted into the air again. *He should be dead.* I'd heard his neck snap.

My blood iced over. "Drop him, Javos," I said. "Something's wrong—"

Bright light spread from both Harvey's hands, scorching up to the sky and burning my eyes. Javos fell back, while Nikolas vanished in a blur of shadow. I froze, a primal terror gripping me, as Harvey landed on his feet once again.

Nikolas had gone. Javos looked at his own hand in disbelief as though in denial that Harvey had broken free.

The celestial stood outlined in white light, his eyes blazing as brightly as his left hand.

Javos snarled and reached out, and Harvey stepped out of the way. The light coalesced behind his shoulders, forming white wing-like shapes.

Shit. Please tell me that's not what I think it is.

There was only one being on heaven's side stronger than a celestial.

"I am reborn again," Harvey said, and grabbed Javos by the throat.

"No," I said. "Don't—"

The massive warlock struggled, but Harvey's preternatural strength held him off the ground. With a swing, he hurled the warlock through the wall of the nearest house. Brick crumbled, glass shattered, and more screaming tore through the street.

"He's an angel!" screamed one of the celestials huddled behind the guild's gates. "The angels have come to save us."

"No, he hasn't!" I yelled at the speaker. "He's on the side of the demons." Never mind that Harvey's aura was as shiny-bright as ever.

"I am reborn," Harvey said, again. His wings shimmered with iridescent light, and he seemed taller, more present.

Faye stood rigid, her face pale. And Nikolas—he must have gone to Babylon when he'd dodged Harvey's attack. An angel's power would burn him alive.

"How the hell did you do that?" I demanded. "You can't turn into an angel. You were human. You can't change species, for crying out loud."

"The Divine Ones can do impossible things, Devi. You should know that."

He must mean the Divine Agents. Apparently they'd stepped up their game.

"How's this for impossible?" I drew back and socked him in the jaw. It hurt like hell, but Harvey's head snapped to the side, red blossoming on the side of his face. "On behalf of heaven and hell alike, screw you. You can't get into the guild."

Or can he? Clover's plans surely hadn't accounted for him turning into an actual angel. The celestials had run for cover behind the gates, but they still thought him a true divine, and might let him inside if he persuaded them.

I drew my celestial blade. In his new form, Harvey didn't have any visible weapons, but that preternatural strength was reason enough to keep him at a distance. A blaze of light at my side told me Faye had drawn her weapon, too, for all the good it did.

I swung my celestial sword at Harvey, and it sailed right through him. *Damn. He really is divine.* The blade only harmed demons. Oh, fuck.

Shadowy lightning exploded from my right hand, bouncing off him as though he held an invisible shield. Even demigod magic couldn't beat an angel? Seven hells.

"It's your choice, Devi," he said. "You could have been Heaven's champion, the way the Divine One intended."

"We both know that was never going to happen, Harvey. Sorry to disappoint you."

He must have spoken directly to the Divine Agents. So much for hearing voices in his head.

Harvey's hands lit up with power, and he blasted it at

me. I dodged, pain spearing my right hand. *Ow.* If he touched the mark, it'd be like when the Devi clone attacked me—his power would burn out the demon inside me. I was way out of my league. *Now would be a great time to show up, Clover.* Only another angel could best one of heaven's foot soldiers. What grade was he? It didn't really matter, since Clover herself had said even a Grade One angel could outdo a Grade Four celestial.

I summoned my blade, feeding power from my demon mark into it. Shadows mingled with light as the magic I'd taken fused with heaven's light. "Get out. You aren't welcome here. The celestials serve heaven. You serve nobody but yourself." I didn't truly believe the Divinities would come along and save us, any more than the guild would. As long as heaven was unaware of the rebellion, we were screwed. And even then—maybe they wouldn't care. They hadn't intervened so far, after all.

"Heaven will have a new leader," he said. "The Divine One will rise once more."

"Who's that, the person who upgraded you?" It must be an angel. Clover had said they had different levels, from heaven's foot soldiers to their leaders, but it couldn't be clearer that Lythocrax wasn't the only one able to upgrade people. We were in serious trouble.

"Our future," he said, his hand lighting up once again. I dodged his attack, swinging my doubled-sided blade. The shadowed edge glanced off his arm, and he moved backwards, his eyes narrowing. Gold blood trickled down, heavenly bright, like the monstrous clone Lythocrax had created.

Hey. I got a hit in. Angels weren't invulnerable, blazing light or none.

Celestial blade out, Faye jumped in, but her weapon passed right through Harvey. Her body collided with his, and he backhanded her, sending her sprawling to the pavement. With blinding speed, he spun and knocked me off my feet, too. Blood trickled into my eyes. *Ow.* I drew on the regenerative magic stored in my demon mark, struggling to catch my breath. I'd landed outside the guild's gates, and terrified celestials watched the show from behind the bars. The shimmering light of their demon-proof defences ignited at my presence. *Dammit, attack him, not me.*

A beacon of light made me start upright, searching for the source. My heart plummeted. The demonglass I'd dropped had lit up again. Purgatory was opening.

Faye lunged at it, only to be knocked back by another blast of light. I tensed, bracing myself, but the blur of light from the portal leapt behind Harvey, grabbing his newly formed wings.

"What the—?"

"Need a hand, Devi?" Clover held Harvey's wings behind his back as she yanked him towards the portal.

"About damned time!" I yelled, back on my feet. "How could you let this happen?"

Harvey struggled, but light engulfed the pair of them once more—and they were gone.

A stunned moment passed. Then the guild's gates opened, a number of celestials approaching the spot where Harvey had vanished. Faye stood still, her expression equally stunned. I shook my head, too breathless to tell the celestials to take cover until the coast was clear. If Harvey got away from Clover, he'd be back in an instant.

A male celestial soldier spotted Faye. "Traitor!"

A dozen weapons came out, all of them pointed at Faye.

"You're the traitor," shouted one of the celestial novices. "You're the one on the wanted posters."

Divinities save me from newbies trying to save the day. "She's not the one you should be after," I said, my head pounding. "Where did the others go? Rachel—and Fiona." My vision swam. *Don't give out on me now, body.* Damn, that angel hit hard.

More celestials came out of the gates to surround Faye. She stood still, unresisting. Outnumbered.

"You're pointing your swords at the people who *didn't* throw a demigod through a building." I rubbed the back of my head, willing my regenerative power to kick in. "Use your common sense. That angel was on the devils' side, if you want a simple explanation."

"Tell Mrs Barrow I'll speak to her myself," said Faye, apparently unconcerned by the number of weapons pointing at her. "It's time I revealed myself to the guild."

My vision kept swimming. A celestial soldier wavered before my eyes. "Hey," I croaked. "Don't lock me in jail again. You saw that angel try to kill me. Where is Mrs Barrow?"

Humans had begun to emerge from the houses. The force of Harvey's attack had knocked a massive hole in the building he'd thrown Javos into. No human could have survived it. My heart dropped. Shaking off a wave of dizziness, I advanced forwards, only to find my path blocked by a dozen celestials.

"You're welcome for stopping him from killing you all," I told them. "Seriously—stop poking Faye, you can tell she's no demon."

"Let me speak to her," said Mrs Barrow. About damn time. The crowd parted, allowing her through. At the edges, terrified-looking humans gathered, their panicked voices jumbling together. My head felt too heavy to lift. I sat down on the pavement, drawing more regenerative power into me, wondering if the celestials would object to me lying down and taking a nap...

Shadows moved in the corners of my vision, and a refreshing jolt of regenerative power spread through my body, bringing me back to alertness. Nikolas was here. *Thank the Divinities. He dodged the angel's magic.*

I sat up, my vision clearing, my head no longer swimming. A few metres away, Javos's body had been laid out in the street. Nobody seemed to want to touch him. Faye and Mrs Barrow were still arguing, though they'd moved closer to the guild's gates, away from the crowding humans.

Shadows enfolded me from behind, and another soothing rush of regenerative power lifted my head. "Nikolas," I whispered. "Damn. I'm so glad you're okay."

He didn't say anything. Though I couldn't see his face, I was sure he'd spotted Javos's body in the road.

"Stay here, Devi," he murmured, and walked forwards, parting the crowd. The celestials moved aside, though I wasn't sure if he'd actually used his psychic abilities or if they were just scared of him. I climbed to my feet and walked behind Nikolas, knowing it was too late.

The divine fire had burned a hole through Javos's chest. He was dead.

"What did you do to the angel?" Nikolas asked me.

"Clover dragged him back into Purgatory," I mumbled. "Rachel and Fiona..."

"Over there."

I spun on the spot, my heart lifting. Rachel and Fiona frantically waved at me across the street, from behind a group of shell-shocked humans. The celestials had pulled back, more interested in Faye's argument with Mrs Barrow than in the fallout of the warlock's death.

Fiona skirted around the humans, and ran to hug me.

"Thank the Divinities," I breathed. "That angel—I was sure he got you."

"No, we were looking for sources," Fiona said, stepping back. "And—it's bad. That explosion we heard? Someone blew up a vampire club."

"Not the shelter?" I said, horrified. *No. Not them, too.*

"No," she said. "Mather's. You know, the vampire bar. There… there were bodies everywhere, apparently."

I swallowed hard. *More people dead… more innocent lives taken.*

Rachel let out a hoarse noise, spotting Javos's body. "No."

"I'm sorry," I said, quietly. "I couldn't stop him."

Rachel sprinted to Javos's body, dropped to her knees, and howled.

Javos's death left more of a gulf than I'd ever expected, considering how few warlocks had actually liked the guy. He'd been manipulative at best even before he'd tried to strangle me, so I wasn't exactly in the depths of grief, but that Clover had been unable to stop the enemy creating their own angels rattled me beyond words. Even if she'd saved us from Harvey, she hadn't been able to finish him off.

Not that I'd know for sure, since no matter where I tried to open a way into Purgatory, it failed every time.

"You can't shut me out," I yelled at the wall of Nikolas's living room. "If you let those bastards in, I should be allowed in, too. You wanted me to be your champion, once, didn't you? You traitorous Divinities—"

"Devi, what *are* you doing?" Rachel moved into the doorway, sucking on her thumb. Her hair was plain and her stature small, like a child of four or five. I'd seen her in that form before, when we were in the tunnels under

Pandemonium, and she'd been that way since Nikolas had brought her home after Javos's death yesterday.

"Trying to get into Purgatory." I dropped my arms to my sides and let the pentagram burn out. "Bastards have locked the place up."

"The angels are running the show," said Rachel, flinging herself onto the sofa. "That means they can keep anyone out who they don't want around."

"Didn't stop them jumping into this realm through *my* demonglass."

"I hope they burn in hell," Rachel said. "How could that shithead turn into an angel? How?"

"I don't know." I sat down on the sofa next to her. "He didn't look like an angel when he crashed through the demonglass in my pocket and nearly crushed me to death. But then—he said he was reborn. He had wings. And his aura was shiny white."

"S'pose those dicks make the rules." She scrubbed her damp eyes with the back of her hands. "They can kill anyone they like. Turn demons into angels."

"He was a celestial. We have angel magic. Maybe that's enough… to be upgraded. I didn't think it was possible, but who knows what we're up against here?"

Lythocrax had cheated at every turn, outwitting me every time. If his last wish was for me to fear using what had once been my best asset, he'd done a spectacular job. I couldn't trust demonglass at all. If it didn't have demon magic in it, it might bring an army of angels into this realm instead.

"Where's Niko?" Rachel asked.

"With the warlocks," I said. "He has to sort out what Javos left behind, and make the…"

"Funeral arrangements?" She sniffed. "Yeah. I know. Niko's trying to pull it together, but the other warlocks are intervening… and then someone has to tell his family. It's a mess."

"I didn't even know Javos *had* family," I admitted.

"He has a brother. A rogue, from what Niko said. It doesn't matter anyway. He's gone."

"Rachel, I'm so sorry."

"It's not your fault. There was nothing you could have done." She looked down, fiddling with her hair. "It's stupid. I know he was a bastard. But he was the first warlock I met in this realm—aside from Niko—who looked at me like I was a person. Not like… not like the ones in the palace, on Pandemonium."

"You don't have to justify caring about someone who was like family, Rachel," I said. "Nobody's perfect. Just look at me. I should have stopped Harvey from getting into this realm altogether. I didn't know he'd…" *Use my demonglass.* No doubt the Divine Agents had specifically told him to do that, so I'd distrust my own source of power. But who the hell had upgraded him?

If I sat here thinking about Purgatory, the Divine Agents or demonglass a minute longer, I'd scream. Nikolas had been gone all morning, and I'd had bloody enough of being outmanoeuvred.

"I need a problem to sink my teeth into," I said to Rachel. "Is—is the way to Mather's bar clear?"

"How would I know?" She shrugged. "I doubt the vamps would want you walking in there."

"I doubt they know who did it," I said. I'd skimmed today's headlines, but most were focused on the ruckus at the celestial guild yesterday. The tabloids were gleefully dissecting the possible identity of the 'Angel of Death' who'd descended to give the warlocks what was coming to them. I'd nearly set the local newsagent's display ablaze when I'd seen the headlines.

"What, you think it was one of the angel's people?" asked Rachel.

"I think it's safe to say it was," I said. "Maybe one of the others is still in this realm. We might get to rearrange his face a little."

Her mouth tightened. "Good enough for me."

It was worth checking out, if just to confirm who'd caused the explosion. But in the end, the answer was always the same.

The Divine Agents.

The angels.

Harvey, his aura as bright as the surface of the sun.

"Maybe put your other form on," I added to Rachel as I got up. "So they don't think I'm bringing a kid with me to a vampire hangout."

"Sure." Rachel turned into her usual teenage-girl appearance, minus the pink hair. Instead, dark curtains hid her eyes from view, making her look deceptively shy. "Is Fiona around?"

"Not at the moment." She'd gone home late last night and hadn't called yet, so I assumed she was with Faye and the vampires, or maybe the humans. She hadn't had the best experience at Mather's the last time, so I decided to drive us there alone.

Last time we'd been to the vampire bar, it'd been night time, and I'd been hanging on the arm of a college-aged vampire pretending to be a lackey in order to get information on the whereabouts of the infected bloodstones.

An age had passed since that day, and seeing the police cars parked on the cordoned-off road made a lead weight settle in my stomach. There wasn't much the human police could do in the event of a preternatural attack, so it came as no surprise that there were more vampires on the scene than police officers. I used some of Nikolas's attention-diverting power to slip through the lingering crowd to get a better look at the bar. The door hung from its hinges, revealing the area inside had been totally gutted.

"This place draws bad luck, doesn't it?" muttered Rachel.

"You're telling me." I had years of experience dealing with magical explosions, mostly of my own creation, but the smell drifting from within the bar was unfamiliar, and the lingering smoke left an acrid taste in my throat. I'd need to get inside the place to see what might have caused the blast.

Two vampires stood in conversation at the entrance. No doubt Madame White, their leader, would already know as much as the police did, but there was no sign of her here. She'd know about Javos, too, so she'd have no reasons to pin the blame on the warlocks.

"Who do you think did it?" Rachel asked. "D'you reckon the person who set off the explosion was caught in the blast? Or did they throw in the explosive from the outside?"

"No clue," I said. "Let's go in."

Rachel transformed into a middle-aged male vampire in a business suit. I raised an eyebrow at her, and she shrugged. "I'm pretending to be one of Madame White's people."

"Good plan." I readied myself with more of Nikolas's

attention-diverting power, but as we reached the entrance, the two vampires moved to block our path.

"Hey," I said to the vampires. "We're here to check the place out, since I'm an expert in explosives."

"What's it to you?" asked one of the vamps.

"I invited her," said Rachel, her voice deeper than usual. "The sooner we find out who did this, the better."

The vampires looked at one another. I hit them with a dose of Nikolas's lure ability, and they staggered back, looking at me vacantly. One of them literally started drooling, his gaze skimming me from head to toe. "Huh," he said. "I never noticed how fuckable you are."

"Good lord," I said, giving him a swift kick in the shins as we entered the bar. "That explains why Nikolas doesn't use that power often. Not exactly subtle, is it?"

Rachel snorted. "I can tell you a few stories."

"I don't really want to know, to be honest."

I swore softly at the sight of the wrecked bar. The reports had said more than twenty people had died in here, but I'd been too stunned by Javos's abrupt death and Harvey's transformation to read all the details. The leather sofas and wooden floor were coated with remnants of a black tar-like substance. The smell of human blood lingered, along with something acrid and unfamiliar. Not brimstone, though I'd expected it. Sprinklings of glass-like black shards lay scattered on the wooden floor.

My heart sank down to join them.

"Damn," I whispered.

"What?" asked Rachel.

"It's demonglass."

Burned-out demonglass, shattered and useless—but destructive enough to reduce this place to a ruin.

"How?" Rachel blinked in confusion. "It's not an explosive."

"It's a source *and* it stores magic. Any kind of magic. One of Harvey's people must have been this way, and…" I stepped back, the taste of burning making me cough. "This seems like… like a middle-finger to the preternatural community in general. *Hey, I can use your valued resources against you.*"

Demonglass wasn't what you'd call a *common* source, but if it was being smuggled into this realm behind the scenes—or already here—it was more clear than ever that Lythocrax's death hadn't been the end of his revenge on me, and Earth. Not by a long shot.

"They moved the bodies," Rachel said quietly. "All the dead were vampires. Do you think one of them might have done it?"

I shook my head. "Maybe, but it could just as easily have been thrown in from outside. If there's no surviving witnesses, I doubt we'll find anything."

Least of all a substantial link to the Divine Agents, if there was one. They covered their tracks thoroughly.

We headed back to the car. I sat behind the wheel for a moment, trying to get rid of the image of shattered glass and screaming. Rachel sat in the passenger seat, fiddling with her phone.

"There's a video on DivinityWatch," she commented. "Someone was filming the bar from outside."

I leaned over to watch. The video was too fuzzy and unclear to make out any faces. The person filming had been in the outside seating area of one of the other pubs further down the road. As we watched, glass exploded outwards from the bar's windows, and everyone in the street began running. Then the film cut out.

I squinted as the video replayed. "I didn't see where the blast came from."

"If anyone was filming inside, they're dead," said Rachel. "Sorry, this is the best video there is."

"Yeah…" I let out a breath. "Right… I'm going to find Faye. I assume Fiona's with her. The celestials didn't jail her yesterday, but it wouldn't surprise me if they tried.

They hadn't even asked to talk to me yesterday, not even for an explanation of why one of their people had transformed into an angel.

"Okay," said Rachel quietly. "Can you drop me off at Niko's place? I… I want to be alone for a bit."

"Sure." I didn't know how to comfort her. I'd spent long enough in the grip of grief myself to know it wasn't something that went away easily. It didn't lessen with time, either. You learned to live with it. Like living with my celestial mark. Every mark on my heart and my soul. I'd never forget them—any of them.

My parents, who'd died while I'd survived.

Rory, killed by a pawn of the Divine Agents.

Gav, killed for finding out the truth.

The Divinities had caused me more grief than hell had.

I dropped Rachel off at Nikolas's house and drove on towards the tower block where Faye was staying. Turning the corner, I muttered a curse under my breath when I spotted a large number of balaclava-clad vampires gathering outside. Not again.

I parked the car at a safe distance away, then walked to meet the crowd.

"Put the cameras away," I said to the vampires, elbowing my way through to the doors. "If any of you would like to admit to writing on my car yesterday, I'd appreciate it."

A vampire caught my arm as I rang the buzzer. "It was me," he blurted. "I wanted to… uh, show my appreciation."

"You can't call yourself my biggest fan and then wreck my paint job, you dick. If I didn't have better things to do, I'd repaint your face to match. Leave the bloody car alone."

I rang the buzzer again, ignoring the snapping cameras and jostling vampires. The door opened and Fiona appeared, ushering me inside.

"Thought I'd find you in here," I said to Fiona, once we were safely in Faye's flat. "I went to the site of the attack at Mather's bar. Turns out it was demonglass they used."

"What, the explosion?" said Faye, from where she sat on the sofa, polishing a knife.

"Yeah," I said. "They must have loaded the glass with some kind of explosive power. But there weren't any survivors to question. I don't know who did it, but I can guess."

Fiona paled, her gaze darting to the door. "Damn."

"Why would they use demonglass?" said Faye. "I can think of a dozen other demonic explosives that would have been way more effective."

"I think killing twenty-odd vamps is effective enough," I said, sinking into an armchair. "It feels… personal. I already had to clear up all the pieces I left lying around, and I can't risk carrying any on me since Harvey decided to use it to hop into this realm. Also, I don't know if you've tried to get into Purgatory, Faye, but it's locked."

"Oh," said Faye. "Thought so. I can't get in, besides. I don't know the fancy ritual or whatever it is."

I kept forgetting she was a celestial grade below me, despite her notoriety. "The guild didn't arrest you?"

"They tried," she said. "But Mrs Barrow saw what happened yesterday. The angel was clearly *not* on our side, and given what he did to that warlock, she's been forced to admit that maybe heaven's got a rogue problem after all."

"About bloody time," I said. "So they just… let you go?"

"That might change when their backup gets here," she said. "I think they're going to ask some of the others from different cities to permanently relocate here, but considering the inspector's disappearance and all the attacks, everyone thinks the city is cursed."

"They're not wrong," I said. "What about your other contacts?"

"Dwindling by the second," she said, her expression darkening. "It's dangerous for me to let too many people find out my identity. Or, it was. It probably doesn't matter anymore."

"Is that what Mrs Barrow said?"

"Not exactly." She grimaced. "I think the only reason she didn't jail me on the spot was because she was afraid I'd bring more angels on her tail. But she's called for reinforcements from outside the city, so they'll be showing up any day now. And Lydia's gone, too. I guess she stayed on Purgatory."

"Damn." It didn't matter how many celestials came here, not when anyone might fall under the influence of the Divine Agents. "I guess it's no surprise. We're officially at the point where the leader of the warlocks can be murdered in broad daylight and people will still swear up and down that the murdering angel is in the right."

"Funny," said Faye. "I think I realised that when the guild pinned a high-level demon summoning on a single celestial who didn't even know how to open a portal."

"Sorry. Slipped my mind."

"Don't worry about it," said Faye. "I often wonder if it might have gone any other way, but the guild—their system is set up to fail. If they give people the benefit of the doubt, they get blindsided. If they don't, hell gets to them anyway."

"Yeah, the guild's pretty much a lost cause," I said. "But I'd like to know who booby-trapped that demonglass. I guess it was one of the other celestials, but I wouldn't have thought they'd just leave without making a huge scene."

Her forehead scrunched up. "Demonglass. Where'd they get it?"

"Who knows?" I said. "This is Lythocrax—I'm certain he specifically asked them to use that particular source as a means of revenge. I can guess which realm it originally came from, but the person in charge isn't exactly on top of things."

Zadok hadn't set up any trade with Earth yet, that I knew of, which meant either the demonglass had been traded before... or someone was acting behind his back.

"Do the rogues have contact with warlocks?" asked Faye. "I don't know the details of inter-dimensional trade, but surely it was the warlocks who actually brought that demonglass into this realm to begin with. Not Lythocrax, either."

"Wait..." I stiffened. "The rogues *did* have contact with

a warlock trader. Harvey told me. Before they ran off to Purgatory. He said they used the guild's back doors, with the help of an outsider warlock collective. I was going to look into it at the time, but then things got a little out of hand."

"Outsider warlocks?" she echoed. "I'm no help there. The guild might think I'm a traitor, but I'm still a celestial, not a demon."

"Shit, maybe I can find them," I said. "I do know the warlocks' hangouts…" A weird pang went through me at the thought of the Harpy's Nest without Javos there.

Fiona shook her head at me. "The last time we went to a preternatural bar, a couple of incubi tried to kill both of us because they thought you were the person murdering them. I'm taking a wild guess that they know you were with Javos when he died."

I groaned. "Yeah, they would blame me for it. Bloody typical. I doubt rogue warlocks will go to the same places as their leader, anyway."

But if I found them, maybe I'd also be able to find the demon who'd turned my own weapon against me. Even if all clues led back to Purgatory, I was in dire need of a face to punch that didn't belong to an angel.

My phone buzzed. Nikolas. "Hey," I said, taking the call.

"Devi," said Nikolas. "Where are you?"

"Faye's flat. You're with the warlocks?"

"Yes, I am. The warlocks are insisting on calling a vote on their new leader this afternoon. I've barely managed to bring them under control."

"You're shitting me."

"Actually, it's a good thing," he said. "Once the vote

goes through, it's final. I'll be their leader and they won't be able to challenge me."

I frowned. "It's that easy?"

"We don't make things as complicated as humans do," he said. "However, there's an outsider warlock collective who've made a petition to oust me as the new warlock leader before I even started. I'd like you to be there for moral support in case they decide to interfere with the vote."

"An… did you say an outsider warlock collective?" *No way. He can't mean the same one.*

"Yes," said Nikolas. "They didn't give Javos too much trouble, but since he died before I could legally win the leadership contest, others have stepped in and are insisting I can't just declare myself leader without allowing everyone else an equal chance."

"Oh *shit*," I said. "Who is this collective, exactly?"

"A group of rogues who live on the outskirts of the city," he said. "They're being fairly insistent. I think they always felt Javos ignored their needs and now they have an opening, they're claiming they want to overhaul the whole system."

The words 'overhaul the whole system' never meant anything good in my experience. "You should probably know what I just found out," I said. "The explosion at the vampires' bar yesterday was caused by demonglass, which was likely smuggled into this realm illegally. And—and the rogue celestials told me, when they lived here, that they had a warlock supplier with access to the guild's back doors, who gave them their demonic props. I can't think of any other way something as protected and dangerous as demonglass might have been sabotaged."

He swore quietly. "I never had the chance to look at the crime scene. Are you sure it was demonglass?"

"Nothing else was left behind. I tried asking around, but there weren't any surviving witnesses. They're stepping up their game. Openly using my own power against me. This is personal. And public." If someone working for the enemy was challenging Nikolas for leadership, too… I didn't believe in coincidence. Not anymore.

"I sincerely hope you're wrong, Devi."

"Me too," I said. "I'll come and keep an eye on things. Even if they're just disgruntled and harmless, I won't let anyone sabotage your chances."

"I'd appreciate it, Devi," he said.

I hope I'm wrong. But the Divine Agents didn't need to hide. They were no longer afraid of being discovered.

Which meant they were ready to declare war.

11

I drove to the house of the warlocks' new headquarters as quickly as I dared, hoping that I was wrong and the warlock collective was just a group of Javos wannabes rather than the alternative. *Please, please say the Divine Agents haven't got to the warlocks too.*

I parked down the road from the house. Nikolas waited outside, his wings out and his aura simmering with shadowy magic. The murmur of voices came from behind the partly open door, punctuated with shouts.

"A little impatient, aren't they?" I said.

"They've been bombarding me with questions all day," he said. "None of them witnessed what happened to Javos, so they got the embellished version from DivinityWatch."

"Since when did warlocks use that site?"

"You'd be surprised. There are videos... someone recorded the incident, and it doesn't paint the celestials in a good light."

"Because Harvey turned into an angel?" Damn. I

should have guessed the warlocks would think the worst. How did you explain to people who implicitly distrusted the celestials that the enemy wasn't actually on heaven's side, despite looking and speaking exactly like they were? Most of them wouldn't believe me. And if Nikolas insisted on telling them the truth, that put him at a disadvantage compared to any warlock who could give them a more believable story and a more obvious enemy to strike at.

"By the way, Rachel was looking for you," I said to Nikolas. "She was pretty much distraught. I don't know how to help her."

He swore. "I'll go and speak to her later, but this is more urgent."

"Yeah. If it's true—if they're the ones responsible… I won't make a scene, don't worry. But what if they win the vote?"

"They won't," Nikolas said. "I have far more experience than any of the other candidates, and besides, nobody knows who they are. I've worked for Javos for nearly as long as I've run the castle on Babylon."

There was the cocky demigod I knew. "I hope you're right, because we don't need any more declarations of war. If the Divine Agents have any warlocks dancing to their tune, what'll you do, execute them?"

"If necessary," he said. "It's risky you being here at all, but as the only celestial demon, I don't want you left out of the negotiations."

"I don't have a great recent record with being diplomatic."

And my attempt to be reasonable with Harvey had met with disaster. Let's face it, a lot of warlocks wouldn't want me in the meeting at all. But if I stayed on the fringes, I might never find out if any of the warlocks vying for leadership had sneakily been helping the rogues on the Divine Agents' orders.

I walked in behind Nikolas, keeping my sleeve firmly down over my celestial mark. At least most people in the room didn't have aura vision and couldn't see my split soul. They *had* witnessed my magic, used in battle, which was reason enough for them to distrust me, but hopefully their fear would hold them back from lashing out.

The main downstairs room had been cleared out and filled with chairs, but most warlocks stood or sat on the floor, looking expectantly at the door when we walked in. I'd sensed Nikolas using his lure ability to stop them from looking at me, but there were too many of them. They were baying for blood.

Celestial blood.

"How dare you bring that celestial traitor here!" shouted a warlock in the front row. "She killed Javos. She deserves to die."

"I didn't kill him," I said. "A rogue angel did, not someone working for the celestials *or* heaven."

"All angels serve heaven," said an incubus in the row behind. "Heaven has declared war on us."

Murmurs to that effect turned into full-blown roars. They'd be throwing the furniture next.

"Hey!" I shouted at the warlocks. "If you saw the video, it's obvious I didn't lay a finger on Javos. And it wasn't the guild, either. Ask any witnesses and they'll say the celestials were nowhere near him."

Nikolas strode to the front of the room. Darkness spread out from his hands, which momentarily stopped the shouts as everyone turned to face him.

"We're here to discuss the matter of leadership," he said. "If war is to be made, it's the leader who has the authority to do so, and last I saw, I had more votes than anyone else in this room. So let's get this over with."

Some of the noise died down. Most of the warlocks present would have known Nikolas for years, which surely counted for something—but if I could depend on anything, it was the Divine Agents' ability to get their way.

"Anyone who wishes to try out for the position as leader of the warlocks in this city is to come to the front of the room and make your argument when I say so," he said. "We've done enough dithering, and it's only served to make us look weak in the eyes of heaven and hell."

"I wish to challenge you, then," said a male voice. A warlock strode forwards—to be precise, the dude who'd once tried to stab me to death with a weaponised paintbrush. "That girlfriend of yours assaulted me."

Seriously?

"Anyone else?" asked Nikolas.

An incubus put up a hand, while a horned demon shoved his way to the front of the room. Apparently, everyone wanted to say their piece.

It became clear within minutes that none of them had any experience in public speaking, let alone trying to wrangle a crowd. Nikolas, who'd taken over the warlocks on Babylon at fifteen, had far more experience than they did. Each candidate sloped off, one at a time, to boos and disgruntled murmurs.

"Nobody else?" Nikolas asked, when the front of the room was clear once more.

"Me," said a gravelly voice. The speaker had cloven

hooves rather than feet, and horns sprouting from his head between tufts of dark bluish hair. He strode to the front of the room, kicking a chair over in the process. "I'm here representing a group of warlocks who are less than happy about how things in this city have been run."

That's him.

"The enemy has had us outmatched for a long time," he said, addressing the room. "I'd say the time is long overdue to stop fearing heaven and take the fight to them. Including those cowardly celestials in charge of the guild."

A rumble of voices rose. With warlocks, it was hard to tell if they were agreeing or just growling at one another.

"The celestials have lived here as long as we have, Talon," warned Nikolas. "In fact, they built this city from the ground up."

"They built on top of a city that used to be ours," said the warlock. "It was never theirs. We have walked this Earth longer than they have, and they've killed too many of us to count."

"If you mean law-breaking demons, then you'd be correct," said Nikolas. "If you wish to live in this world, then obey the laws of the place you choose to be your home or stay in the netherworld. It's always been that simple."

"No," said the warlock. "It's not simple. Not when they bring angels and heavenly light into this realm and use it to destroy us. Javos died because of them."

"The celestials weren't the ones who killed anyone," I said. "A rebel angel killed Javos. Tried to kill me, too. If I were on his side, he wouldn't have. There were witnesses."

"What witnesses?" said the warlock. "Celestials. How

convenient. Maybe their rules need to be thrown away for the good of us all."

Several murmurs of agreement followed. Damn him. He was playing on their hidden anger at the guild. Because let's face it, the celestials had often made bad calls, especially recently. Locking up warlocks. Callously leaving infected vampires to die. Letting the Divine Agents sneak in under their noses—not that anyone in this room would believe *that*. No, they'd lay the blame at the feet of the guild. Always.

"I'm *not* saying the guild is perfect," I said. "Nikolas doesn't like them at all, for the record. Just ask him."

"I think the guild is flawed and doomed to fall of its own accord," Nikolas said. "It doesn't need our help to do so."

It wasn't the first time he'd said that. It *was* the first time I almost hoped he was right.

"There is no point in marching to war on the celestials," Nikolas went on. "The rebel angels aren't on Earth either. They're in Purgatory, and even the celestials are unable to reach them. Their rebellion is heaven's mess to fix, not ours. If we go against this city's laws, all we do is make life more difficult for ourselves. Javos was killed because the rogues had no intention of negotiating with either the celestials or the warlocks."

"Then what do you propose we do?" demanded Talon. "Let Javos's death go unpunished?"

"If they come here again?" Nikolas looked more demonic than before, his eyes glowing gold, his wings dark as night. "If they come here again, we will meet them with an army, make no mistake. But I will not let them allow us to destroy ourselves in the meantime. If the false angels return, I will lead you to war against them."

Damn, he was good. All eyes were on him now, and the other warlocks seemed to have forgotten I was there at all. *Please. Take his word for it.* The most important thing was getting the warlocks under Nikolas's control. Then he could tell them the truth, when they were ready.

When Nikolas called the vote, a clear majority raised their hands in his favour. And that was that.

The noise died down, and the warlocks got to their feet, leaving the room. More than a few glared at me as they passed by. They'd voted for Nikolas, not me, after all. I remained standing against the wall, one eye on the corner of the room where Talon and his followers gathered.

Even if they weren't acting on orders from outside this realm, what they'd said about the celestials made me suspicious they wouldn't let one defeat hold them back. If they launched an attack, there would be deaths on both sides, and the Divine Agents would stand there and let them destroy one another.

Nikolas moved to my side, following my line of sight. "I'll handle it," I murmured to him.

He gave me a brief nod and left the room. Finally, the only people left in the room were me and the small group of warlocks following Talon.

The hooved warlock scanned the room, his gaze snagging on me. A glow lit up his hand.

"Hey there," I said, approaching him. "Not thinking of doing anything stupid like attacking your new leader or his partner, are you?"

12

"Get out, celestial," growled the warlock. His two buddies—apparently even warlock bullies needed hangers-on—murmured agreement, cracking their knuckles threateningly.

"I didn't see a sign on the door saying, 'no celestials here'," I said. "Also, I'm as much a demon as any of you, and more than some. And for the record, I'm not with the guild. I'm a free agent. So if you get any ideas about striking down your new leader, you won't be able to pin whatever I do to you on the other celestials."

"Your magic is nothing compared to ours, celestial."

He raised a hand, and I did likewise, his magic rushing into my demon mark. "I can steal your magic," I told him. "That's my demon power."

"Thieving bitch," he hissed. "You gained your magic through trickery and deceit. You betrayed both heaven and hell."

"Who told you that?" I asked. "Not a celestial, surely. Because that would involve admitting you were involved in a scheme to bring them down yourself, and that you know perfectly well who my powers came from. Wouldn't want the others to know about that, would you?"

He flushed all the way to his horns. "What are you accusing me of, celestial?"

"Treason, obviously."

He raised a hand, and his magic rushed into my demon mark once more.

"We can do this all day," I said. "There's no limit to how much of your power I can take. And if you decide to do anything stupid like declare war on the guild, then I'll stop you."

"You claim not to belong to the guild any longer, yet you still defend them?" he growled, and his two warlock buddies growled in agreement.

"Do you really want them to fight back?" I asked. "Because that's what you'll get if you strike them: armies of celestials in the streets, burning every warlock they see. Doesn't seem a great outcome for you."

"Heaven's forces as good as declared war on us."

"You can cut the charade." I let Abyss's magic flow through my demon mark, transforming me into a mirror image of the hooved warlock. The warlock gawped at me, rendered speechless at the sight of his own reflection come to life. I probed the surface of his thoughts, just for a second—long enough to determine I was right.

"What... are you?" he growled.

I turned back into Devi again. "You gave the warlocks' supplies to a group of rogue Grade Four celestials in the hope that they'd replace the guild and make it easier for you to drive them out of the city."

He opened and closed his mouth, his face ashen. I'd

read his mind, and he had no argument to defend himself with. No rehearsed story. I'd bet that he hadn't been able to resist the opportunity to seize control of the warlocks and wipe out the celestials in one go, and now he was severely regretting that decision.

"They told you," Talon said, his voice quieter, his aura darker.

"Because they're the ones who killed Javos," I said. "And I can make that information public, if I want."

The warlocks all backed away, their fear almost as palpable as the magic I'd drawn into my demon mark.

"You're lying," said Talon. "The rebels' enemies are the guild, not the warlocks. They intended to establish a new order in which warlocks are allowed the freedoms they rightfully deserve. No celestials will be permitted to harm us again. If heaven is allowed to have its own foot-soldiers here, then so should hell."

"The celestials don't kill warlocks," I said. "They're not supposed to, anyway. If they do, they face the law. Just like you will if anyone finds out what you did. Besides, the rogue celestials wanted to take over the guild for their own gain, and they don't give a shit about you. Anyone with half a brain could figure that out."

"Do not mock me, celestial," growled the warlock. "We are more than a match for a few rogues. I refuse to believe they killed Javos so easily."

"The rogues are now angels, not simply celestials," I informed him. "One of them is, anyway. Ever met Lythocrax?"

His blank expression answered that question. So he'd been operating completely in ignorance. It shouldn't surprise me, given the Divine Agents' ways.

"Lythocrax was a fallen angel who fell on purpose to infiltrate hell," I told him. "A rebel. He tricked warlocks, celestials, demons—anyone he could reach. He never spoke to them in person. Every single person he tricked believed they were acting of their own free will. I suppose it was a demon who told you to help the rogue celestials a few weeks ago?"

"The celestials contacted me themselves." He stepped back, and his hangers-on did likewise. "Stay away from me, celestial, and if you tell anyone what you know, I'll kill you."

And he ran, fleeing like hell itself was on his tail.

Shadows appeared beside me, and Nikolas stepped out of them. "I can *convince* him to stay," he said. "Or send someone after him."

"No need," I said. "He's running scared. Besides, I can easily find out what else he knows without having to interrogate him."

I drew on Abyss's power and transformed into Talon again. His small, terrified mind wasn't hard to probe, and was much less unpleasant than Lythocrax's—though not fun to be in. I felt his annoyance, anger, but not burning rage. It didn't hold a candle to mine, anyway.

I turned to Nikolas, still wearing the warlock's skin. "He's pissed, but he's not actually going to try to bump me off now he's seen what my magic does. Pretty sure he's scared of both of us, especially now we know he traded behind the warlocks' backs."

"He also lives on the city's outskirts, not far from where those celestials set up their base," Nikolas put in. "I suspected he might try something if he didn't win the vote, so I'm intending to send people after him.

"Good plan. I didn't know warlocks lived that far out. I don't know if any of the celestials' resources are still in this realm, but maybe…"

I dug deep into the warlock's mind, pushing for answers. Harvey and the others hadn't moved outside the city until recently, so the trade had started *after* I'd killed the vampires trading behind the guild's back on Pandemonium. The vampires weren't responsible. This was more recent.

A clear image appeared in my mind. Five glowing points of a pentagram, gleaming in celestial light on the ground. Beside it, several celestials carried a sheet of demonglass out of the portal, reflecting the celestial light back at them. The warlock whose eyes I watched through stepped backwards as though scared the light would burn him.

Then I spotted someone else in the portal, a familiar horned head poking out from between the glowing lines. A demon, watching the celestial rogues and warlocks carry the demonglass onto Earth.

"Dienes," I said, blinking the memory away. "I should have guessed he'd go from one set of traitors to another."

He'd been there from the beginning. I should have killed him when I had the chance.

Crap. He's still in the palace, with Zadok. Maybe whispering in his ears, urging him to start wars on the Divine Agents' orders.

Nikolas turned to me, his eyes widening. "Dienes traded the demonglass? Did you see who put their magic into it?"

"No, I didn't see any demon magic in the memory. I'm

guessing it was done before it was smuggled to Earth, but I might be wrong."

More to the point, a sheet of demonglass that size shouldn't be hard to track. But in all the last few months hopping around the city, I'd never run into it. *What did they do with it, then?*

"Are you going to question the demon?" Nikolas asked.

"I'll have to. Now." That's what I got for trusting anyone from the netherworld to turn over a new leaf. I'd known Dienes was working with the enemy and let him live, and look where it got me. "Is anyone else inside this building?"

"The warlocks who actually own the house live upstairs," he answered.

"Okay. I won't do anything too drastic." I burned five pentagram points onto the wall. "Hey, Dienes, get the hell out here."

There was a burst of fire, then shadow, and Zadok's head appeared. He smiled widely, his dark red hair reflecting the light.

I scowled at him. "I asked for Dienes."

"He's currently being used for target practice," said Zadok. "Devi, do my eyes deceive me, or is that my brother behind you?"

"Zadok," said Nikolas. "What have you done with the messenger demon?"

"It's spectacular to see you, too, brother," Zadok said. "What do you want with the little demon?"

"He's a traitor," I said to him. "He traded with rogue celestials behind the guild's back."

"Rogue celestials? Intriguing."

"Don't you start," I said. "The rogue celestials are dead

set on using Earth as their personal battlefield, and that little shit of a demon handed them the ammunition."

"Remind me why I should care about the fate of the guild?"

I groaned. "Not you, too. Look, it's your property he's sneakily trading behind your back."

He tilted his head. "The demon hasn't left the palace since I took power, Devi. Are you sure you didn't just miss me?"

"The palace is made out of demonglass," I said. "Dienes can get to any realm from there, you know that. Besides, this happened weeks or months ago."

"Then if the supposed props are in your realm, shouldn't you be looking for them?" he said.

"The celestial rogues must have hidden them before they jetted off to Purgatory. Besides, I want to talk to him in person. Maybe he's betraying you, too."

"Well, when you put it like that..." Zadok's head disappeared from the pentagram.

A moment later, a struggling horned demon appeared, Zadok's grip tight on his arms.

"Devi!" Dienes squirmed and squeaked, terror suffusing his features.

"Watch it," I said. "You didn't think you'd get away with betraying me twice, did you?"

"I have not betrayed anyone, Devi, I swear it!"

"Spare me," I said. "You're the person who traded supplies to the rebel celestials. You handed demonglass to them, Dienes. You know that's a restricted substance on Earth. Don't deny it."

"We had plenty of demonglass and no use for it," he squeaked. "Why, I thought they were with the guild."

"Like hell. Fool me once, shame on you. Fool me twice, burn alive."

He screamed as I fired off a bolt of celestial power, narrowly missing him. Grinning, Zadok dragged him back into view. "Finish him off," he said.

"Please, Devi," sobbed Dienes. "I'll tell you anything—anything. Ask me anything and I swear I will deliver."

"I doubt there's anything you can give me," I said. "Unless you know how I might go about getting a demon name? Or the names of anyone on your realm who might have dealt with Lythocrax?"

Zadok tossed Dienes into the light of the pentagram. The little demon's body fell, crumbling into ashes.

"What was that for?" I said.

"I would have thought you would know better than to hesitate, Devi," he said.

"I was that close to learning how to get a demon name, idiot," I retaliated. "How many other demons would give that information away for free?"

"Any demon, given the right pressure." He eyed my uncovered hand.

"Zadok," Nikolas said warningly. "The demon deserved to die. That doesn't mean you have the right to manipulate Devi."

"Oh, this is standard," I said, rolling my eyes. "All right, genius. *You* tell me how I'd go about getting a demon name." I moved my celestial hand to point directly at him.

Zadok narrowed his eyes. "You wouldn't kill me."

"I would if it turned out *you* were allied with the rebels, Zadok."

"I have no need for rebellion, Devi," he said, his burgundy eyes glowing. "I have everything I need."

"Don't speak too soon," Nikolas said.

"Never mind," I said. "I'd like to know where they hid the rest of that demonglass, but since Pandemonium's esteemed ruler is as unobservant as the last two—"

"It sounds like Abyss is the one who let the demon trade with Earth without her knowledge," Zadok said. "Nobody has traded behind *my* back, and I executed Abyss's former advisers personally."

"Of course you bloody well did." I groaned. "Great. I don't suppose you've seen any celestials in the palace?"

"None aside from you, Devi, and my offer is still open." He smiled. "Was that all you wanted? I thought you'd seen sense and decided to ally with me to take on the guild. You can hunt all the little demonic traitors you like, but someday you'll realise that nothing will satisfy you other than the sweet taste of revenge."

"Nothing would satisfy me more than hearing you shut the fuck up. You can stay right there in infernal hell, Zadok."

"But I'm right."

"Keep telling yourself that," I said. "You should probably check nobody else is trading behind your back. The demonglass is being booby-trapped with explosive magic, so you'd better hope the people responsible *aren't* on your side of this pentagram. Because you're standing in a palace completely made out of the stuff."

The moment the colour drained from his face, I killed the pentagram.

"What a waste of time."

"Devi..."

I turned to Nikolas. "What is it?"

"You don't think the person who booby-trapped the demonglass is in the palace, do you?" he asked.

"For his sake, I hope not. But I want to find out where they hid the stuff. A source that big... *how* have I not found it yet? I thought I gathered every source in the city, except Javos's old demonglass stash."

"Maybe we should have questioned Talon more carefully," Nikolas said. "I might not know about Pandemonium, or the guild's back doors, much less the rebels—but when it comes to the warlocks living legally in this city, there is little I don't know. I can certainly find where he and his allies live."

"Good," I said. "I'm getting tired of the Divine Agents' allies being one step ahead. Anyone would think they wanted to me to perish in a fit of frustration before I ever laid eyes on them."

"I'll send someone to 'invite' those warlocks back in for questioning," he said. "It's a pity that current warlock law forbids me from executing anyone on the spot for betrayal, but I'll see how they like the inside of a jail cell. In the meantime, we'll go and investigate Talon's house."

"Sounds like a plan," I said. "Maybe Rachel will be up for hunting down some traitors with us."

13

"You bet," said Rachel, when I asked her. "I'd like to smack around some of the idiots who tried to take leadership from Niko. Did they ever think they'd get any votes?"

"They tried," I said, walking to the lab in Nikolas's living room to grab some props. "Instead, three of them are on their way to jail. Turns out they helped the rogue celestials when they lived in this realm. They traded with Pandemonium, and they have a load of illegal demonglass hidden somewhere. Problem is, only Harvey and his friends know where it is, and they're not exactly accessible at the moment, so it looks like we're going to have to search all their houses."

"Can't you just use your ability to jump around between pieces of glass until you find it?" she asked.

"I should be able to," I said. "But I've hopped around the city all week looking for fragments and haven't found a giant piece of it anywhere. Besides, we need to see if the warlocks were keeping anything else illegal at their base."

Considering how many hours I'd spent demonglass-hopping, it bothered me that I hadn't picked up on such an obvious source, but unless the celestial rogues had taken it with them, it must still be in this realm somewhere. Not knowing how they'd infused it with demon magic bothered me, too. At least the humans didn't seem to have suffered any adverse side effects from the magic they'd gained, but it was a glaring reminder that the Divine Agents were still several steps ahead of the rest of us.

I hesitated before picking up the last of the demonglass pieces I'd kept in the lab, locked up in a container where they couldn't be used as a portal. I was shooting myself in the foot if I carried none at all, and the pieces I'd gathered were direct from the warlocks' stores, uncontaminated. Wouldn't stop Harvey from materialising on top of me again if he felt like it, but I refused to run scared from my own power source.

I drove to Talon's house, following Nikolas's directions until the houses thinned out and the roads became bumpier. Like a lot of the celestial cities, Haven City had been built on top of another, older city, which wasn't obvious until you got to the outskirts and found abandoned buildings and pothole-ridden roads. The sinking sun followed us across the darkening sky, melting over the rooftops like liquid demonglass. Maybe I had the stuff on the brain, but I was positive I'd missed a clue somewhere. A piece of demonglass as big as the one I'd seen in the vision didn't vanish into thin air.

I winced as we hit another pothole. "I don't think my tyres can take much more of this."

"We're almost there." Nikolas indicated a turning on the left. "Talon's house is just around that corner."

"About time." I parked at the road's side, next to a convenience store that'd seen better days.

"What a dump." Rachel wrinkled her nose. "Smells foul. Like dead demons."

"Better hope he hasn't left anything nasty behind." I opened the door and got out of the car.

"Be on your guard," Nikolas said from behind me. "There's a chance he might have alerted his friends before being jailed."

"Bring it," I said. "Maybe they'll give me a clue where the rogues stashed that demonglass."

A tingling in my left hand warned me my celestial mark sensed something demonic. Movement behind the curtains in the window of the brick house confirmed Talon hadn't left it unattended.

Rachel kicked the door in, and the three of us moved into the hall to face down the two warlocks inside. One was a horned half-demon with hooves who might have been Talon's sibling. The other was a big brutish green-skinned menace with gaps in his teeth when he bared them at me. "Who are you?" he demanded.

"You know who I am." Nikolas gave them a humour-less smile. "I'm assuming your associate told you to leave town?"

"Dunno what you're talking about, mate," said the horned warlock.

"Sure you don't." I folded my arms, eyeing the bag

slung over his shoulder. "So if I don't search you, I won't find any illegal demonic props... right?"

"What do you want with us? Why are you breaking into my brother's house?"

Nikolas's aura turned jet black. "Your brother is in jail for conspiring against the leader of the warlocks. Hand over everything you have or spend the night in the shadow realm. I can't promise you'd survive it."

"I didn't do anything, I swear."

I'd heard *that* before.

"Smuggling from the demon realms puts the safety of everyone in this city at risk," Nikolas said, shadows folding around him into the form of huge wings.

Swearing, the horned warlock threw the bag at me. I caught it one-handed and pulled it open. "There's no demonglass in here."

I thought not. The giant piece I'd seen in the vision had been way too big to be carried by hand, except perhaps for the massive green demon, and he wasn't carrying anything.

"Demonglass?" The warlock blinked in unconvincing confusion.

"Ring a bell?" I said. "Talon had some of that, too. What did you do with it?"

"Nothing!" he said. "We handed it over to the trader and left."

"Uh-huh." I drew on some of Nikolas's shadow magic to join with his, and the room filled with darkness.

The green-skinned demon paled and stumbled back. Scared of the dark, huh. As for the horned demon, he edged towards the window.

"Nice try." Rachel appeared from the shadows, wearing

her demonic form. "You're not getting away until we confirm you didn't steal what we think you did."

"I'm sure you two won't mind if we search your property and then torch it to the ground?" I said.

They did mind, but one look at Rachel's unhinged jaw and three sets of teeth shut them up. While she kept an eye on them, Nikolas and I searched every room, picking up every demonic prop we saw. Unfortunately, there did seem to be no sign of the demonglass, even in the attic and the basement.

"I wonder if I can probe your memory about where your fellow warlocks took that demonglass?" I said to the horned warlock when we returned to the living room. "Did they by any chance have weapons that looked like this?" My left hand ignited with celestial power.

"You're no demon!" said the green-skinned warlock, who seemed a little slow on the uptake.

"I'm worse than a demon," I said. "And if you don't tell me what you did with that demonglass, I might change my mind about not burning this house down with you already inside it."

"The celestials had it!" yelped the horned demon. "They took it. I dunno where it is."

Well, then. Bolt Street it was.

Five minutes later, we left the two of them tied up with their own rope in the alley beside the burning house. Nikolas called on some of his warlock allies to come and pick them up, while I drove us out of the dead-end of town and back in the direction of Bolt Street.

"Didn't the celestials burn down their hideout?" Rachel asked from the back seat.

"Yeah, but maybe they left a clue about where they

relocated their props. I don't *think* they took it to Purgatory." Though I might be wrong. "The demonglass I saw in the vision was huge, but maybe they're breaking it into pieces and hiding it that way. The pieces that made the portals… even the glass that caused the explosion at Mather's wasn't that big."

I parked the car down the road from Bolt Street.

"The weird thing is, I'm sure I left some demonglass of my own here," I said. "When I tried hopping here with Faye and Clover, though—it didn't work."

"Does your power have a limit?" asked Nikolas. "A geographical one?"

"Huh," I said. "Maybe. I haven't tried using it to get outside the city before." But now I thought about it, I could only travel to places in demon realms which were close to the city itself.

"Maybe if the demonglass source is somewhere out here, you can't reach it from within the city," Nikolas said.

"You can cross realms, though," said Rachel.

"Only places that directly overlap with the city," I said. "I've tested it. Pretty extensively. Shit, maybe you're right. It could have been out here the whole time, beyond the limits of my reach."

But that meant—the glass might be anywhere out here, and I would never have known it.

"When exactly did Talon smuggle the demonglass into this realm?" asked Nikolas.

"Before Lythocrax died," I said. "I bet he knew my limits and planned for it. Lythocrax is the one who *gave* me that magic. If you took a piece of demonglass out into the countryside, I wouldn't be able to reach it."

"You can't drive around the whole country, Devi," said Rachel.

"I won't need to." I looked up and down the street. The house on Bolt Street was a burned husk, nothing more. "It's a massive piece of demonglass, they won't have taken it far."

"The building's completely gutted," Nikolas commented. "I don't think the glass is in there."

"Thought not." I gripped the demonglass fragments in my pocket in my right hand. "I'm going to find it. If it's anywhere within my limits, I'll land on top of it."

"You sure?" asked Rachel.

I nodded. "I have to know what they did with it. If I land in a nest of demons, I'll send up a smoke signal."

"Use your celestial mark," Nikolas said. "I can fly in and find you."

"Flying in this realm? Whatever next?"

"Warlock leader's privilege," he said, with a smile.

Rachel pulled a face as he briefly hugged me. Then I stepped back, gripped the demonglass, and disappeared in a flash.

———

My feet hit the ground, my knees buckled, but the glaring white light didn't go away. A whistling sounded in my ears, and my blazing hand showed me the walls of a warehouse.

I rotated on the spot, facing the giant piece of demonglass from the vision. Its edges were fixed to the wall with bolts that shimmered with light.

How was I supposed to move the thing when it was locked down with magic? The sheet of glass was a good ten centimetres thick and as wide as two Devis put together. It would require a crap-ton of power to turn it into a proper portal, at least, but a source that size was dangerous enough on its own. And if Harvey came out of it…

I pressed my right hand to the glass, wondering if it was possible to sense if it had any magic stored inside it. A humming sensation rippled under the skin of my palm, and my heart jumped in my chest. My demon mark vibrated, my pulse fluttering against the glass. A similar fluttering came from within the glass itself, like something living beat within it.

I jerked back, an inexplicable rush of terror chasing down my spine. The blinding white light on my left-hand side wasn't from the glass. My left cuff had slipped, and my celestial mark was ablaze, as though I stood on top of an arch-demon.

"What did they leave you in here for?" I muttered to the glass, my voice quiet, scared. *Really, Devi.* It was only a chunk of glass. There was no reason for me to be so freaked out. I gave my left hand a vigorous shake, willing the celestial light to die down, but if anything, it grew brighter.

I stepped back, looking around the warehouse into the darkness. My Grade Four celestial light didn't appear for no reason. It was a warning, etched into our skin along with the celestial mark, to react to any dangerous nether-world presence. No demons were in here. It was warning me about the glass. There *must* be demon magic inside it… but how could I get it out?

I rested the knuckles of my right hand on the glass and pushed some shadowy power at it. Nothing happened. So I couldn't get it to absorb power that way. Or take the demonic magic out of it. Maybe the handmade mechanism holding it against the wall stopped me from doing that.

I drew demonic power into my right hand, and zapped the contraption with Nikolas's lightning.

Sparks flew from the glass, and my body left the ground as a vicious current slammed into me, lifting me off my feet. Somehow, I landed upright, gasping, my hair standing on end. Laughter spiralled around me, echoing off the walls. *Holy Divinities, that's creepy.*

"Who the hell are you?" I gasped. "Show yourself."

"I'm right here, Devi," whispered a voice.

I stiffened, my blood turning to water. That was Lythocrax's voice.

"He's dead," I said, the warehouse's high ceiling catching my voice and throwing echoes back at me. "Whoever you are, show yourself."

"I'm here, Devi... I never left."

His voice came from the glass.

I jerked back, my heart free-falling. The voice... it'd come from inside the glass. But it wasn't an active portal. It couldn't be. And besides, Lythocrax was *dead.* His body had disintegrated into ashes right there in Haven City's street.

Was I losing my mind? Quite possibly.

The demonglass lit up, showing my reflection. Half light, half dark. From this view, the light side gleamed brighter, but that only served to make the darkness more potent.

I scowled. So did my reflection. Okay, not a Devi clone this time. That voice I'd heard… it was some kind of demon trick. Or an illusion spell, another demon hiding out of sight trying to freak me out.

Nikolas's lightning magic shot from my hand, hitting the glass. Not so much as a dent appeared.

"No demigod's magic can destroy demonglass," whispered the voice. "You know that, Devi."

"Who are you?" I demanded of the disembodied voice. "If you really are Lythocrax, you picked a hell of a weird place to haunt."

Not that I believed in ghosts. They didn't exist, demonic or otherwise. And I couldn't move the glass, let alone destroy it. I reared back, slammed my foot into the glass, and yelped with pain. Well, that was confirmation I wasn't dreaming. Either I was hallucinating, or a demon was playing a shitty practical joke on me. Based on past experience, I'd bet on the latter.

Celestial light rose to my left hand, and I burned a point of light into the ground. I couldn't move the glass, and any type of magic involving a source was incredibly dangerous, but if the enemy planned to use it to open a portal, I could at least make their lives difficult.

"You're wasting your time, Devi," said Lythocrax.

"Piss off."

I burned another point into the floor, then another, until five points surrounded the glass. The light would keep any demon contained, but wouldn't stop a swarm.

Or an arch-demon.

"In two days, I will rise," said Lythocrax.

"That would be creepy if you were actually him, but

you're talking out of your arse," I said. Maybe he'd slip and give away his identity if I talked for long enough. "Invisibility magic doesn't last forever, and neither do illusions."

"I'm not invisible. I'm right here."

A ripple passed across the surface of the glass. Despite myself, I found my gaze following the movement, as the light disappeared, sinking into shadow. Within, a pair of furnace-like eyes momentarily appeared.

Mother-fucker. I wouldn't forget those eyes in a hurry.

What if he was right? If part of him had survived...

Don't be stupid. I'd slit his throat with his own demon-glass, for the Divinities' sakes. His body had turned to ashes right there in the street. And yet...

A creeping sense of dread filtered through. Maybe... maybe, like Azurial, part of him had survived after all.

Triumph that wasn't mine rushed through me, and the sensation of wings behind my shoulders flickered in and out of existence.

I tripped backwards away from the glass, my own fear momentarily swamping the weird rush of emotion that wasn't mine. "You shouldn't be in my head. You shouldn't be here at all."

Some demons could affect emotions. Rarely, but they did exist. Maybe I faced the fear version of an incubus, which took my own fear and multiplied it tenfold. But that *voice*—

"I am creation, Devi. I cannot be killed. And I *will* return to finish you off."

"Stay in hell where you belong." My voice trembled, despite my best efforts to calm it. Hearing his voice from the glass, feeling his emotions in place of mine—it was like looking into a vast gulf and knowing I was about to fall into it. And not being able to stop it. "I suppose it was you who turned Harvey into an angel. That's cheating, you piece of shit."

"Nothing is cheating in this war, Devina. The Divinities chose to limit their servants: I chose to let them shine."

Seven hells. Either someone was playing an elaborate joke, or he really—

I swore, hitting out at the glass. Pain splintered my knuckles, and rage and fear fought for dominance. I wanted to run. I wanted an enemy to slay face to face rather than a disembodied monster. I was built to kill demons, not phantoms which didn't, *shouldn't* exist anymore.

"Do you fear me, Devi?" he whispered from the glass.

I snarled and drew on Abyss's power, turning into the winged arch-demon I'd destroyed. Lythocrax's feelings swamped mine—righteous anger, depthless as the abyss... and below that, unmistakably, *fear.*

"You're the one who's afraid," I said, in disbelief. I'd destroyed him, reduced him to nothing and the idea of looking into oblivion terrified him beyond measure. He was clinging onto existence by a fragment—but he was still here, still alive. I'd been looking for faceless Divine Agents, when my true enemy had never died after all.

"I am everywhere, Devi," he growled. "Every piece of demonglass I touch contains a piece of my magic. When I died, my power dissipated..."

"Bastard," I whispered.

His magic was in this realm. Infecting humans... infecting *Earth.*

No wonder he'd let me kill him. I'd sown the seeds of my own world's destruction without him needing to survive. When I'd spread that demonglass around the city, I had no way of knowing it contained Lythocrax's own essence.

"You can't turn the glass into a portal," I said, my voice raspy. "You'd need a thousand bloodstones to power a source this size."

"I don't need bloodstones when I have the divine light on my side."

Oh, seven hells. Celestial light could power a portal, and he had no shortage of willing celestials waiting to help him. Who knew how many others he'd turned into angels?

"You're a demon," I said. "You shouldn't be allowed to turn anyone into angels."

"I was once divine, and that magic lingers still, Devi." His triumph flickered through me again, unencumbered by fear. "You will feel what I feel when your world dies, Devi... I will make sure of it."

"I won't."

My fist hit the glass, over and over. Blood streamed from my knuckles, on both hands, but I couldn't break it. Not with my own power.

"Two days," whispered Lythocrax. "Two more days until I will be reborn, and Earth will fall. Two days, Devi..."

His voice faded away. Nothing remained but blood-stained demonglass, showing my own shell-shocked reflection.

The doors crashed open behind me, and a different kind of light flooded the room, the light of a setting sun. Two people strode in: Nikolas and Rachel.

"You were supposed to send up a smoke signal," said Rachel. Then she saw my face. "What is it?"

"I can't move this source." My voice sounded distant. "Guys… we're in serious trouble."

14

I t took most of the drive back for me to explain what Lythocrax had said. My hands shook so badly, Nikolas had to take the wheel. At least they didn't think I was going mad, but the alternative was worse. For me—and for Earth.

"The snake," said Rachel. "He shouldn't have survived. You killed him."

"He did," I said. "He's a demon of creation. That's how he brought *me* back. He did the same to Harvey, too."

"If he was going to be reborn, surely it would have happened right away?" Nikolas said. "That's usually how it is."

I shook my head. "I don't know why he didn't come back right away, but I used his own power against him. Maybe it weakened him. Or maybe it's because he died on Earth, which isn't a demon realm. He turned to ashes, and I guess whatever was left of him latched onto any piece of demonglass it could find. That's what it sounds like."

"So he's *in* the glass?" said Rachel, from the back seat. "That's crazy."

"Crazier than maggot demons possessing people?" I said. "Or him creating a glass clone of me? This is the netherworld we're talking about."

Nikolas steered the car around a corner. "Exactly, but it sounds like he was severely weakened."

"He still said it'll take two days for him to come back," I said. "And he's in the source. It's a hell of a powerful one."

"He can't use the source to create a portal, though," Nikolas said. "Like you said—it'd require a significant amount of power. And if he *is* reborn, he wouldn't be able to manifest in a realm like this for long."

"If he had a portal, that wouldn't be an issue," I said. "Besides, he has a bunch of celestials who'll do whatever he says. Celestial light can power a portal."

"I'm not sure even they can power the rebirth of an arch-demon," he said, though his hands clenched on the wheel. "I called my contacts and they took Talon's associates in for questioning. They claimed ignorance about other sources."

"There might be others," I said slowly. "Outside the city."

"Then we'll find them," said Rachel. "Drive all night if you have to."

"Not if we can't destroy them," I said. "I think it's safe to say he planned this way before he actually died. Without a body, though—you're right, Nikolas, he'd need one hell of a boost of demonic magic. It was only his consciousness that survived. Kinda like Azurial, but he didn't need saphor demon eggs or vampire bites to do it."

He survived. I should have known that the arch-demon who'd brought me back from the dead would have had one final trick up his sleeve. It'd seemed too easy to take him down. His own source of power might be his weakness, but it was also his greatest strength.

Damn him.

"But what did he mean by two days?" asked Rachel.

"He said it'll take him two days to regain his lost form," I said. "I guess that means getting his body back or making a new one. Or he plans to take someone else's. If he can create a clone of me out of demonglass, creating a new body isn't beyond him. Demonglass is his power source. I guess it kept him alive—"

"In the road!" yelled Rachel. "Stop the car!"

Nikolas hit the brakes and we skidded to a halt. There *was* someone in the road—a human, his hand glowing with white light.

A celestial. One of the rogues stood in the middle of the road, jerkily swaying to the side as though drunk or injured.

Rachel gagged. I turned on my own celestial light, warily pushing the door open. Then I gagged, too. The light from my hand illuminated blood splattered around the celestial's feet, and the reason he was stuck in that position was because someone had hammered glass shards into his feet. Not regular glass, either.

"Help…." He gasped. "He's here… he's here."

I swallowed bile. "Lythocrax is fucked in the head."

The celestial turned to me, his eyes glowing with divine fire. "He said… he said tell her there are five, five points. When five ignite, so do I."

"The hell does that mean?" I moved closer, but even if I

removed the glass from his feet, his wounds were too deep. He wouldn't survive.

"It means you're too late," Lythocrax's voice whispered in my ear. The light at the celestial's feet gleamed brighter, then there was a horrible crack. The celestial fell backwards, blood spilling into the road, his legs destroyed. He was dead.

I heard Rachel vomiting and gagged again. Nikolas moved behind me, wrapping an arm around my shoulder.

"I'm okay," I said, shuddering. "More than he is, anyway. Rachel, I recommend you don't look at this."

I swallowed hard, squeezing my eyes shut. Then, gritting my teeth, I approached the dead celestial. At his feet, the glass had exploded into fragments. Like at the warlock bar, there was nothing left. It'd burned out from the inside out, leaving no traces behind.

"Nothing there," I said, returning to the car. "I guess Lythocrax is going to keep leaving me creepy messages for the next two days delivered by his unfortunate followers."

"Five points?" said Nikolas. "There are five points on a pentagram."

"There are." I cast my mind back to the odd metal contraption the demonglass had been trapped in, fixed to the wall. "If they wanted to turn that thing into a portal, they'd need to use something similar to a pentagram to contain it."

An image entered my mind—five celestials, each holding a burning light as they transported Faye and me into Purgatory. Five points on a pentagram could also be five separate sources, if it was a particularly big portal. If five celestials surrounded that glass, they'd be able to turn it into a portal…

When five ignite, so do I.

"Figure it out later," said Rachel, from the back seat of the car. "That guy is giving me the major creeps."

"Seconded." I got back in the front passenger seat. "You two heard him then, right? Lythocrax."

"Yes," Nikolas said darkly, taking the wheel. "He wasn't trying to hide his presence."

"No kidding."

We found the second celestial on the outskirts of town. This one had been nailed to a wall by a shard of demonglass deep in his shoulder. As he spotted our car, he choked out the words, "Two days, Devi…"

"Fuck off, Altheare."

He didn't react to my use of his true name. Lythocrax's creepy laugh tore from the celestial's throat, and when Nikolas stopped the car, a burst of light engulfed the celestial's right-hand side. *The glass exploded again.*

I leapt out the car and sprinted to his side, but the entire right side of his body was a bloody mess. The celestial teetered on the spot, falling to his knees. With his last breath, he gasped, "Look below, not above, for heaven was built on hell's ruins, and light and dark are both divine."

"What the hell does that mean?" I stepped back as the celestial fell onto his face, his body still. Dead.

"He said, 'look below'," said Nikolas. "Underground? The netherworld?"

"Maybe the netherworld," I muttered, turning away from the celestial's body.

Once again, I climbed back into the car. I didn't appreciate being toyed with, and Lythocrax was getting on my last nerve. What the hell was he killing off his own people for? It wasn't like I'd mourn their deaths. But if the celestials found them, it'd freak them out even more than it did me. After all, the missing celestials were supposed to be dead. You'd think he'd have more sense than to sacrifice his own people, but when it came to Lythocrax, nobody seemed to *stay* dead.

"Heaven was built on hell's ruins," said Nikolas, getting behind the wheel. "This city was rebuilt by the celestials. Heaven's soldiers. Maybe he means the city itself."

"Maybe, but it wasn't hell's to begin with," I said.

I don't think so, anyway. I hadn't exactly paid attention in the celestial academy's history lessons. And the celestial cities *had* traditionally been built on sites where the demons had waged war and lost.

Talon's words came back to me. *They built the city on top of what used to be ours.*

"It wasn't hell's," Nikolas said, "but it wasn't the celestials' either."

"Never mind that," said Rachel. "Lythocrax is toying with us. It wasn't the Divine Agents at all, was it? Not even screwing with the rogues and promising them power."

"Nope. It's him, all over again. It's always been him."

The celestial's words echoed in my mind. *And light and dark are both divine.* What the hell did that mean? Both heaven and hell's rulers were both divine? Not hardly. Arch-demons were the polar opposite of the Divinities. Unless Lythocrax still saw himself as divine despite falling from grace. He was certainly egotistical enough.

"Two days seems too generous," said Rachel.

"Don't speak too soon," I said. "I'll bet he has other

plans in motion. Like those humans with celestial powers. And even then, we can't destroy the portal, not without…"

"Without what?" asked Rachel.

"There's only one way to destroy that glass," I said. "The shadow arch-demon's magic."

———

We pulled up at Nikolas's house, and Rachel shook her head at me. "That's not just a bad plan, it's suicidal."

"Got a better idea?" I looked at Nikolas. "Believe me, if there's another option, I'll gladly take it. Casthus's power can destroy the glass. If I get my hands on some of it, I can drive right back to that warehouse and wipe the source out."

"I doubt robbing the shadow demon will go as well as the last time did, Devi," he said. "You were exceedingly lucky."

"When I took the fallen?" I asked, an uneasy flutter going through me. I'd been sure I'd got them safely out of the way, and yet… Lythocrax wasn't supposed to survive. All my plans to keep them safe had hinged on him no longer being alive. I couldn't even keep the people on Earth I loved safe, let alone anyone else.

Two days. Two days to save the world.

"I'll look at my resources," said Nikolas, getting out of the car. "Devi, you're worn down. If you try to confront anyone tonight, you'll make careless mistakes. Besides, it may be that there's a solution that doesn't involve the shadow arch-demon at all. I got the impression Lythocrax was giving you a hint."

"Or just screwing with me." I climbed out of the car,

sighing. "I can't make heads or tails of what those celestials said, which is probably the point."

"Don't let him get to you, Devi," said Rachel.

I turned to lock up the car. "He crept up on me and killed two people. And he's supposed to be dead. Also, I can still sometimes feel what he does, and it's creepy as hell."

"I didn't know you could still feel it," said Nikolas, waiting beside the unlocked door to his house.

"Not all the time." I walked in and flicked the light switch in the hall, making for the living room. "He's scared shitless of dying. That's why he's hanging on so hard. I guess being the demon of creation isn't necessarily a failsafe."

"Guess not." Rachel flopped into an armchair. "Okay, what clues did he give you? Five points... he must have meant a pentagram."

"Everyone knows you need a more than a source to power a portal, though," I said. "That isn't news."

"No." Nikolas turned the kitchen light on and approached the shelf above the cabinet where he kept his collection of old books. "I don't think an arch-demon could possibly come through a source even that size, however. He'd need a far bigger portal to come to a realm with as little demon magic as Earth. Bigger even than the one that covered the guild's headquarters when the vampire king created that bridge on Babylon."

"How big?" I asked, a new possibility hitting my heart. "The size of a building?"

"Bigger." Rachel lifted her head, her gaze connecting with mine.

"The size of a city," I whispered. "Five… he didn't mean a pentagram around *that* source. He meant five sources."

The demonglass itself wasn't the portal. The *city* was. And if it was true… if his power was inside the glass, waiting to ignite… maybe five sources, powered by celestial light, would be enough to bring him back.

Rachel drew her knees up to her chin. "That would take some major planning."

"He's had ages to plan this," I said. "That source at the warehouse has been there for weeks. I'd need to see a map to figure out where the others are… does anyone have a map of what the city looked like in its original form? Before the celestials modernised everything?"

Rachel frowned. "They did? I thought the city was built over fifty years ago."

"Seventy," I said automatically. "Give or take a few. Okay, maybe I do remember a bit from school. The five sources must be spread out like the points on a pentagram, otherwise the portal wouldn't work."

"That's way too far apart," Rachel said. "The city… he'd need to connect the sources to make them join."

"He has a whole team of celestials," I said. "And he's *in* the glass, powering it himself. I don't know which demon realm he plans to link to, but it doesn't matter. He's already here."

He'd always been here. I'd been chasing an enemy who didn't exist, when my real nemesis—the demon who'd ruined my life—had never left at all.

"What about the humans with demonic power?" asked Rachel quietly. "You don't think he'll use them?"

"He would if he could," I said. "But I don't think he can when he has no body and little power. When he comes back, though… it's the bloody saphor demons all over again."

"He's not exactly like a saphor demon, though, is he?" said Rachel. "They don't harm humans. I don't think his magic can actively harm the people it infected. Otherwise, it already would have."

"True." I sank onto the sofa. "I guess it'd be a different story if it was celestials he'd infected, but he knows I can drain the virus out of them and I can probably do the same with his influence. It's the fact that he's stuck in the *demonglass* that's tripping me up. He shouldn't be able to move around like that."

"He can't," said Nikolas, returning to the living room with an armful of books. "Even with saphor demons, the person has to have actually made physical contact with the demon—or its egg—to be infected with the parasite. The only demonglass he's actively had contact with are the pieces that came directly from the sources he's stored around the city."

"Yes, but I can't destroy them without shadow power," I said. "Unless there's another way. I'm all ears. Walking back into Casthus's realm is at the bottom of my bucket list, believe me."

Rachel's mouth twisted. "They can be used as sources, right? Individually? Couldn't you open a portal on top of one of them, drag the source into another realm, and then close it before it does any damage? Even getting rid of just one source would stop him from linking all five of them."

"It's not possible to open a portal of that size without *something* getting through," said Nikolas. "Not an arch-demon, but a demigod, for sure. And that's assuming that activating one of the sources won't trigger the others to switch on, too. Don't forget, they're already arranged in the form of a pentagram, if we take Devi's theory as correct."

"So… you don't think I'm talking crap?"

"No, it makes sense," said Nikolas, holding up a faded map of the city. "No arch-demon can enter this realm without a source to sustain them, not without causing damage to this realm and the one on the other side of the portal. I would hazard a guess that he plans to link up his own realm with this one—"

"I never should have left those fallen there," I said. "But —he can't get into that realm from Purgatory. It's not possible."

"The demonglass didn't come from his own realm," Nikolas said. "Did it?"

Now I understood. "It came from Pandemonium. And that realm was definitely linked to Lythocrax's realm. Twice over."

My hands curled into fists. I didn't have a damned clue how Lythocrax's ability to survive death actually worked, but if he could transfer his consciousness between bits of demonglass, there was little doubt he could hop through a portal into another realm, too. And with his own realm one step away, rebirth would follow.

I got to my feet. "I don't see a way out of this. I can't single-handedly destroy even one demonglass source that size. I suppose since that source was fixed in place with magic, the others will be, too?"

"Do you want the 'Fiona' answer or the 'Rachel' one?" asked Rachel.

"Ha." I lay back down on the sofa, exhausted beyond measure. "To be honest, there aren't all that many places you can hide a massive treasure trove of demonglass. Someone else might be able to find them. But—"

"Nobody else can destroy them." Nikolas flipped through the book in his hand. "Devi… I wish I had answers. Your own power comes from demonglass, too. Maybe there's a way to leverage that and use it against him."

"I already tried that," I said. "Didn't quite work out as planned. Besides, he's *in* the glass. I'm what, a Grade Three demon, magically speaking? He's an arch-demon."

"He's also literally in pieces," put in Rachel. "You know, I think he's in the process of regenerating from scratch. That takes time and a hell of a lot of power. If you can keep him from linking to his own realm, stall for time, maybe you can stop him regenerating."

"If his power is inside the source," said Nikolas, "can't you drain it yourself like you did with the vampire virus?"

"I tried draining whatever magic he put in the glass," I said. "Didn't work. He's too strong. I doubt I can do what I did to the saphor demons with magic on an arch-demon's level. And if the humans' power upgrades… I can't stop him from hurting them, too."

"Put the humans out of mind," said Nikolas. "When you destroy Lythocrax, they'll be fine."

I sat upright again. "He even shut me out of Purgatory. I wonder if Clover knows he's alive. I guess he's the disembodied ghost Harvey keeps talking to." I forced a brittle laugh. "And he made him into an angel. Why did I ever think I'd killed him for good?"

"He shouldn't have been able to do that," Rachel said. "He's an arch-demon."

"Once a Divinity," I said. "Light and darkness were

both divine… he claims he still has his divine magic. I guess that's what he meant."

Nikolas turned the page of the book. "According to all sources, the realm with the most demonglass on it is Pandemonium. There's nothing here about storing magic in the glass, though."

"Maybe Zadok knows," I said. "He stored his own power in demonglass cuffs when he took Abyss's throne. Hell, maybe he knows how to reverse the process and drain someone else's power out of the glass. I sure as hell don't."

"He can only do that with his own magic," said Nikolas. "I did look into how he did it. He siphoned off his own magic—which is extremely dangerous, I might add. Not his consciousness. Few demons would take the risk and store their magic in a proxy, let alone separate their consciousness. The saphor demons that become parasites usually die off quickly."

"Lythocrax's magic *is* mine, though," I said. "I still couldn't drain his power from the glass. Pretty sure I'd need to be the same level as him to do it." I could store a little arch-demon magic in my demon mark, but not much. Not enough to drain the consciousness of an arch-demon determined to cling to life. Lythocrax's will to live was too strong to break.

No… the only way to wipe out that demonglass was to risk ticking off the shadow arch-demon who'd barely spared my life when I'd swiped the fallen out from under his nose.

I stood. "All right. Let's go visit Casthus."

"No," said Nikolas. "It's too risky—he'll kill you."

"Relax, I've got this. I'm not going to him directly, except as a last resort."

I drew on Abyss's power, calling to mind the overwhelming sight of the shadow arch-demon the first time I'd seen him. I wouldn't forget his face in a hurry. Two eyes, burning in a shadow-black aura…

Shadows blurred my vision, and then pain shot up my spine, as though I'd trodden on an open wire. I yelled and fell to my knees, pain racking my bones like an electric shock.

"Ow." I groaned, rising to my feet. "Okay, that went wrong."

I called on Abyss's magic again, willing the shadow arch-demon's form to take over me. Again, pain speared me through the lower back, spreading to each limb. Like someone was trying to pull my bones out of my skin. I let the magic go, gasping for breath.

"Devi, stop," said Nikolas. "I don't think it's going to work."

"Why can't I turn into him? It worked with Lythocrax."

"Lythocrax isn't a typical arch-demon," said Nikolas. "His power is in your demon mark. Maybe that's why you can turn into him and not the others."

"Great." I sat back on my heels. "Would have been nice if Abyss had told me that. I guess if we want Casthus's magic, we'll have to sneak up on him. Or make a deal with him, but that never ends well."

"No," said Nikolas. "Absolutely not."

"The world dies in two days if I don't destroy that demonglass," I said. "Unless I make a deal with another demon, but who could possibly know how demonglass works except for Lythocrax himself?"

"Turn into him again," Rachel said. "Maybe he's hiding more secrets."

"I don't think it's doing Devi any good to keep using that power," Nikolas said.

"That's what he wants me to think," I said. "He wants me to feel helpless. But the first time I met face to face with him, I was weaker than I am now. I won't be afraid of him. I can't afford to be."

I let Abyss's magic flow from my demon mark, and became the arch-demon once more.

Lythocrax's thoughts swamped me, as potent as ever, yet hard to grasp. Almost as though his mind was… split. Like his consciousness. *Tell me how you did it. Tell me how to beat you.*

Images flickered through my mind, of portals and pentagrams, celestials surrounding pieces of glass. "Ow," I groaned. "I was right, he's planning to use the city, all right. Not that it matters if I know where the sources are if I can't destroy them."

No… only he could destroy them. He was inside them, after all.

I swore loudly. *No. There's got to be another way.*

I dove deeper into his mind, past the pain, past everything. Anger flared, and fear, and pain. Decades of it.

"Devi, are you okay?" Rachel's voice sounded distant, like it came from far away.

"Yes," I said. "Damn, he's *pissed* that Abyss gave me her magic and let me access his thoughts like this. I'm not sure even she knew I'd use her power to steal his secrets. Or maybe she did."

"Right," said Rachel. "Can you please stop making

those faces? He's hideous and freaky enough without you making it look like he's about to wipe us out."

"Ah. Sorry." I turned back into myself again, sifting through the information I'd gleaned. "He survived in the demonglass, but I think it cost him the best part of his power. He's breaking apart, but I—I can't find any other way to destroy the glass than using his own power. And I already tried that. It didn't work."

I turned into him again, gritting my teeth. It was harder this time, as though part of him was actively fighting against me trying to gain control. My voice was my own when it tore from his mouth—"He turned himself into a parasite at the last moment, but I don't think losing his body was part of the plan. He's not in all the demonglass, only the bits he's touched. Those five sources. And I can't destroy them with my own power. It'd just end up giving him more."

As I'd feared.

"Devi," warned Nikolas. "I wouldn't hang onto his mind for too long. He's an arch-demon—"

I let go, turning into myself again. "Damn. You know, I was wondering if he left part of himself behind on his own realm, since he needs to go there to reform, but now I think about it, part of him must be on Purgatory. Has to be. Harvey's wandering around talking to himself like a crazy person, and someone's definitely giving them orders."

Small problem: the damned place was completely locked up.

"Then we'll go there tomorrow." Nikolas tossed the book onto the table and pulled me to my feet, his arms steadying me against his body. "Not Babylon. You know

Casthus will see it as an act of war if you step into his realm, let alone take his power."

"I bet that's why Lythocrax wants to force me into it," I said. Divinities above, it felt good to be held like this, even if the world was breaking apart. "He wants me to ask the one person for help who'd wipe out Earth on a whim without even giving me a shot at a deal."

It wasn't like I had a bunch of celestial rogues to manufacture a distraction this time around, either. Unless I asked Zadok, which was extremely unlikely. He wanted to stay away from Babylon, probably forever.

Nikolas's arms tightened around me. "Devi. We'll figure this out."

"He has us backed into a corner," I murmured. "Either we tick off the shadow demon or we sit here and wait for Lythocrax to regain a body with no way to stop him."

"There'll be another way," he said. "You're worn out, and I guarantee that the solution will come to you if you give it time. You always think of something."

"We're a little short on time at the moment, to say the least." I looked around the living room, my gaze snagging on the lab set up on the table. Everything I'd invented had started as nothing more than the spark of an idea. Since a demon of creation had marked me, no wonder I'd always felt an affinity for invention. But I couldn't for the life of me figure out how to concoct a way to make a shadow arch-demon bow before me or stop Lythocrax from returning from death. "I wish a full-body blister attack could destroy the bastard."

"You'll think of something," Nikolas repeated. "I've asked my warlock advisers to question Talon closely, so we're likely to be able to track down the other sources by tomorrow. And after that, we'll work out how to destroy them."

"Yeah." Rachel yawned. "I'm going to sleep. Try not to invite any more demons into the house."

She made for the stairs, while Nikolas continued to hold me against him. I rested my head on his chest, wishing I could stay here and someone else could sort out the demons' mess for a change. "Bloody arch-demons. Who made me the only person who can keep them out of the city?"

"You're not alone." He swept my hair over my shoulder with one hand, leaning to brush his lips over mine. "I have every confidence in you."

"What are you doing?"

"Distracting you. You can't help the world if you don't help yourself."

"Hmm." I kissed him back, enjoying the feel of his arms around mine, chasing away the threads of Lythocrax's presence. "Maybe you're right."

"I'm rarely wrong."

"You have enough self-confidence for both of us." I stepped back from him, aware I was still wearing my jacket. Demonglass and all. I shrugged it off and threw it onto the sofa. Behind it was the picture of the Northern Lights I'd moved here from my room at the warlocks' old headquarters. "I should move the rest of my stuff here."

"What, from your flat?" he asked.

"Yeah, all the stuff I bought when I used to travel for the guild. Sentimental value is stupid, but…"

But we might die in a day or two. I'd danced on the edge of danger since I'd joined the guild, but it'd been a long while since I'd had so much to lose.

"Are you implying that you want to relocate here permanently?" Nikolas said, one eyebrow raised. "You might want to make it clearer."

"You're supposed to ask *me* that," I said, smiling despite myself. "It's that or get our own place… I'm assuming you mean to say you're not completely opposed to the idea."

"Oh, I'm absolutely horrified at the idea of spending any more time with you than I have to," he said.

I swatted at him. "Ha ha. I practically live here anyway. And *I* won't be spending any more time than I have to at the warlocks' new headquarters. Not sure what to tell Fiona, but she mentioned moving to another flat, closer to this part of town. She still hasn't been able to find another job in the human world since she got her demon mark."

"I thought so," Nikolas said. "Things are still a little volatile with the new warlock council, but if she wants to continue teaching the humans magic, I can make it into an official position."

"I'll see what she thinks of that," I said. "With her demon magic… I know she wants to use it. Demon magic doesn't give you a choice. Look at me."

"And what do you want, Devi?"

"I want…" I paused, trying to get my words in order. "I don't want to work for the warlocks. Not the way Javos ran things, anyway. And I'm not working with the celestials, either. Not sure I'm cut out for a quiet life, to be honest, but there aren't a ton of options that won't piss off one side or the other. But I would like to be able to afford to travel again. And not just to the demon realms, either. I miss it."

I missed waking up to a new sight every morning. I

missed every day being full of possibility, not the potential end of the world.

Nikolas frowned. "I wouldn't stop you."

"It's not you," I said. "It's the paperwork."

His mouth curved in a grin. "Really."

"You know, I didn't hate being a freelancer," I admitted. "I just wasn't great at it. My skills weren't in high demand."

"They are now," he said seriously. "People know your name. I think you could make a go of it, if it's what you want to do."

"Yeah… I think it is." I'd got one thing right in the last two years: I never wanted to be tied to the guild, or any other organisation again. "Not that I'd object to you helping me out if necessary," I added. "Got to keep up good relations with the warlocks."

"Very good relations." His hands slipped around my back. "Why would you think I'd stop you?"

"Force of habit," I said. "I spent most of my adult life trying to wriggle out of being controlled by the guild. Being a celestial soldier was supposed to be my life's calling. I have no family. Aside from Fiona, I have no human friends. And I can't—" I broke off. "You know celestials and warlocks can't have children, right?"

He nodded. "I assumed you'd bring it up if it was an issue for you."

"It isn't. Can you imagine me hauling a kid around when dodging rogue demons?"

He tilted his head. "Devi, at no point since we met have I ever thought your lifestyle is remotely suited to involve small children."

"Believe me, I don't see the danger factor ending anytime soon."

"Good. Wouldn't want life to get boring." He tucked a curl behind my ear and kissed me softly, slowly. I leaned into him, wrapping my arms around his back. My phone buzzed.

"Dammit." I pulled it out of my pocket. "Fiona. I'll tell her… shit, I can't do this now. I'll give her the story in the morning."

"Leave it here." Nikolas took my phone and tossed it onto the sofa along with my coat. "Just for tonight."

"I'm on board with that." My hand slipped into his as we headed upstairs into the darkness. I couldn't shut out the world forever, but I just wanted to forget. For one night.

Nikolas pushed the door to his room open, and was kissing me again before we reached the bed. I tugged at his clothes and he obliged, shrugging out of his T-shirt so I could run my hands over his muscled shoulders and chest. His hands slid up my shirt, undoing the clasp of my bra, and I wriggled out of my trousers. His hand dropped to my waistband, skimming the top of my underwear, the other sliding down my leg.

"Demon mark," I murmured.

He obliged, taking my right hand and caressing it. Shadowy power rubbed against me, and I gasped as his other hand moved in tandem between my legs. Pleasure fractured my mind, and I fell back onto the bed. "Get over here."

"If you insist." He removed the rest of his clothes, his erection hanging loose. "I hope you have enough energy left to get through the night."

"Oh, I'm just getting started." I reached for the bedside table and grabbed a condom, sliding it onto him.

He slid inside me with a single thrust, moving slowly, then faster. His lips caressed my neck as we moved against one another. My nails dug into the bed as he pushed me to the edge of pleasure and over, and I came again, seconds after he did.

"Did I mention you're divine?" he murmured, his lips chasing a path over my breasts.

"Several times." I rolled to the side to give him room to lie down next to me. "We really need a bigger bed."

"I take it I've distracted you enough?" He planted a kiss on my neck.

"Not by a long shot." I wrapped my arms around him, holding him close to me. Holding on as tight as I dared.

Chasing away Lythocrax's whisper that this might be our last night alive.

15

Nikolas had it right: I did feel a little better about our chances of survival in the morning. Not that there was much improvement on 'we're doomed', but hey, I could dream.

When I retrieved my phone from where Nikolas had tossed it onto the sofa, I had a dozen missed calls and a huge backlog of messages, mostly from Fiona. Apparently, Rachel had decided to give her the bad news last night, and she'd passed on the message to Faye. Now, the entirety of DivinityWatch was packed with 'evacuation tips'.

"Uh, Fiona," I said, when she picked up the phone. "Did you tell anyone apart from Faye about Lythocrax? Because he's going to be pissed if he finds out everyone knows. Besides, evacuating the city won't stop him."

"You can't keep it quiet, Devi," said Fiona. "This is bigger than Haven City."

"I know that. But there are still several million people living here, and I don't want them to die because

Lythocrax threw a hissy fit about his image showing up in a thousand memes on the internet."

"I'm pretty sure he can't use the internet if he's a disembodied spirit, Devi," said Fiona. "You know, that's why Faye created DivinityWatch to begin with. It's a fool-proof way to spread information and completely avoid leaving a trail for the demons to follow. And the celestials —the ones in charge, anyway."

"Yes, I'm aware," I said. "But he's a disembodied soul just like the piece of Azurial who nearly destroyed you. You don't want to know what he did to those celestial helpers of his. He's killing them for sport."

"I know he's a dick," she said. "I think it's worth making an evacuation plan, though, in case whatever you do to stop him has side effects."

"You're way too calm about this," I told her. "Also, you're assuming I have an idea of how to stop him. I don't."

"You've got out of worse situations before," she answered. "Faye thinks you can do it."

"Faye has been listening to vampires proclaim that I'm a Divinity in human flesh for the last few months. To be honest, Fi, I *don't* have any ideas." Much as it pained me to admit it. "Aside from stealing some magic from the shadow demon, but I'm not sure even destroying that demonglass will finish him off for good."

"Bound to be worth a try, though."

Her faith in me was heartening, but I doubted Lythocrax would let the city be evacuated before he staged his comeback.

"I'm on my way to your place. I'll pick up Faye on the

way," Fiona said. "Believe me, you'll think of something. Put your inventor's mind to the task."

"My inventor's mind can create interesting and painful ways to stop demons getting their paws on me, not keep a vengeful arch-demon from smiting everyone in the city into oblivion in the name of revenge. But thanks anyway."

I ended the call and turned to Rachel and Nikolas, who occupied the sofa. "Please tell me one of you has a plan?"

"No, but I have people looking out for the other four demonglass sources," said Nikolas. "I told them that someone illegally smuggled them into this realm for the purposes of making a portal. On the off-chance that a demon *does* break through, they'll find warlocks waiting to challenge them on the other side."

"What if Lythocrax attacks them if they get too close?" I asked. "I mean, he *is* in the glass."

"He can't get *out* of the glass," said Nikolas, as calm and confident as ever. "He's taunting you because he's harmless in that form. He never intended to be humiliated and stripped out of his body."

"He still plans to revive from death in two—no, one and a half—days," I reminded him. "And a few warlocks won't be able to stop him, trust me. Look what he did to his own people."

His casual slaughter of the celestials shocked me not because of the unnecessary cruelty of it, but because it was a genuine waste of talent he'd recruited himself. Either he was confident he'd have a proper army soon, or he didn't intend there to be enough of Earth or Haven City left for him to rule over. And despite the secrets I'd read from the depths of his mind, he remained ten steps ahead of me.

"Weren't you going to Purgatory today?" asked Rachel.

"Earth is locked out," I said. "I'm sure what's left of him is hiding out there, though. Someone's telling Harvey what to do."

Whatever form he existed in was undoubtedly weakened. His thoughts had been unhinged, desperate, and terrified. Maybe it was the effect of splitting his consciousness, but he'd felt somewhat less substantial than before. I'd shaken him up, forced him to split his soul just to continue existing. Didn't mean he couldn't give me grief, of course, but I had to remind myself that he wasn't an all-powerful mastermind but a weakened shell of his former self.

"You can't get to Purgatory from Earth," she said. "But what about other realms?"

"The demon realms?" I looked at Nikolas. "I don't know. Purgatory is at heaven's gates, not hell's. But maybe it's worth trying."

"Which realm?" asked Nikolas. "I think... being a between-realm, it might be possible to link to Purgatory from the netherworld. But I wouldn't count on it."

"Pandemonium has more than enough sources," I said. "Not sure Zadok would appreciate us using his palace as a portal, but he wouldn't appreciate Lythocrax using his palace to come back from the dead, either. Maybe I can make him see how serious the situation is."

"I wouldn't count on it, Devi," said Nikolas. "If you tell Zadok what's going on, anyone might find out."

I raised my left hand and burned a pentagram into the wall. "I think Lythocrax *wants* everyone to know, to be honest."

Zadok appeared in the pentagram almost immediately,

as though he'd been expecting me to call him. "Devi," he said, smiling. "Am I to understand I've become the person you consult when you're in need of assistance?"

"Actually, I wanted to ask you a question," I said. "Is it possible to access Purgatory from the demon realms?"

"Heaven's gates?" he asked. "I've never tried it, but since it's not actually *in* heaven, possibly. Why?"

"I may need to use your demonglass."

He cocked a brow. "Oh?"

Nikolas stepped in behind me. "Would it create a two-way connection between your realm and there?"

Zadok tilted his head. "I suppose it would. Any reason, brother?"

"Shit." I glanced back at Nikolas. "There are some seriously nasty rebel angels on that world. Not to mention it's the place with the exploding demonglass. I don't think you want that in your palace."

Assuming it isn't already there.

He scowled. "No, I certainly do not. Is that the only reason you decided to disturb me?"

"It's not always about you, Zadok." I killed the pentagram and sighed. "Anyone got a demon realm to nominate which can link with Purgatory without bringing in a swarm of rebel angels?"

Nikolas's mouth pulled. "Only one which wouldn't end badly for the people who live there."

Oh, damn. "Babylon. Your father could smite all those angels in one go."

"I thought you weren't going there," said Rachel. "Since, you know, Casthus wants you dead."

"He doesn't have to know he has visitors," I said. "Right, Nikolas?"

Nikolas didn't look too pleased, but he nodded. "I can fly us away from the castle to set up the portal without being seen. I think it's the only realm that can potentially link to Purgatory without giving Lythocrax another opening to get to Earth."

"Yeah, I thought so."

"I'm not exactly in favour of linking Babylon with Purgatory either, since it's a bridge to Earth," he said. "But Purgatory and Earth are already linked, regardless."

"Yeah. I bet he'd be thrilled if I opened the link to Pandemonium and gave him another way in," I said. "I'd never forgive myself if I let him sneak onto Earth."

And I wouldn't give him any more time. I gathered my weapons, hoping the shadow arch-demon wasn't particularly observant today.

"We'll fly a long way from the castle," said Nikolas. "Are you ready to go over there now?"

"No time to waste," I said. "Literally. I don't know what I'll find on Purgatory—hell, it's risky going right into Harvey's lair, but I feel like Lythocrax must be hiding out of sight. He wouldn't want his followers to know he's weak."

"And Clover's there," added Rachel. "What in hell is *she* doing, anyway?"

"That's what I'm planning to find out," I said.

"Rachel, wait in reserve for my signal." Nikolas took my hand. "I've told the warlocks I'm away on nether realm business today. With luck, we won't be long, but just in case, I'll leave a portal open so you can get in after us."

"Sure," said Rachel. "Don't get thwacked into oblivion by a shadow demon."

"Wasn't planning on it." I squeezed Nikolas's hand, and we crossed over into the shadow realm.

Babylon really was beautiful, for a realm that had once been a dead end and now hosted the most powerful shadow arch-demon in all the realms. Its perpetual midnight sky glowed velvety blue, studded with stars, and the huge luminous moon hung behind the castle. I'd often wondered if whoever had built the place had positioned it to get that exact effect. Spires and towers were etched against the sky, though the separate tower that had once been Zadok's home was noticeably absent since Casthus had torn it down.

Nikolas didn't stop to admire the view. Shadows flowed from his hands, reforming into wings at his back, and he lifted me into the air. My stomach dropped as the ground abruptly disappeared and the star-studded sky loomed ever-closer. I didn't feel particularly secure dangling beneath Nikolas's hands, but from the way he flew, he could easily be mistaken for a flying bat demon from a distance. We swooped over the landscape without pause, which appeared to be nothing more than barren Earth for miles around.

The wind blew my hair back, and my heart leapt in my chest. I'd enjoyed flying as Lythocrax. It'd been the only pleasant part of the experience. Below, dark canyons and cliffs and crevices marked the desolate landscape, with little around except for wild demons. The war on Babylon had left scores of demons and celestials dead. The only survivors, if you could call them that, were the fallen. With them gone, the sole inhabitants of the castle were the few warlocks who'd survived Casthus's purge—all that remained of Nikolas's army. Not that he'd have much time to run an army now he was in charge of Haven City's warlocks, but it was easy to forget that we were now trespassing in someone else's territory. And if our plan went wrong, both of us might be the next to have our heads mounted on pikes along with the other warlock traitors.

I swallowed a shout of surprise as we dropped without warning, landing inside a gulf below an overhanging cliff. Nikolas put me on my feet and blasted the surrounding area with his lightning attack. Several wild demons scuttled away.

"This is miles out," I said, my teeth chattering from the cold. "Better hope we don't get stuck."

"I have every confidence in you." Nikolas leaned close to me, his hand on my demon mark. His power hummed into me, chasing the cold away.

"Don't overdo it," I said.

"I can recharge my power here," he said. "I doubt Purgatory will allow me to enter, much less leave."

"I thought not." I stepped back, burning a pentagram into the ground. "Wish me luck."

"I'll be waiting on the other side. And I believe you can do this."

Bolstered by his faith in me as much as the power he'd loaned me, I leaned in and hugged him. "I'll be back before you know it.

He brushed his lips over mine. "Don't do anything too risky."

"It's the apocalypse. Anything goes."

I stepped into the pentagram. "I, Devi Lawson, celestial soldier, request entry to Purgatory to speak to heaven's angels." *Or whoever's running the show over there.*

Half of me didn't expect it to work, but white light

bloomed from my left hand, mingling with the pentagram's burning edges, and swallowed me up.

The dark ground became lighter, though just as barren. A hard rock face loomed above me, not unlike Babylon, except the sky here was blood-red and streaked like flames. Not nearly as scenic. I stepped to the side, and as the light faded, it became clear that it wasn't a cliff I faced, but a building with barred windows. A jail.

"Devi." Clover leaned out between the bars.

"Divinities!" I jumped backwards, nearly tripping into the pentagram again. "What—they locked you up?"

Part of me, small though it might be, had been clinging onto the faint hope that Clover had been devising a way to beat the rebel angels during her time here. Finding her a captive made my heart sink into the Earth. Not least because I had no idea where I was. I'd never seen any buildings on Purgatory when I'd been here before.

"You shouldn't be here, Devi," said Clover. "You're not strong enough to defeat him."

"Who, Harvey? I'm not here for him. I'm here to wipe out what's left of Lythocrax."

Her expression went still. "Lythocrax isn't here."

"He survived, and part of him is here. In the demon-glass." I looked down at the barren ground, then up at the sheer face of the prison. "Is there anyone else in there?"

"In the jail? Yes, they have other prisoners here. I can't get out. The place is made of—"

"Demonglass." The bars gleamed with it, set between the stone. "Oh, damn. I'm sorry."

I thought you had a plan. I'd honestly thought she'd come here with a strategy. Not to mention, if anyone had known Lythocrax had survived, I would have put her top of the list. But then again, he'd duped the best of us.

"Lythocrax shouldn't be alive," she said. "But if he is—it explains why I've seen no signs of the Divine Agents."

"None at all?" I drew in a breath and told her what we'd found last night—and the impossible challenge now facing us.

She watched me, her face impassive, as I talked.

"I came here because part of him must be here, with Harvey," I explained. "I need to destroy every piece of him, to stop him from reviving. It'd help to know how to destroy his demonglass, too."

Clover leaned forwards, her reflection rippling oddly in the glass bars. "I wish I knew where he might be, but Devi, if you go up against the angel as you are now, you'll lose. If it was Lythocrax, it should have been impossible for him to revive Harvey as an angel."

I shook my head. "This is Lythocrax we're talking about. He fell on purpose and brought his divine magic with him. Anyway, he's going to be reborn right on top of Haven City tomorrow night unless I find a way to destroy five oversized demonglass sources, preferably without robbing Casthus in the process."

Her mouth pinched. "If you confront the shadow arch-demon, he'll likely retaliate by attacking Earth."

"No shit," I said. "Lythocrax's strategy seems to be to force *me* to destroy the world. He booby-trapped my demonglass. And now he's *inside* the stuff, and if I can't destroy it, he's going to turn the whole of Haven City into a pentagram. The celestials are planning an evacuation, but that won't stop him. Please tell me you have a clue, because I'm all out."

She gave me a long look. "I'll think about it, Devi, but —you shouldn't be here."

"It seems awfully quiet. Aren't they guarding you?"

"They don't need to," she said. "My power is limited, and the intention is for me to die here or serve them. The angel locked me up days ago."

I swallowed, hopelessness rising within me. "I wish I could break you out, but you know. I can't destroy demonglass."

I leaned forwards anyway, resting my hands against the glass bars. My left hand tingled, and I pulled back, frowning. The glass *felt* different to the source Lythocrax had infected, purer somehow. Brighter. So was Clover—a faint glow surrounding her body. I was sure she had more power left than she let on, but for whatever reason, she refused to use it to break out.

"Please," I whispered. "Tell me how to destroy the glass. Casthus isn't unique, is he? Can't I find someone else with similar magic?"

"There may be a way," she said. "Devi, your own demon magic comes from demonglass, does it not? But you're not on his level."

"Tell me something I don't know."

"I've often wondered, Devi, if you can take any power into that mark of yours. It reminds me of something... I'm sure I've encountered something similar before."

"In your past life? Would be nice if you remembered it."

"Yes," she said. "It would. However, I'm certain that if you managed to destroy him once, you can destroy his demonglass using his own power against him."

"Already tried that. Didn't work. But—I'm Grade

Three, on a demon level. Do you think that if I upgraded to Grade Four, I might be able to? That's still nowhere near arch-demon level…"

But in the heat of battle, the Devi clone had shattered under my hands. If I upgraded—tapped into that vast power myself—maybe I'd stand a chance. He'd made me with that power. I *should* be able to turn it against him.

"Tell me how it's possible to upgrade," I said to Clover. "Do you know? There isn't a demonic equivalent to Purgatory, is there?"

"This is the entry point to the heavens," she said. "The demonic equivalent is the gates of hell. You learned of that realm in your training."

I pressed a hand to my forehead. "Of course I did."

The gate that led to the seven hells. It was a realm all on its own, and part of the upper-level celestials' training took place there. Just like Purgatory.

"Hell's gate is the place Divinities are sent when they fall," Clover said. "If you create a portal, I have power enough to send you there… but I can't promise the demons there will help you."

"Figures," I said, my heartbeat kick-starting again. I remembered all too clearly how the fallen angel who'd upgraded my celestial magic had taunted and tricked me… and offered me a favour for succeeding.

The favour I'd asked for had been Lythocrax's name. A name alone couldn't destroy the glass, but if I asked for direct advice, maybe I'd learn something useful.

Or maybe the demons would smite me on the spot.

I'd failed more than I'd succeeded lately. And I might not get a second chance this time. Even if I upgraded my demon magic, I'd be Grade Four, which wouldn't hold a candle to an arch-demon. But Clover was right—my own demon magic linked to the glass. Lythocrax had made me, and he'd also given me all the tools I needed to win this.

I burned five points of a pentagram into the ground, and stepped into the centre. "I'm ready."

Clover's magic hummed through the demonglass, into me. There was a flash of light, and the world faded out.

———

I stumbled forwards on bare ground, blinking at a red sky almost identical to the realm I'd just left. All I could see was an expanse of rocky ground extending all around me for miles.

I'd come this far. Nothing to do but walk.

Within a few minutes, the shimmering on the horizon resolved into a shape that resembled a set of gates, stretching between two high cliffs. Hell's gates. It didn't look like any Divinities had fallen recently, judging by the bare, empty landscape. Lythocrax had been here, too, even if he'd since ended up stuck on his own realm, unable to go into the other hells. *Just as long as he hasn't been here recently...*

"State your purpose, human, or die," said a voice.

16

I turned on the spot, my skin prickling, but I didn't see the speaker. Clouds rolled in overhead, turning to smoke on ground level. Thick, white smoke masked my surroundings, wrapping around me.

"Who are you?" I asked, realising that the speaker had addressed me in Higher Chthonic. The language of Pandemonium.

A current of air stirred the smoke and ruffled the otherwise bare ground. Then, a male figure descended before me. Dark feathery wings sprouted from his shoulders, the same colour as the armoured clothes he wore. He looked maybe my age, but I'd bet he was centuries old. Must be a fallen angel. Like the one in Purgatory who'd upgraded my celestial powers.

"Not going to give me a name? Mine's Devi," I said. "I'm a human, marked by an arch-demon, and I'm here to ask how to upgrade to Grade Four level. I'm guessing that type of thing happens here?"

He looked down at me, hovering a few metres above

the ground. "A human cannot become one of us. We are not celestials, like you. I see your aura."

"It's half light, half dark," I said. "The light side hasn't done much for me, so I'm picking the dark. I'm told it's possible to upgrade my demon magic. I've done so already—twice."

"Our magic does not work like yours, celestial."

"Try me." Shadows flowed to my right hand at my command. "If it wasn't possible to upgrade, then this mark wouldn't exist."

His eyes glowed faintly as he looked at the shadows in my hand, and a smile curled his lip. "Right you are, Celestial Devina Lawson… but you're in the domain of the demons. We make the rules. And if you take on a trial, you may live to regret that choice."

"How'd you know my—" No shit, Devi. "You're with the Divine—"

The fallen angel smiled, and his wings beat, carrying him out of reach of my magic.

The fog shifted, and I lunged back, just in time. Three roak demons, horned and deadly, appeared where I'd been standing, spear-sharp horns stabbing at the air. Their main method of attack involved impaling their prey on their horns. Damn, that would have hurt.

I jumped into the air as my celestial speed kicked in, and I landed on my feet at a safe distance from the demons. I called my celestial power, but my left hand burned with sudden pain, forcing me to dive to the side as one of the demons charged. The beast collided with its neighbour instead, and the two of them fell into a heap. They might be big, but they weren't bright. Problem: my left hand felt like it was on fire. I grimaced, grabbing for my celestial blade.

Another bolt of pain shot up my left arm to the elbow. *Something's wrong with my celestial mark.* Wincing, I rolled across the bare ground and was on my feet once more, using Nikolas's lightning attack to spear the demon in the head. I risked a glance at my left hand, and saw the celestial light had gone out.

Oh, *damn.* If this was a true test to upgrade my demon magic, I wouldn't be allowed to use my celestial power to win. Thanks for that one, fallen angel.

Fine with me. I had more than enough power stored in my demon mark to make these Grade One demons flee into whatever hell they'd come from. More lightning blazed from my palm, and each demon collapsed, turning to ashes.

Almost immediately, the next round of demons took their place. Venos demons spraying venom, web-spewing kerith demons like oversized spiders crossed with lizards, swarms of biter demons. The system exactly matched my celestial upgrading trial. Though I didn't see the fallen angel, I'd bet he was watching closely. I guess like all of Lythocrax's people, he hadn't been able to resist turning my suffering into a game. When I felled the vaug demon that came with the Grade Three testing, I stepped away from the body, my demon mark humming with power.

I'd beaten a Grade Three demon. That meant a Grade Four one was coming next.

Thump.

A tremor rocked the bare rocky ground.

Thump.

My heart caught in my throat, and dirt sprayed everywhere as a huge armoured body erupted from beneath the ground, its horned head swaying. A full-grown saphor demon.

The last time I'd faced a giant worm demon, it'd been a convincing fake. This one was the real deal. Its body was entirely covered in dark red spikes, sharp enough to gore a human with a single flick of its tail. Bristling spines extended down its back. Its mouth gaped, emitting a foul smell that made me cough and gag.

Holding my breath, I blasted the demon with lightning. My attack bounced off its armour, and its tail lashed up, out of the Earth. I leapt aside, aiming my next lightning blast for the demon's huge mouth. Teeth snapped—too many teeth to fit inside its mouth, rotting and falling out. I picked up speed, weaving in and out of its lashing tail. A blast of lightning from my palm knocked another tooth loose.

I aimed blast after blast at its open mouth, dodging its writhing, spiked body. Its spikes were rock solid but its teeth easily loosened, and black demon blood splattered the ground with each blast that reached its mark. In a lunge, it dived below the Earth, tail still thrashing.

I landed on my feet. "Get out and fight me, you coward!"

The beast's tail shot into the air. I caught it in my demon-marked hand, using it to launch myself off the ground. When the saphor demon's head reappeared, I landed on the brim of its mow and blasted magic right into its open mouth.

Blood and spikes flew everywhere as my attack blasted a hole through its head. The beast sagged, and I jumped out of range as it slammed back to Earth.

The fallen angel appeared above the dead demon, dark wings beating. "One more challenge awaits, Devina," he said, his voice echoing.

"What, I have to face you?" I asked. Did he know that the fallen angel who'd upgraded my celestial powers had tried to trick me by parading images of Rory in front of me? Had he planned something similarly sadistic? It wouldn't surprise me.

"Not quite." The winged man landed beside the fallen demon, and in a blaze, its corpse vanished from sight. "You have bested foes of all levels. But killing demons does not further your skill in using our magic."

He waved a hand. Two more angels appeared in the lingering fog, hauling a female human between them. Their silhouettes faded in and out of view, then solidified as they grew closer. When the two angels were directly in front of us, they let her go. The woman stumbled forwards, her hands chained together, her head down. Her blond hair was matted with blood.

Lydia.

"What the hell?" I stepped forwards, my heart sinking in my chest. "What's she doing here?"

"She's your final challenge," said the fallen angel. "If you fail, you'll lose your chance to upgrade your demon magic. If you win, you'll gain all the power you need to defeat your adversary."

"I won't fight one of my allies." How had they even brought her here? *Damn you, Lythocrax.* He must have guessed my plan. Again.

"It's simple, Devi," the angel said. "All you need to do to become a full demon… is kill a celestial."

A heartbeat passed. Lydia lifted her head, but didn't quite meet my eyes. My demon mark tingled, power humming within. I'd taken so much magic from all the demons I'd faced, striking down a celestial would be child's play.

"That's ridiculous," I said. "I'm not killing her. Nobody had to die in my celestial training."

"You conveniently forget you killed so many demons, do you?"

"Demons aren't—" I broke off. "You're just screwing with me on purpose, aren't you? Did Lythocrax think it was funny?"

"I imagine a large number of the demons you've killed would be interested to see how you'd react to this particular dilemma, Devina."

"Get fucked," I said. "Lydia has nothing to do with this. I won't kill her for your entertainment."

"The rules are rules," he said. "If you want that demon mark of yours to reach its full potential, it must go up against a worthy celestial opponent of the same level as you and win."

"Lydia isn't Grade Four."

One of the angels reached and yanked Lydia's left sleeve up, exposing the blazing light of her mark. She'd upgraded. And whether this guy was working with Lythocrax or not, he'd picked someone who I didn't want to kill. At all.

"Look, say I do kill a celestial," I said. "The rule means any celestial, doesn't it? It doesn't have to be her." He was screwing with me on purpose, knowing that I wouldn't want to kill an innocent to save my own life.

But to save Earth?

My hands clenched. If I chose to destroy Lydia, I'd never be able to forgive myself for it.

"Go on," said the fallen angel. "As the Divine One told me, one must die so the other can live. Your life is worth more than hers in your own doctrine…"

One must die so the other can live… such are the rules of divine magic.

The same magic that had killed Rory.

My celestial hand ignited as my fury peaked. "You're lying to me. Rory didn't have to die. The Divine Agents killed him because they knew it would cause me to break ties with the guild. Or maybe they just wanted to break me. Whichever it is, I didn't kill Rory myself."

"Yes, you did, Devi." The angel gave me a smile. "It was your demon magic his celestial power reacted to. When you returned from that realm, you were reborn, and you sealed his fate as well as your own."

"Who told you that, Lythocrax?" My throat was dry, my heart pounding. "It's a lie. Every word of it. Just like everything else he says."

Isn't it?

The two angels yanked Lydia's shoulders, forcing her upright, and she screamed. Their hands lit up with infernal light. The message was clear—kill her, or they'd do so for me.

"I'll even make it easier for you to finish her off," the leading angel said, raising his own hand.

"Actually, it makes it easier for me to finish *you* off." I lunged at the angel, blasting him with celestial power. He dodged, his mouth twisting with anger, but my second attack reached its mark. He recoiled with a snarl, my infernal blast singeing the edge of his wing.

At the same time, Lydia twisted around, hitting one of the angels over the head with her cuffed hands. She leapt, using her celestial speed, and kicked the second one in the head. He keeled over, knocked out cold.

"Great job," I called to her, and sucker-punched the leading angel in the face.

Hitting an angel hurt as much as hitting a human, but damn, it felt good. The fallen angel swore, his mouth bleeding gold, and struck me in the chest. I tumbled head over heels, my demon mark blazing with fire, and took aim at the last angel beside Lydia. The angel screamed, ducking out of reach of my magic.

Behind me, the leading angel roared in fury. Power blasted from his hands, and the ground trembled as his two fellow angels were flung off their feet.

I swore, throwing myself flat to avoid the force of his attack. "Don't you care about hitting your allies?"

The fallen angel leapt into the sky, wings beating, forcing me to flatten my body against the ground. When I jumped to my feet, he had Lydia in his grip, his arm around her throat.

"Let her go," I warned.

"You failed the test," he said, and tightened his grip.

Infernal flames rose to engulf her body. Lydia didn't even have time to scream before the fire burned out the light in her eyes, and she went limp.

I let out a hoarse scream of fury as Lydia's dead body slipped from the angel's hands.

"Get out of this realm, Devi, or you'll be next."

I ran at him, but light flared around my feet, swallowing me up.

————

The next thing I knew, I lay outside Purgatory's jail, in the same position where I'd vanished. The pentagram was where I'd left it, and Clover watched me from the window of the prison, the demonglass bars reflecting her shining aura.

"Devi!" said Clover. "Did you succeed?"

I shook my head. "No, he killed—" I broke off, my eyes stinging. *Dammit.* Lydia hadn't deserved to die in a fallen angel's twisted game.

A growl at my shoulder made me spin on the spot. A demon stood in the portal to Babylon I'd left behind, its teeth dripping drool onto the barren ground.

"I wouldn't," I told it. "I'm not in a generous mood."

My hand ignited with white light, telling me my celestial power was back as though it'd never left—but I'd still failed the test. I snarled, blasting the demon into pieces. Ashes engulfed its body, leaving emptiness behind.

I'd lost my chance. There was no way I'd ever be able to upgrade my demon magic now. Lythocrax had seen my decision coming. He'd known I'd try to give my demonic power a boost in order to stand a fighting chance of wiping out that demonglass before he could be reborn.

"Is there... is there another way?" I whispered to Clover.

"Not to my knowledge, Devi... I'm sorry."

Anger ignited, at the demons and angels both. With a snarl, I kicked the barren Earth and stormed back into the pentagram. Who knew, maybe the shadow arch-demon was feeling reasonable today.

The portal to Babylon swallowed me up, banishing

Clover's shout of warning. In an instant, I landed back in the canyon where the other side of the portal had been set up.

Blood streaked the ground on either side of the pentagram. Thick black streaks of demon blood, but not just that.

No. Divinities... no.

Human or warlock blood stained the cliff's side, as though someone had been dealt a terrible wound. And there was no sign of Nikolas.

"No," I whispered. "Tell me he didn't."

Shadowy magic brushed my hand. I jumped, scanning the sky, but he wasn't there. Merely the trace of him.

Casthus had caught Nikolas.

17

<hr>

Shuffling noises and growls came from the clifftop. I looked up, seeing dark shapes moving above. Tensing, I ignited my celestial hand and jumped, using my celestial speed to propel myself out of reach of the biter demons' snapping teeth. A familiar stance took hold as my instincts kicked in, putting my growing panic over Nikolas momentarily on hold.

I summoned my blade and slashed through the nearest biter demon, severing its head, and spun on the spot to intercept another. The blood on the cliff had drawn them here. I'd bet Casthus had left it there on purpose.

Damn him.

A huge spiny demon with porcupine-like spikes appeared over the cliff's edge, its teeth bared. The leader of the biter demons lunged, batting at me with paw-like hands. I dodged easily, my blade severing its head. An impatient snarl tore from my lungs and I raised my blade at the remaining demons. "Get out or die."

The survivors fled, leaving bloodstains on the remains

of the pentagram, but my rage remained undiminished. If I blasted my celestial power to the heavens, Casthus would spot me instantly. I was miles from the castle. I'd never be able to sneak in there without him spotting me, and a direct confrontation would be a suicide mission.

I can't leave here without Nikolas.

More growling noises came from close by, and I swore under my breath, spotting another group of biter demons in the distance. Now I understood why Zadok had lived in an impenetrable demonglass tower. Everything out here wanted to eat me alive.

Hands grabbed me from behind. I struggled, twisting on the spot to access my blade.

"It's me, Devi," Rachel hissed in my ear. "We need to get out of here."

She released me, and I spun around. Fiona stood at her side, her eyes wide and her face pale under the luminous moon. "Devi—I'm sorry."

I could hardly speak. "Did he really take—?" I pointed at the distant dark shape of the castle with my blade.

Fiona nodded, biting her lip. "We had to hide. He would have killed us otherwise. He has his bat demons flying around looking for trespassers."

It's my fault. I should have known Casthus wouldn't leave his territory unwatched. Not after I'd stolen the fallen from him.

"We have to go," Rachel said. "Before he comes back."

"I can't leave him here." But I knew I'd lost. I didn't have the resources to mount a rescue mission. I was dead the instant I walked in there. To beat the arch-demon, I'd need to use my brain, not my blade.

Rachel and Fiona all but dragged me through the

canyon to the place where they'd left the pentagram Nikolas had set up while I'd been gone.

We reappeared in Nikolas's living room, where the full impact of my failure hit me like a freight train. I swore loudly at the ceiling, not much caring if anyone heard, and sank to my knees.

Lythocrax wanted this. He'd wanted me to make an enemy of the shadow arch-demon. I wished I'd opened a door to Purgatory from Pandemonium after all, but who knew what Lythocrax would have done with an entire palace of demonglass? There was no way to get out of this without sacrificing lives. Humans, demons, angels and otherwise.

I won't let Nikolas be one of them.

"What happened out there?" Fiona asked, her voice soft.

I lifted my head. "I failed the test. I tried to upgrade my demon magic—Clover implied that was the only way I could destroy the demonglass without borrowing Casthus's power—but the dickhead in charge of the testing forced me to kill an innocent celestial in order to upgrade."

Fiona clapped her hands to her mouth. "Did you—?"

"What do you take me for? Of course I didn't. I tried to kill *him,* and he kicked me out. And then I got back to Babylon and found out Casthus stole his son back. So we're in twice the amount of crap as before."

The door rattled as someone knocked on it. Oh, today just got better and better.

"Make that three times as much," said Rachel. "Uh, I don't think the warlocks bought Niko's story about him being away on business for his first day as the warlocks' leader."

The knocks grew louder. Fiona winced. "Can't you fob them off with an excuse? Say he's busy with important nether realm business?"

"They don't trust a word I say." My nails bit into my palms. "Maybe I'll scare them off. We *have* to get Nikolas back, and I'd rather not get torn to pieces by angry warlocks before we can think of a plan."

"I don't think scaring them will do us any favours," said Rachel.

"They think he abandoned them," I said. "It's hardly worse. I can't exactly tell them the shadow arch-demon kidnapped him, can I? They'd elect a new leader by the week's end and free Talon and his dickhead friends from jail."

"Can't you transform into Nikolas with that arch-demon's magic?" said Fiona.

"You're seriously overestimating my acting skills," I said. "I'll go and get rid of them."

I marched to the door, too furious over my failure to care when the three warlocks on the doorstep shrank away from my glowing hands.

"Nikolas is at an urgent meeting with the shadow arch-demon," I told them. "If you want him to help you, go in there and ask Casthus why your business is more important than the nether realms."

The warlocks looked at one another, and I let the glow on my hands brighten.

"If you'd prefer to wait for him to return, I'm in the middle of an experiment, and I wouldn't mind having a few volunteers." I gave a manic grin, my hands gleaming.

This time they backed off.

"Never mind," one of them muttered. "Tell us when he's back."

I closed the door behind them as they walked away. "Is it bad that I kind of wanted to throw them into Babylon as bait?"

"Nope," said Rachel. "They're whining about unimportant council crap and have been driving us both out of our skulls for a week. I'm pretty sure Niko is gonna appoint me as his assistant, but—"

"We have to rescue him first." I turned my back on the door and stalked into the living room.

"Let me guess," Fiona said. "You have a wild and risky plan?"

"I do, but it's a long shot," I said. "There's *one* person who knows the castle as well as his brother does, but considering Casthus nearly burned him alive last time they saw one another, Zadok might not want to volunteer to help."

Rachel pulled a face. "I wish you weren't right, but I bet Zad does know how to get in and out of the castle without being detected."

"The shadow arch-demon will be expecting us, won't he?" said Fiona.

"No way around that," I said. "All we can do is outsmart him or be really fast."

He already had Nikolas. I wouldn't let him take the others, too.

I set up the pentagram, not bothering to do any fancy rituals this time. I didn't have time to play verbal tennis: I'd walk right into Zadok's palace and make him listen.

Fiona stepped up beside me. "Ready?"

"Fiona, I don't think Zadok wants you to come into his palace."

"What, you think he'll throw me out a window?" She set her jaw. "He can just try. Devi, there are demonic assassins after you and Lythocrax will do *anything* to stop you from getting around his plan to revive himself. I'm not leaving your side."

"Likewise," Rachel put in.

I sighed. "Don't make me regret this. And don't forget Zadok is an unstable element, too. For all we know, Lythocrax got to him as well."

I couldn't believe I was depending on Nikolas's unreliable brother to save his neck. Especially as he had very good reason to want to avoid his father. No demigod could outdo an arch-demon. But if anyone was slippery enough to know a way into the castle to get Nikolas away without being caught, it was Zadok.

I walked into the pentagram and landed in Pandemonium's throne room again, stepping out of one of the pillars. Zadok turned on the spot, his brows rising in apparent delight.

"Zadok," I said. "I need your help."

"Any reason you've brought an entourage?" He eyed Rachel and Fiona behind me. "I take it your quest on Babylon didn't go according to plan?"

"Casthus took Nikolas prisoner while I was in Purgatory." No need to mention my little excursion.

"Dearest Devi, please come and talk to me alone. I'd prefer not to discuss delicate matters in front of the mortals."

"I'm mortal," I pointed out. "So are you."

"No deal." He stepped towards a door at the back, between two pillars. "Talk to me alone, or not at all."

I rolled my eyes. "Fine. Guys, wait for me here. Zadok, if you harm them, then I'll make you wish Casthus had taken you instead."

"That won't be necessary," he said.

I shot Fiona and Rachel an apologetic look as I walked after Zadok, hoping he didn't plan to set his demons against us. The last time he'd seen Fiona, he'd wanted to recruit her, not harm her. Besides, it wasn't like they were incapable of defending themselves.

Zadok pushed the heavy gold door open, revealing... a laboratory.

I blinked in surprise. While the hall looked more or less the same as it had when Themedes had owned the place, and then the vampire king, this was new. It was like Zadok had transplanted his lab from Babylon here in its entirety, demonic equipment and tools included.

"Wow," I said. "Did you have someone sneak all your equipment over here before or after you sent Abyss packing?"

"Before, naturally," he said, picking up some pieces of metal and moving them around the heavy wooden desk. Multiple half-finished contraptions filled the available space. I couldn't tell if they were decorations or torture instruments. "I initially set up a safe house to store my possessions and some of my army until I was able to take control. I planned to stay here long-term, after all." He moved a huge sheet of a rippling luminous metal behind the table. Where had I seen it before? *Oh. The pentagram.* He'd once made a pentagram which enabled the person who used it to summon their target anywhere they liked. Including another dimension.

"You planned this takeover well," I said. "So, I assume you have just as elaborate a plan to get back into the castle on Babylon, right?"

He finished placing the metal on the floor. "Not at the present moment, no."

"Come on," I said. "I know you."

He shook his head. "Do you, Devi? I think not. I have no intention of provoking my father. I was forced into doing so before, and I'd prefer not to repeat the experience."

"I don't need you to actually go into the castle," I said, abandoning all pretence. "Is there a way to get Nikolas out? I can get back to Earth from any dimension if need be. You've had more experience dealing with Casthus than I have."

"I suppose I have," he said, with a casual shrug. "Not with being his prisoner, I have to say. I assume his death will be quick."

I seized a hunk of metal from the desk and threw it at his head. Zadok dodged, his mouth curving in a scowl. "That wasn't necessary, Devi."

"He's your brother!" I snapped. "I don't care how many years the two of you have spent trying to do one another in, he'd come for you if you were captured. He would. I'm not even asking you to show up in person."

"No, you're asking for the impossible. I have no way of knowing what changes my father has made to the castle since I was last there, let alone what trap he might have devised to hold my brother. Unlike him, I don't have his convenient ability to quickly travel between realms, though I'm sure Casthus locked that down first."

Damn. He was probably right. "You know him, though. The shadow arch-demon. You must know how he thinks."

"Arch-demons are largely incomprehensible even to us, Devi. You should know that."

"He's your father. He created the place, for crying out loud. And you've escaped Nikolas's attempts to lock you up in the tower a thousand times."

He tilted his head. "I suppose I have. But the answer's still no."

"Look, Zadok. The enemy is going to destroy Haven City tomorrow. You'll be next. I bet even your demonglass palace can't keep out rogue angels."

"I'm prepared, as is the rest of my army, for any number of attacks on the palace, Devi. They won't catch us unawares."

"Dammit, Zadok," I said. "I don't know what game you're playing, but—"

"You know perfectly well what game I'm playing. It's the same one every demon has played for millennia."

"What, the one where you betray, kill, conquer and destroy everything?"

"I suppose that's one way of putting it."

I released a frustrated noise. "Your brother's life is in danger. I'm going to go out on a limb and assume that you actually have a way to beat the shadow demon here somewhere. Do you?"

"I'm not interested in open conflict at this particular moment, Devi. I'd prefer to issue a challenge in my own time.'

"Look, your brother—"

"Is a bloody fool, and far too human to survive in our realms for long."

"He's a better person than you."

"Ouch," he said, mockingly. "As a matter of fact, I have several strategies, none of which involve suicidal rescue missions. I'm interested to hear your theory about these angelic traitors coming here, though. What makes you think they're formidable enough to overcome my father?"

Damn him. "Fine," I said through gritted teeth. "I will enlighten you on the nature of the overpowered fuckers coming to conquer the netherworld, if you agree to help me free your brother. Deal?"

"Tell me first," he said. "You're asking me to put my life at risk, and I value it highly. More to the point, if my father decides to declare war on me as a side effect, then you're putting this realm in as much danger as any. Unlike you, I won't let it be collateral damage."

"I opened the way into Purgatory on Babylon to avoid you and your followers being collateral damage, dickhead," I said. "But fine, whatever. I'd be prepared for the possibility of your people working with Lythocrax either way."

Zadok stepped towards me, his expression cool. "The arch-demon is dead, you told me. You killed him."

"I thought I did," I said. "Not only is he still alive—in a manner of speaking—he killed the angels on Purgatory and is now in possession of a rogue army of angels, fallen or otherwise. He's an arch-demon of creation, the only one of his kind."

"An arch-demon of creation?" he repeated. "This is the demon who marked you, correct?"

"Yep," I said. "He tied his soul to the demonglass he

smuggled from this realm, the same way a saphor demon can latch onto a human. His magic comes from demonglass, and he has five pieces all around Haven City. The moment he turns it into a pentagram, he'll be revived, and a portal will open on top of the city."

He stilled. "That's not possible. To make a portal that size, he'd need—"

"An angelic army? He has one." I gave him a level stare. "I went to Purgatory to try to stop him, but—"

"But you failed and let my brother get captured by our father instead," he said. "Interesting. So this divine conspiracy is a result of your meddling, is it?"

I glared at him. "I didn't ask to be marked. You were partly responsible for backing me into a corner and forcing me to go directly to Lythocrax for help when you let Abyss and the vampire king take over your realm. It was Lythocrax who sent them. He's been playing on both sides longer than I've been alive. Even Azurial played into his hands, though it was the vampire king who told *him* what to do. The vampire king was marked by Lythocrax, too. See where I'm going with this?"

"Every bad thing that's happened in the last year is down to a single divine rebel?" he asked. "That seems unlikely."

"He didn't start it." I hadn't the faintest clue where the other Divine Agents might be, but Lythocrax hadn't started off working alone. Not that it really mattered at this point. "I might add that the only way I can destroy his demonglass is to borrow some of Casthus's power, which is what I was trying to avoid doing by going to Purgatory to begin with."

Zadok's mouth twisted. "Devi, I'll be blunt. The

shadow arch-demon can't be fooled, and if you thwart him again, you won't be as lucky as last time. The only way to get my brother back from him in one piece is to trade him something he wants very much, but there are very few things you can offer… except for the obvious."

"Earth." I clenched my fists. "Why is it always Earth?"

"Your realm is a free resource."

"Not to me, it isn't. Or the other seven billion people living on it. Besides, if I don't stop Lythocrax, it blows up in a day anyway."

"I thought not," said Zadok, moving behind the desk again. "As it happens, I'm working on something at the moment which *might* be able to circumvent my father's magic."

He lifted the metal sheet, revealing a rough framework set into place with five crude points.

"A pentagram," I said, a memory stirring. "That—"

"This is a version of the trap I used to draw Abyss out of the palace so I could kill her," he said. "It works, Devi, as you remember from when you used a similar device of mine on that abomination of a vampire king. And with your help, I may be able to make a version that contains enough power to imprison an arch-demon."

Damn. He'd remade his demon summoning device— the one Nikolas had taken from him and then later destroyed so it couldn't be used again. "Have you lost your wits? You know what happened last time."

"You need to trap a demon, don't you?"

"An *arch-demon,*" I corrected. "It's not the same. Besides, if we summon him, he'll break out in two seconds and kill everyone in sight. I suppose I can try to summon Nikolas instead, but for all I know, the castle is warded against summonings."

"You're not wrong," he said. "My father will doubtlessly have upped the defences. But if you were to summon Nikolas *within* the castle, he'd be drawn out of whatever trap my father has designed and the two of you would be able to leave the place—"

"Without him knowing," I finished. "Yeah, no. If Nikolas disappears from under his nose, he'll know I did it."

"Allow me to offer an alternative," said Zadok. "You can use this to summon *any* arch-demon. Including, say, an arch-demon who's hidden part of his essence in another source."

My gaze snapped to the metal sheet. "No way."

He smiled. "You'd be able to draw what's left of Lythocrax directly into my father's hands. I imagine it would result in him being swatted like an ant, if past experience serves, and if you're correct in assuming this arch-demon is powerless the way he is now."

"I wouldn't call being able to blow up Haven City on a whim 'powerless', Zadok. But would this work? For definite?"

"I thought you had more confidence," he said. "I assume you're willing to give your life to the cause, which is likely to be the case when my father is finished with the arch-demon. But if all else fails, this Lythocrax creature won't be reborn if he perishes in the pentagram."

I stared at him. "Would that really stop Lythocrax regenerating?"

Zadok gave a sigh, as though he thought I was too dense for words. "Clearly, Lythocrax relies on his source to stay alive. If you destroy his essence when it's imprisoned in a trap—without carrying any demonglass in your pockets for him to latch onto, I might add—then he'll likely expire permanently. It's up to you. Rescue my brother and leave our father to assume you were responsible—or give him a little distraction in the form of someone you'd like to expel from existence."

Was that possible? Lythocrax *was* weakened. And Zadok's trap had worked a little too well when we'd used it last time. Hell, Nikolas and I had even summoned the former inspector into it when a Grade Four demigod had masqueraded as him. Sure, Nikolas had since destroyed the pentagram, but if anyone could rebuild it, it was Zadok.

I can't believe I'm doing this.

So this was what my life had come to. Teaming up with a demigod, putting our brilliant minds together, and hoping we didn't kill everyone in the process.

18

As I'd predicted, both Rachel and Fiona reacted with horror at the very idea of using a penta-gram on an arch-demon.

"You want to summon Lythocrax on purpose?" asked Fiona.

"He's following me anyway," I pointed out. "Better he materialises in front of Casthus than on Earth."

"It's too risky," said Rachel. "Just summon Nikolas without Casthus seeing."

"I doubt he's that stupid," I said. "We flew miles from the castle and he still found us. If I use that pentagram, I need to make it count. And you know, we never did solve the issue of not being able to destroy the demonglass on Earth, let alone destroying what's left of Lythocrax. There's no other way."

Unless I got back to the gates of hell with the blood of a celestial on my hands, assuming the fallen angel didn't strike me dead on the spot. Besides, even if I reached the highest class of both celestial and demon, I'd still remain human.

"Done arguing?" asked Zadok. "It sounds like my brother doesn't have all day."

"Come on," I said to Rachel and Fiona. "Zadok, let the others help. It'll be quicker."

"It certainly won't." He eyed Fiona. "Are you offering your friend up after all?"

"She volunteered to help you of her own free will," I said. "You know, that thing demons conveniently seem to forget about as far as humans are concerned. Is this all a joke to you?"

"Certainly not," he said. "Don't be so touchy, Devi. I've wanted to work with you for a long time. Your skills are second to none."

"You nearly killed me the first time I tested one of my inventions on your face, if you remember."

He smirked. "Yes, I do remember. I feel I didn't give you enough credit for inventiveness at the time."

"You tried to kill me and Rachel for it. And you know, the reason I did it in the first place is because you trapped me in your shadow magic."

"I suppose I did," he said. "I was curious. I'd never met a celestial before, let alone one like you."

"I'm choosing to take that as a compliment." I turned to the others. "Let's do this."

Rachel caught my arm as he turned away. "You're sure he's not gonna sabotage you?"

"Never a hundred percent sure with Zadok, but you know, take what you can get. Besides, I'll know if he tries."

As we entered the lab, Zadok turned to face us. His gaze lingered on Fiona a second too long, and I gave him a warning glare. Then he nodded to Rachel, his jaw tense.

"I'll allow you access to my equipment if you don't break any of my possessions. I'm not good at sharing."

"No, you really aren't, are you?" I rolled my eyes and made for the sheet of luminous metal. "We won't break any of your toys, Zadok, don't worry."

"Fine. Devi, help me with the framework. Fiona, stand behind and maybe juggle some fireballs."

"Zadok."

"Fine, help Rachel fetch those props from the corner over there."

If I didn't know better, I'd say he was trying to get a rise out of me so I'd focus on building the pentagram rather than on the impending apocalypse and Nikolas's fate. Because if playing nice with Zadok ended up being for nothing, I'd be pissed beyond measure.

While Zadok hammered at the metal piece, I busied myself stirring ingredients for the base in a cauldron.

Rachel moved closer to the table. "How'd you make that armour?" she asked Zadok.

He scowled and didn't answer, continuing to hammer at the metal sheet. Now she mentioned it, it did seem odd that every inch of him was covered in armour despite the relative heat. Guess you couldn't be too careful on a demon realm.

"She's not trying to steal your ideas, she's just making conversation," I said.

"I *am* trying to steal his ideas," said Rachel. "I want a suit like that."

"None of the materials I used to make it are found on Earth," he said.

"Ooh," she said mockingly. "I know what I'm doing, you know. I made Devi's super-stealth boots."

"She did," I confirmed.

He grunted. "Get on with the job and stop bothering me."

"You don't have to try so hard," I muttered to him, planting the cauldron on the desk.

He tilted his head. "What?"

"To be a dick to her." He'd always claimed to dislike Rachel personally, but from the way he watched her wander around his lab, it couldn't be more obvious that she was the target of his jealousy, too. After all, Nikolas had chosen her as a sibling and hadn't tried to distance himself from her the way he had with Zadok. Sure, Zadok himself hadn't exactly helped the situation, but I'd wondered before if he'd lashed out at her not from malice, but because he envied her close relationship with his brother.

Still, unless he was putting on an act, he wasn't the same warlock who'd thrown me off a bridge rather than admit defeat. Didn't mean he'd actually come along to rescue Nikolas, but between the four of us, we might just have a chance at thwarting the shadow arch-demon.

If I had faith in anything, it was the power of invention. Even if Lythocrax had given that to me as well.

Then I'll use it to destroy him.

When the framework of the pentagram was in place, Zadok and I covered the frame in pieces of demonglass. I didn't like using the same substance that Lythocrax had used to hurt me, but Zadok seemed certain that it was the best source to summon the arch-demon. And keep him contained. The glass's glow made the pentagram look silver-white, more like a heavenly device than a demonic one. Like a miniature cage, fitted with the same magical expansion spell that Zadok had used on the last penta-gram he'd created. We'd fused his magic with mine, the power of shadows with light.

Almost like a fusion of heaven and hell.

"Are you sure it will hold an arch-demon?" I asked.

"Not quite yet." Zadok stood back to survey his work. "The shadow arch-demon can break demonglass because it's weaker than he is. I suspect the same must be true of Lythocrax. But if we melded it with the magic of an arch-demon, it'll be strong enough to hold him, and certainly Lythocrax."

I swore. "You're telling me this now? It's not like I have another arch-demon on standby."

"I was under the impression you had the power of one of them inside your demon mark."

"Abyss." If I gave up what was left of her power, I'd no longer have a shortcut to the demons' side. Not that I'd learned a ton from transforming into Lythocrax in the end. His mind was too scattered, too slippery, and besides, I already knew his weakness. "If this works, I'm perfectly content to let Lythocrax and Casthus destroy one another."

"They deserve nothing less," Zadok said.

"Never thought I'd agree with anything you said, but they do," said Rachel. "Let the arch-demons kill one another, then the rest of us get to live."

I doubted things would be that simple. Sure, Lythocrax was weakened and Casthus wasn't, but that didn't mean the arch-demon of creation didn't have another batch of tricks waiting in the wings. I never thought I'd find myself cheering for the shadow demon who'd stolen Nikolas's castle from him. Then again, we had maybe thirty hours until the end of the world anyway.

I stepped up to the table, gripped the pentagram's edges, and tapped into my demon magic. With the edges of the pentagram trapping any magic that went near, it had one place to go—into the glass. Demonic power made my right hand tremble as I held it still, echoing with remnants of the other magic I'd taken.

I gave it all. Abyss's power left me, flowing into the glass, followed by the other demonic magic I'd stored in there. I needed to make the device as strong as possible to stand a chance of keeping an arch-demon captive.

Even then, a thread of fear remained, telling me it wasn't enough. No man-or-demon-made device could permanently contain an arch-demon. And even if I summoned Lythocrax straight to Casthus, he might just kill us all anyway.

Nikolas's magic was the last to leave my hand. Shadow power, mingling with light as bright as heaven, flowed into the glass. The surface glowed, then dimmed as I turned off the switch on the back. *Here we go.*

Fiona and Rachel stood and watched me pick up the pentagram. It was deceptively lightweight.

"Wow," said Fiona. "That's—that's not like anything that's ever been created before, isn't it?"

"Don't write about it on DivinityWatch," I told her. "At least not until after we win."

She grinned. "Don't worry, I'll keep quiet."

"I'm going to the castle alone," I said. "Divinity knows how many traps Casthus might have set. I won't let any of you get caught. Even you, Zadok."

"I'm flattered that you'd even consider me, Devi, but I

have no intention of dealing with my father face to face at this particular moment in time."

"Figures," I said. "All right. I'm ready."

"Your great destiny awaits," he said.

"Fuck destiny," I said, with feeling. "The guild uses fate as a means of control. Hell does the same. I won't let that ever happen again."

A smile curled his lip. "We might make a demon out of you yet, Devi."

I *wasn't* ready. I was scared out of my wits. If our plan didn't work—the shadow arch-demon would be able to strike directly at me, and possibly take out Earth in the process. Lythocrax would be able to come back. And Nikolas would pay the price for my mistakes.

I'd never been inclined to make the sensible choice, but usually there was a failsafe. This time, nothing would stop the arch-demon from tearing me to shreds before I could utter a word. And then, Earth would be at his mercy.

I didn't operate on faith alone, but hope… as long as there was hope, I'd believe I could do this.

I held the pentagram in my hand. "Guys, I can take you back to Earth. I'll leave a portal open so you can get back into the palace if you need to, but there's a chance Casthus might trace the pentagram back here and guess you helped me."

"That's very trusting of you," said Zadok. "Maybe I don't want you walking into Babylon directly through my palace."

"It doesn't matter either way," I said. "Casthus and Lythocrax already know the way here."

"Then I'd advise you not to let either of them follow you."

"If they do, assume I'm already dead." I raised my right hand and burned a pentagram into the nearest pillar. "Rachel, Fiona, go back to Earth if I'm not back in… say half an hour. Whatever you do, don't follow me."

Fiona stepped up and hugged me, then Rachel did the same. "Kick both arch-demons into next week," Rachel said.

"You can do it," Fiona said.

"Can't make any promises, but I'll try."

I burned a second pentagram into the neighbouring pillar, and stepped through to Babylon.

The ground fell out from underneath me. I dropped like a stone, tumbling head over heels, too stunned to think. *Where'd the ground go?*

Rachel's boots cushioned my fall onto hard stone, in the middle of a circle of five burning lights.

Oh, *shit.* I wasn't the only one with a summoning pentagram. The shadow arch-demon must have had a similar idea. But his pentagram wasn't made out of demonglass. It was too dark to see much, but the five lights were odd and shimmering, and judging by the open space, I'd landed in the castle's entrance hall.

Nobody was within sight. Not even the arch-demon. I ran to the edge of the pentagram, trying to see the source of the burning lights, and a scream ripped through the air.

Nikolas.

"No." I threw down my own pentagram, though I

doubted I could summon anything within another penta-gram. Not like I had a choice, though. "I summon—"

Shadows blasted into me, knocking me onto my back on hard stone. "Come to rescue your lover, Devi?"

He was here.

Darkness fell, so complete it was like night itself had gained form and strode into the hall. Casthus's eyes burned like furnaces, his wings spread to the ceiling, his body cloaked in shadow. His aura took up twice the space —menacing, relentless, breath-stealing.

The shadow arch-demon reached out a hand and picked up the handmade pentagram. His shadowy magic lapped at my demon mark, which urged me to draw it in.

What the hell. I'm going to die anyway.

Shadows punched through me, and blood spurted from deep wounds in my chest. I groaned, and felt a familiar shadowy power flow into my demon mark, healing my injuries.

Nikolas...

Casthus"s burning eyes watched me. "Take it in. Take everything he has left."

"Damn... you," I gasped.

The shadows shifted aside, revealing Nikolas tied to a stone pillar by the wide staircase. His clothes were torn to rags. Two other bloodied warlocks stood beside him, holding crude weapons.

Casthus spoke. "I had them slaughter him a few times, but demigods are notoriously resilient."

I swallowed hard. "Let him go. He's your son, and the castle is his. He's allowed to travel here whenever he likes. I'm the one who trespassed."

"Both of you humiliated me and stole what was mine.

You will suffer for it." He gestured to one of the warlocks, who picked up a bucket. "Wake him up."

I ran forwards. "Stop!"

The warlock threw some sort of liquid at Nikolas's face. He roared in agony, twisting away, and went limp once again.

"Let. Him. Go." I stepped up to the pentagram's edge, only to collide with an invisible shield. The shadow arch-demon had stolen the device Zadok and I had made—my last hope of getting us out of here. "Don't you have an empire to run and a bunch of worlds to conquer?"

Nikolas struggled limply, and I gagged when I saw his face. His skin had melted off, revealing the bone and muscle beneath. What the hell had the warlock thrown at him?

"His weakness," Casthus said, from behind me. "A very rare substance, but one I made sure to have on hand. There's little other use for demigods. Too weak to rule, too powerful to be allowed to run around unchecked. I assumed both he and my other son would perish in weeks if I left them behind, but I underestimated that pathetic human family of his."

"Fuck you." I kicked helplessly at the pentagram's edge. I'd need to knock out the source powering it to escape, and the shimmering lights were out of my reach. "There's another arch-demon who wants to conquer the nether-world, and Nikolas and I are the only people with a slight chance of stopping the bastard. If you want to know anything about Lythocrax, the arch-demon of creation, you're more than welcome to ask me. But I guess I'm too much of a pathetic human to know information that might save your worthless life."

He didn't know Lythocrax—at least, he'd never mentioned him—but it was in Casthus's interests to protect his empire. If I convinced him that Lythocrax would be here next, I might be able to win us some time.

The shadow arch-demon paused before saying, "Your tenacity impresses me, if nothing else, Devi. I wonder how many times I need to kill *you* before you permanently leave this world?" He turned the handmade pentagram over in his hand. "Did you plan to trap me?"

"Not you," I said. "The arch-demon of creation, Lythocrax. He survived, and he wants to meet with you."

It was my last desperate hope. I didn't believe for a minute that Casthus would give a crap about Earth, but I never did find out if he and Lythocrax had ever met before. If I could somehow draw them together, maybe Nikolas and I would be able to escape.

"Arch-demon of creation?" he said. "There's no such thing."

"There is, and he's coming here," I said. "He can't die. He preserved his soul in demonglass, on Earth, and he'll be here next."

Casthus crossed the room in a wingbeat, grabbing Nikolas around the throat and giving him a shake. "Well? Is she speaking the truth."

"Yes," he rasped. "Yes, she is."

"And you decided to warn me out of the goodness of your heart?" queried the arch-demon.

"No, because your power destroys demonglass," I said. "Lythocrax tied his soul to it. I got the impression that's not a common ability, even in the nether realms."

The arch-demon's attention focused on me. "Do you

know what demonglass is, Devina? I assumed you did, but perhaps I was mistaken."

Now he wants a chat? "Yes, I do. Demonglass is from the nether realms, and it's the source of Lythocrax's power."

"Very interesting," he said. "Maybe I shouldn't have been so quick to forgive you for ridding this realm of the fallen."

"What?" I blinked, startled. "What does that mean?"

"Maybe I will talk to this… Lythocrax, if that's what he calls himself," said Casthus. He held up the pentagram. "It always amazes me what humans devise to make up for their lack of power, as though they would ever be our equals."

Keep bashing humans. I don't care. He'd offered us a lifeline. If the two met face to face—if nothing else, Lythocrax would get one hell of a surprise. Unless he'd anticipated my plan, like he did everything else.

"I think I'll let you be the one to summon him, Devi," Casthus said, holding the pentagram out.

I hope he burns you alive. It was hard to say who I hated more, in this moment. Looking at Nikolas's ruined face made my heart twist.

I swallowed, closed my eyes, and told myself that I was doing this for both of us.

"I summon the arch-demon Lythocrax, otherwise known as—"

There was a flash of light, burning the backs of my eyelids. My eyes flew open. A glassy golden substance spread across the handmade pentagram's surface, and Casthus laid it on the floor. The golden substance rose into the air, solidifying into a sheet of glass. Within it, Lythocrax's face appeared in the glass. Smiling at me.

"Did you really think I could be contained, Devina?"

"Not me. Someone else wants to talk to you, and he's not playing nice."

The glassy form of Lythocrax turned slowly to face the huge, monstrous shadowy arch-demon.

Casthus gave him a long look. "So this is the form you take now?"

"A temporary one," said Lythocrax.

"You *know* one another?" I said disbelievingly. They both ignored me. Then it hit me—Casthus hadn't recognised Lythocrax's name, but it wasn't a stretch to imagine they might have known one another as Divinities.

"What argument do you have with the realm the divines call Earth?" queried Casthus. "It never held any interest for you before."

"None," Lythocrax growled. "I plan to recreate it once the celestials are razed from existence and an example is made of the one who defied me."

"This one?" Casthus stabbed at me with his shadowy magic. I jumped out of range, the edge of his pentagram pushing me back. Damn. I was still trapped. So much for sneakily freeing Nikolas while the arch-demons were squaring up to one another.

Lythocrax's voice grew louder. "If you rob me of the delight of killing her, Casthus, I will not rest until I have destroyed every inch of the empire you possess."

Whoa. If ever I had proof that his motives were entirely built around revenge on me... yet he didn't scare me. Not nearly as much as the shadowy monstrosity who held me captive.

Casthus looked down at him. "You have such strong feelings for a mortal? What did she do?"

Lythocrax's voice vibrated with fury as he spoke, making the glass tremble. "She destroyed my body, conquered my home dimension and infected it with abominations, stole my magic and obliterated my armies."

"Oh, come on, I did some good things, too," I said. "I saved millions of lives. I gave you a taste of your own power when you thoughtlessly handed it over me. I rescued the fallen. You've never done a decent thing in your centuries-long life, have you?"

"Decency is for the weak."

"That explains so much." I took a few steps backwards as Casthus turned his full attention on Lythocrax again. Nikolas still hadn't moved. He'd be healing, but since Casthus had hit him with his weakness, the process would be slower than usual. I wouldn't be able to get him out alone. Worse, the two warlocks who'd been torturing him seemed to have slipped away. Cowardly bastards.

"You seem a little less substantial than you once were," Casthus said to the other arch-demon. "Do you plan to conquer Earth in that state? I suppose you have much fewer of your resources than last time, though your old method of relying on mortals doesn't seem to have changed."

"How the hell do you two know one another?" I looked from the huge shadowy form of Casthus to the gleaming glass showing Lythocrax's glittering eyes. "As Divinities?"

"He can tell you himself," said Casthus. "If finishing Devina off yourself is so important to you, then I will offer her to you in trade. In exchange, I would prefer it if you would leave this world intact when you destroy Earth."

"How about not destroying Earth at all?" I said. "And for that matter, you can't trade me to him. I'm not yours."

"You will be," he said. "Otherwise, my son dies."

No.

"Devi…" Nikolas's head lifted a fraction.

"We had a deal," I snarled at Lythocrax. "You said two days!"

"One day, now, and the deal is still in place," he said. "I will accept your offer, shadow demon. The girl is mine. I will leave Babylon alone, since it has long fulfilled its purpose. I have to admit, I never expected to find you here on this dead-end of a world, Casthus."

"No?" said Casthus. "I suspected the divines were planning to make a move, but I never expected to see you again, much less as you are now."

"You're not seriously just handing me to him!" I yelled. "I thought you wanted to kill me. Or are you too much of a coward?" Goading him was my last shot. They'd trapped me. And how did they know one another if they'd both been in heaven at different times?

"You or him, Devi," Casthus said, giving Nikolas another shake with a shadowy hand. "I will send him back to Earth if you go. He's far too troublesome to keep around."

Damn him.

"Fine," I choked out. I'd have to find some other way to wipe out Lythocrax—and escaping from him seemed less impossible than escaping the shadow arch-demon's clutches.

One way or another, I will end this.

Casthus's aura surged black, my demon mark burned, and the pentagram swallowed me up.

19

I landed on hard stone, which tore the skin of my knees. Red sky, dead ground—and someone peering down at me. I jumped violently away from the other person who'd appeared in the pentagram next to me.

The creature looked human, but it was small, emaciated, weak. Like a fallen. But the eyes that stared out of his face were as furnace-bright as ever.

This was the part of him he left on Purgatory.

"Lythocrax?" I said.

"This is a temporary form," he said. "It won't be for long. You are mine now, Devi."

"You wish." My hands ignited, Casthus's power whispering to the surface. "You made a huge mistake bringing me here when I can overpower you so easily."

"But I'm not alone, Devi," he said.

Wings fluttered, and angels descended to surround me. Snowy white wings formed a blinding wall of light, and Harvey landed directly in front of me. My hands clenched.

"I will break you for what you did to me, Devi," he said.

"If you wanted to break me, you're too late." I gave Lythocrax a blistering glare. "I was broken long ago, and I'm never going to be afraid of you. You'll lose. I'll make sure of it."

Divine light dazzled my eyes, and agony ripped through my demon mark. The angels closed in, their hands glowing, burning me alive. *The mercy of angels indeed.*

I screamed, half in pain, half in anger, punching at anyone who came close, but there were too many of them. Too many fists striking me. I sucked in a breath, desperately clawing for whatever was left of my demon magic. I had to live through this, otherwise—

I can't let him win.

Blackness filled my vision. The darkness came and went, taking the pain along with it. I clung to life, breathing shallowly, my right hand a torrent of pain. Lights sparked before my eyes. The bright light of heaven… no. It was a lie.

Darkness turned to light once more, and I passed out.

———

When I next awoke, I lay on hard stone, curled in on myself, bright light prickling my eyelids. No pain. *I'd better not be dead.*

I opened my eyes a little. My body had healed, and the light…

Demonglass.

I forced my eyes open. I was in a cell like the one Clover had occupied the last time I'd been here. They hadn't finished me off. For some reason, Lythocrax had kept me alive.

A cough drew my attention to the neighbouring cell. Bars divided the two cells, made of demonglass. Another source of the shimmering light came from the window in the cell next to mine, where what passed for sunlight here peeked through the glowing golden bars. The dicks hadn't even given me a window. But the person in the cell next door… wasn't Clover.

The former Inspector Deacon sat against the wall, his eyes on his feet, his hair greyer than it'd been the last time I'd seen him. He was alive? Lythocrax hadn't killed him?

"We both die tomorrow, Devina Lawson." He spoke without looking at me.

"The whole of Earth does, too." I dragged myself into a sitting position. "I thought you died out here. The guild… well, I'd say they're going crazy looking for you, but I think Mrs Barrow's over her hysteria about that by now. If she has any sense, she's planning to evacuate the city."

Fiona had seemed confident that Faye could use DivinityWatch to mobilise people to evacuate, but Lythocrax must have prepared for that possibility. Worse, now the shadow arch-demon knew his plan, and was doubtlessly coming up with schemes of his own. I hardly believed he'd traded me away so easily. He must have decided my suffering would be worse at Lythocrax's hands than on Babylon. That, or he'd just wanted rid of me forever.

My demon marked hand tingled. Huh. They hadn't

removed my demon magic. I still had Casthus's power… and the bars were made of demonglass.

I grabbed the bar in my right hand, calling my demonic magic to the surface—but the shadows simply bounced off the bar. Climbing to my feet, I blasted more shadows at the bars, then tried my left hand. Celestial power was even less effective. Of course, it only burned out evil and sin, and even the inspector apparently didn't count. His aura was as squeaky clean as ever.

"It won't work." The former inspector sat upright against the wall, dignified even in imprisonment. "Devina, this building has been constructed using the same type of defences we use on our celestial cells. It is, after all, where we got the idea."

I ignored him and tried my demon mark again, but with no result. I'd been able to heal, but no magic would let me get out of here. Nikolas would live another day, but considering Earth was scheduled to explode tomorrow, he might have been better off staying on Babylon.

The inspector leaned forwards, his hands clasped against his knees. "Devina, you must know I had no intention of any of this happening."

"Being captured?" I shook my head. "Yeah, I can't say that was on my itinerary for today either. I sort of hoped I'd be saving the world."

Not watching it burn from afar. How much time had I lost? How many hours had burned to nothing while Lythocrax prepared to be reborn and bring Earth to ruin?

"Not that," said the inspector. "I meant to say I had no intention of allowing the guild to fall into chaos or myself to be captured at the crucial moment. I was misled into thinking the angels would help me here. But it was them. These Divine Agents."

I faked astonishment. "Not blaming me this time? Not saying I'm a corrupt influence on everyone and the Divine Agents were somehow spawned from every rule I've ever broken? I thought you were with them from the start."

"No..." He moved forward into the light. He looked tired. Resigned to his fate. "Never. I served only the guild."

"They got the guild a long time ago," I muttered. "They set us all up. I suppose you know it all now. Lythocrax... he was the one who wanted to destroy the guild. Him, and the other Divine Agents. Divinities."

"He is no Divinity," the inspector spat. "Never. He betrayed his brethren and the rest of his soldiers in the worst way."

"Yeah, sure." I was in too bad a mood to appreciate him railing against the demon who was actually responsible for this crap. Deacon's epiphany about the real nature of the war had come entirely too late. "We die tomorrow, he's reborn, and then... who even knows. Maybe he'll start a charity for starving orphans and surprise everyone. I'm not sure he even wants to destroy the guild, more replace it with his own nest of willing puppets."

Like Harvey. The idea of *him* being in charge was somehow worse than the inspector. And I could think of countless people I'd have been happier to spend my last hours alive bonding with rather than Inspector Deacon. I'd almost prefer Sammy Groves. Okay, maybe not, but still.

We die tomorrow. How time passed here, I didn't know, but the light coming in from the inspector's cell persisted.

Sunset, or sunrise? It didn't matter. Time was running out.

"I tried everything I could to stop hell from infiltrating the guild, Devi," he said. "I was just looking at the wrong target. By the time I got here, it was too late."

"I'm not going to forgive you, you know," I said. "I almost thought I'd find you here serving them. I mean, you've always hated me. You drove me away from the guild to begin with."

"I suppose I did. Your partner's death…"

"Was your fault. Yeah. And a dozen other people's. Including your own partner's. I know you did something to put Inspector Angler in the enemy's line of fire and then freaked out when he came back from the demon realm with an aura like mine."

He paused. "You aren't wrong."

"Honesty, now? Suppose neither of us has anything to lose."

It'd be the Divinities' last laugh if I had to spend my last moments alive with the person who'd ordered Rory's death. But I had little rage to spare for him, and despite everything he'd done, I'd still lay the blame solely on Lythocrax.

The inspector hesitated for a long moment. "I dismissed your report on the mission where your partner died, because I did know those demon eggs were planted at the scene. In the same way, they were on a dozen other missions in the same time frame. Most of those missions ended with fatalities, too."

"Why are you telling me this?" Did he want me to spend my last moments alive raging mad at him?

"The messages from heaven, such as I received them,

said that the Divinity who marked yourself and your partner had fallen, and that the mission was required as a test of your loyalty to heaven. I never questioned—"

I leaned back against the wall. "Of course you didn't. The directive came from heaven, after all."

"Devina," he said.

"You can call me Devi, you know. We're going to die either way." I stretched out against the wall, too exhausted for words. "So you dismissed my report because you didn't want anyone to find out you had him killed on heaven's orders."

"I was not aware of that at the time, Devi, believe it or not," he said. "And I did not dismiss your report out of malice. When I heard you survived the mission, I hoped that the same demons that took Kenneth hadn't found you, too. But I saw the mark on your aura even then. I took that as confirmation that the directive was right and that you would fall into hell's grip whether you stayed at the guild or not."

"You might have told me."

"What would that have achieved? I was never your favourite person, Devi, and you were in desperate search of a target to blame for his death."

"I already hated you. And the guild." I'd enjoyed killing demons, travelling on missions, taking every opportunity to spend time with Rory. I'd detested every other part of being a celestial soldier. "Because the guild doesn't give anyone the option to make something of their own life rather than following heaven's directive. That's why you're losing the war."

He didn't answer, and we fell into awkward silence for a bit. The light outside brightened, suggesting the sun was rising after all. A new day in Purgatory. My last day alive.

I rested my head against the wall and closed my eyes. "Wonderful. We've exhausted all other conversation topics. Unless you have any other scandalous confessions to make, aside from the gambling? More debauchery that nobody knew about? Slumming with Lucifer? Dancing with the devil on Babylon?" I winced as light pierced my eyelids. "Damn, that's bright. They don't do sunrises by halves here, do they?"

"It's not the sun."

I opened my eyes, frowning when I saw the inspector had moved so that he stood against the bars between our cells. He'd pressed something metallic and small against the stone wall, and beneath his fingers, the stone was eroding away.

"What is that?" I asked. "How did you—?"

"Harvey's people neglected to check if I brought any props," he said. "I can't do the same to the windows—they're doctored with something that repels magic—but I can blow a hole in the wall, given enough distance."

I frowned. "You don't know how to make an explosive."

"I thought you knew better than that, Devi. I once saw you blow a table to pieces with a few drops of ruith demon ichor."

"Oh yeah." I'd taken my own eyebrows off in the process. "I thought you were too busy yelling at me to care how I did it."

He pulled the metal device off the wall. Half the stone came along with it, leaving a gap wide enough for a person to crawl through. With a glance at my cell, he moved to the window, pressing something to the bars. "This is likely to react badly with the building's defences."

Smoke began to pour from the wall. "You're not wrong."

The inspector took a step back. A tremor ran through the floor. "Uh, Inspector. You might want to get out of the—"

The wall exploded. The inspector leapt through the gap between our cells, his body slamming into mine. The bars dividing the cells toppled over as their foundations fell to pieces. The inspector's weight pressed into me, forcing the breath from my lungs. I gasped, trying to shove him off me—then dampness soaked my hand. Blood.

Blinking dust from my eyes, I feebly shoved at the inspector again. He'd shielded me against the blast, but— that was a lot of blood. I inched upright, and he flopped over onto his back. Some of the bars were still in place, but others had broken loose, lying where they'd fallen like sharpened poles. Even the explosion couldn't destroy demonglass.

"Devi..." The inspector coughed feebly. His clothes were drenched in blood. A pole had impaled him through the back. "Please..."

He wouldn't survive. He was asking me to finish him off so he could die with dignity.

I leaned forwards and grabbed one of the demonglass bars, now unsupported by stone. Sharp enough to cut.

"Divinities have mercy on me," he gasped.

"Better hope they will." I slit his throat, swiftly, easily. His blood soaked my hands, and he was silent.

I climbed to my feet, stepped between the remaining

bars into his cell, and leapt out of the gap in the wall. The light was so bright, it hurt to look at. I turned around, seeing no signs of Clover. She must have been moved to another prison… or killed.

The pentagram was still there, though—the one that led to the gates of hell. My hand dripped with the inspector's blood. Celestial blood.

"All right, you bloodthirsty bastards. I met your requirement. He's dead. I killed a celestial."

My voice rang into the silence. I moved closer to the pentagram, wondering where Clover was. Maybe she was already dead.

The gates of hell were safer than here. The ground inside the pentagram was scorched slightly, as though I'd brought part of that realm back with me. Maybe I had. I still had its dust and dirt on my clothes, along with the dirt of Babylon and here. I didn't know if that would be enough, but anything was worth a shot at this point.

I stepped into the pentagram, and spoke. "I request entry to the gates to the netherworld to speak to the angels of hell." Like entering Purgatory, or any realm for that matter, the words didn't matter so much as the intention. "I request entry to upgrade my magic." Blood dripped from my hand as I clenched my fist around the demonglass bar. Demonglass was a source. Enough to power a portal. "I demand entry to the gates of hell."

There was a flash of light, and the barren landscape vanished. A moment later, the distant shape of hell's gates wavered before my eyes. "That's more like it. Hey, you feathery bastard, I met your requirements."

"Did you?"

In a beat of wings, the fallen angel landed in front of

me again. Or, beat of wing. One of them hung limply at his side, while the other was missing several handfuls of black feathers. His face was bruised, too.

"Yes, I did," I answered. My hands dripped with the inspector's blood. My body ached with exhaustion. I had less than twelve hours to get back to Earth in time to save it, and if the angel didn't upgrade my demon magic, I'd rip his remaining wing off.

"Get out," said the fallen angel.

"I met your requirement," I said. "We had a deal." I held up my right hand, which continued to drip blood. My demon mark hummed, reminding me I still held the demonglass bar, its sharp edge glittering. Reflecting my dark aura.

Hate simmered in the fallen angel's eyes. "You dare to have the audacity to claim a deal with me after you tried to take my life?"

"Working for Lythocrax is fun?" I eyed his battered wing. "I don't want to make a deal with you. You killed Lydia for no reason. But I earned the upgrade. If it's true that I have to kill a celestial to earn Grade Four demon magic, then I deserve it. I wouldn't have bothered coming back to this shithole if I didn't need that power. And you'll be in more trouble if I don't stop Lythocrax."

"You won't stop him," he said, his eyes glittering. "He slaughters angels for sport. You're a mere human."

"Trust me. I killed him once already. I'm telling the truth."

His jaw tensed. "You cannot upgrade your magic until you go into his own realm, celestial."

"And what then?" I asked. "I get a favour, right? In that case, I request my own demon name."

He gave me a long look with those fathoms-deep eyes. It struck me that he was fairly young, for an angel. And Lythocrax had crippled him.

"When you upgrade," he said, "you will be permitted to choose your own demon name. Once you do, the name is set, and cannot be used against you unless someone hears you speak the name aloud."

A demon name would prevent me from being summoned using my given name. It wouldn't save my neck if I walked onto an arch-demon's territory, but what the hell, maybe it'd be another layer of protection against Lythocrax. It made sense that if I picked the name and told nobody, then no one would be able to steal it from me unless they bribed or tortured me into telling them. Nobody had known Lythocrax's true name, after all.

"Get out, Devina Lawson, and never darken the gates of hell with your presence again."

I gripped the demonglass bar. "Fine with me."

Was there even any demonglass left on Lythocrax's realm? I shouldn't need a portal to travel there, not when it was the source of my own power. I raised the bar, seeing a city reflected crookedly in the glass. A city I knew.

Dusty ground replaced the gates of hell, a paler sky replaced the red one, and the distant form of a city came into focus. I'd expected more fanfare, but then again, I hadn't even noticed my demon power upgrade the last two times. I transferred the demonglass bar to my other hand and flipped my right wrist over. The demon mark had darkened, its lines spreading to cover my entire wrist, like it'd gained a life of its own. Lines crept to my elbow, like shadows, and darkness spread across its surface, swirling within, depthless, angry.

Grade Four demon power.

Clover had said it'd be enough to kill Lythocrax.

And I can choose a demon name.

"Shadow," I whispered, thinking of Nikolas. I needed to find him. Destroy the demonglass before Lythocrax did, and before he had the chance to be reborn.

20

I squinted into the distance. The blurred shapes resolved into buildings, the sky above them over-cast, almost black. I walked towards the city, curious despite myself. I hadn't come back to check up on the fallen since I'd left them here on Lythocrax's former world, not wanting to bring any more trouble on them. But it seemed awfully quiet.

"Devi," gasped a voice.

A head popped up from behind a rock. One of the fallen. Like the others, he was pale, his form skeletal, his aura the colour of a demon-infected wound.

"What are you doing out here?" I asked him.

"He… he came back."

My heart lurched. "Lythocrax did?" Oh, no. I should have known he wouldn't leave Purgatory without good reason.

"No… him." He pointed at the shadowy sky above the buildings, which cast them into darkness.

Wait. That wasn't a thundercloud.

Casthus.

My heart gave another jolt. "No." *No. Damn him.* He'd said he'd leave Earth alone… but hadn't said anything about the fallen. "How did he get here? This world was cut off from the other demon realms."

"He used a device to summon one of us."

"The pentagram." I never should have taken it near Casthus to begin with.

The fallen. This was his revenge on both me *and* Lythocrax. No wonder he'd let me go so easily. I was beginning to see where Zadok had got his cunning nature.

"Does he still plan to open a bridge?" I asked.

"Maybe." The fallen looked at me, his gaze dim. "With him here… I remember, Devi. It was the one who calls himself Lythocrax who abandoned us on Babylon."

I frowned. "What—he did? I thought he was lying. You mean when he was a Divinity?"

He'd been to Babylon before. Was that when he and Casthus had met?

The fallen pushed himself upright with his frail arms. "We were half angel, half celestial, chosen by the gods. There were some realms that used to be in harmony between both heaven and hell. Demons lived alongside celestials and warlocks and angels. Not unlike Earth, if it were a little more divine. One of those realms was Babylon."

I gaped at him. "Uh. I thought—damn, okay, that makes sense. Celestials and demons wiped one another out on that realm, right? And… and Lythocrax and Casthus were involved in the fighting."

So Lythocrax hadn't been talking complete nonsense

when he'd claimed the fallen were his own children after all.

"On Babylon, peace turned to destruction almost overnight," said the fallen. "An angel killed the demons, and hell retaliated in turn. Casthus claimed that realm for his own with the help of his demonic allies. And we were unable to die, and so we remained behind."

"Damn," I said. "So… Lythocrax—I suppose if he was still a Divinity, he just flew back to heaven. Babylon ended up a dead end… and he couldn't go back there even if he'd wanted to."

Or to Earth, for that matter. So to have his revenge on hell, he'd needed to fall.

"No," said Casthus. "He couldn't."

My blood iced over. The arch-demon's shadowy form blotted out the sky as he descended, hovering above me. I backed up, gripping the demonglass tight, but even my newly acquired magic was no match for his.

"I see you've managed to free yourself, Devi. And you're trespassing."

"This world doesn't belong to anyone but the fallen," I said, a tremor in my voice. "Can't you leave them in peace? They've done nothing to you."

"They did me a great deal of harm, once," he said, his dark wings beating.

"Oh. *Oh.* They fought against you in the war." No wonder he'd enslaved and tried to sacrifice them. "But I still I claimed them from you. I won."

"Now I've conquered this world, they are mine by default."

"You conniving bastard," I said. "Why bother letting me win, then? Or is this supposed to be fun, toying with people's lives? You and Lythocrax are as bad as each other. What do you want to do, create another bridge?"

"Not quite," he said. "Eventually, perhaps. Babylon wasn't the right timing. I thought someone was manipulating events, and I was right."

"You…" He'd guessed the Divine Agents were trying to manipulate him. So I'd had it right when I'd suspected he'd let me claim the fallen after all. "You can't go back on your word."

"Oh, can't I, Devi?" His aura grew, dark and endless, swamping the city. A threat. He'd kill them all if I acted against him, and as they couldn't die, they might well suffer forever.

I can't let him do it. But I couldn't leave Earth to Lythocrax's wrath, either. "Babylon… it wasn't always your domain, was it? It was him who wrecked it. Lythocrax, and his angelic army."

Seven hells. Clover had *told* me Babylon was the realm where she'd died and was reborn, and that it was the last realm to fall. She'd also said the celestials had made a deal with the angels in order to prevent any other realms from falling. As a result, the Divinities had left, leaving the fallen trapped and the world to turn to decay…

But the divines hadn't been true Divinities. Not all of them, anyway.

"The angelic snake hasn't changed with the centuries," Casthus said. "I knew him for a traitor long before I fell myself. It shouldn't have surprised me that he decided to try to bring down my empire."

I'd guessed right. *An angel killed the demons, and hell retaliated in turn.*

"But you won the war," I said. "Right? You killed the celestials, the angels… everyone."

"Yes, we did," he said. "My armies slaughtered heaven's warriors by turning their own weapons against them. The other arch-demons and I formed an alliance against heaven, but Babylon paid the price."

"The other arch-demons," I said. "Was one of them Themedes, by any chance?" Nikolas had told me they were allies, if not friends.

"Themedes was one of many demons who offered their help against heaven's abominations. He took a large share of the prize, which was his right."

"And you kept the fallen imprisoned after you won because you knew if they somehow turned into angels again, they'd beat you," I said.

"No, I kept them because they could not die, and I had to find a way to destroy them without inviting *him* back into my realm."

"You said, *so it is you,* when I beat you. Is that because you recognised his power in me?"

"You carry a bare fraction of his power," he growled. "The one who calls himself Lythocrax is the embodiment of heaven and hell, and you will lose this war, Devi."

"Wait, so you're not going to kill me yourself?"

His dark wings beat, the sky lightening as his aura drew in. "Why would I need to? One life means nothing in the battle of heaven and hell, Devi."

That's where you're wrong. One person could destroy an empire, or decide the outcome of a war.

But he'd given me an opening to leave. It was a mere few hours until Lythocrax made his dramatic rebirth. I had to use the magic I'd taken to destroy that demonglass.

Time to see if Clover was right.

I gripped the demonglass bar in my right hand, focusing as hard as I could on the image of Lythocrax's hateful face reflected in a sheet of demonglass trapped in a warehouse. With my power upgraded, new doors were open to me.

And like it or not, Lythocrax and I were bound.

Take me to his source. Take me to Lythocrax's source.

A flash of light engulfed me, and I landed hard, on my knees, on the warehouse floor.

Well, crap. It worked.

"Ow." My knees throbbed. My whole body ached, telling me I hadn't taken in nearly enough regenerative power. But my demon mark exuded smoke, as dark as night. I'd taken on some of Casthus's power.

I could destroy the demonglass, and Lythocrax's portal along with it.

Turning around, I faced the glass, trapped in the mechanism affixing it to the warehouse wall. Shadows wreathed my reflection. I'd never seen my aura like that before, and to be honest, it sort of freaked me out. I wasn't a shadow demon, right? Maybe my mark had taken my new name literally.

I transferred the demonglass bar to my left hand and pressed my right one to the glass. Casthus's power brimmed at the surface, and dark shapes appeared within the glass.

I jerked my hand back, my heart pounding. The source was active. Lythocrax had already turned it on, or one of his angels had. If I used demon power on it, it'd turn into a portal into hell there and then. *He planned this.*

Nice try. Lythocrax had *wanted* me to take the power.

On the off-chance that I survived, I'd be the one to bring about Earth's end.

It won't happen.

But… what was I supposed to do to the demonglass? I couldn't leave it here, not with hours at most until Lythocrax's rebirth. *Think, Devi.*

My left hand tingled, reminding me I still held the blood-stained demonglass bar. It glowed brighter than the source behind me. I raised the bar, frowning. Beneath the blood, it showed the image of Zadok's new palace, which he'd fashioned into the mirror of his old tower on Babylon.

When I'd first started to use demonglass, the tower had kept calling me back. Like part of me was bound to it… bound to the source.

Celestial light bloomed at the surface of my left hand, mingling with the glass's light. Bright… more like heaven's than hell's.

My armies slaughtered heaven's warriors by turning their own weapons against them, Casthus had said.

Babylon was last place heaven and hell had lived in harmony.

"Light and dark are both divine," I said, half to myself. My reflection was split. And so was the glass.

Demonglass wasn't hell's weapon. It was heaven's, too. *Light and dark are both divine.* The glass absorbed demonic magic… could it absorb heavenly magic, too? I'd used it as a shield against the clone he'd created. I'd made it into a weapon.

I passed the still-glowing bar to my right hand, and pressed my left palm to the sheer surface of the glass before me. In all this time, I'd never touched a piece of the source using my left hand. After all, it'd been my demon powers that enabled me to travel through the glass. I'd never thought it could possibly work with my divine magic as well.

Immediately, the glass's surface brightened, chasing away the shadows that darkened it. My celestial mark vibrated, glowing ever-brighter. *Is it taking in the power? Or cancelling it out?*

Celestial magic burned out anything demonic. That was the whole *point* of it.

I called the light to the surface of my left hand, and pushed it towards the glass. The shadowy shapes in the glass began to disappear. *It's working.*

Heaven burned out hell. Divine light destroyed demonic. And he'd burn along with them. He wouldn't rise.

You lose.

A scream of rage erupted from the glass.

"You were supposed to destroy it," Lythocrax howled, his eyes flickering in and out as the divine light burned the glass. "You were supposed to bring the shadow demon here... even your angel was fooled."

"Isn't it lucky I don't trust a word any demon says?" I continued to feed power into the glass, watching its glow brighten. The shadows faded, and divine light replaced them, bright as the bar in my hand.

I broke the connection and stepped back, watching for any traces of Lythocrax's presence. Then I pressed my left hand to the glass once again. Instead of the taint of demonic magic, heaven's light hummed against my hand. I'd burned him out—destroyed him.

And I'd do the same to his other sources.

I moved the bar to my other hand, my right palm brushing the glass. I'd already travelled further than ever before. With my power upgraded, I wouldn't fail.

I stepped through the demonglass, emerging into a basement. I hadn't the faintest clue where I was, but I'd found one of the other sources. I turned to the glass I'd stepped out of, seeing shadows blurring the light, just like the other source.

I pressed my left palm to the glass, and celestial light flowed from my hand. The mark was overflowing with magic. More than enough to cancel out Lythocrax's presence.

The shadows died out, leaving the glass bare, crystal clear. My body hummed with energy. I'd never felt so alive.

Once again, I stepped through the glass, willing it to take me to the third source. This one appeared to be inside a large, empty hall.

"I can still manifest, you foolish girl," Lythocrax rasped from the glass. "I cannot be destroyed."

"I beg to differ."

Once more, I lifted my left hand, and burned the demonic influence out of the glass. The shadows, and Lythocrax, disappeared, buried under gleaming light. *Three down, two to go.*

For the fourth time, I stepped through the glass, reappearing in a room with whitewashed walls and another sheet of demonglass.

"You seem so confident that those you care for are safe, Devi," Lythocrax said, his voice a grating whisper. "You haven't even checked on them since their return."

"Nice try, but you'll have to do better than that." I

raised my left hand, transferring celestial power into the glass. Lythocrax's eyes blinked, his mouth twisting.

"You're too late," he whispered. "I already transferred part of myself to Pandemonium."

"Like hell you did." I pushed more power into the glass —and it exploded.

21

I jumped clear of the blast, gripping the demonglass bar. Shards of glass cut into my skin, the bar falling from my hand as its light drew me in. I fell through the source and landed on my knees—and looked up to find myself surrounded by warlocks.

"Ah." I jumped to my feet, scattering pieces of broken glass. I'd fallen out of the fifth and final source, and by the look of things, the warlocks had got here first.

"Devi?" Nikolas strode to the front of the group, clad in battle gear, no longer weakened and bleeding. My heart lifted. His face had healed, and he looked as strong as ever.

"Thank the Divinities. Wait, don't thank them, they did fuck all." I rose to my feet shakily, looking at the other warlocks. "What are you all doing here?"

"Waiting for an attack," said Nikolas. "We found the other sources."

"I shut them down," I said. "Except one. He blew it up before I could shut it down. I don't know if it can still be turned into a portal or not, but I need to shut this one off, too."

"How did you shut it down?" he asked.

"I'll tell you later," I said, conscious of the curious warlocks watching me. "Everyone near that source needs to be evacuated—I don't know how far the explosion went. The room had white wallpaper."

"I know which source it was," he said, beckoning to another warlock. "Take a team to Southfield Avenue, but be careful. Devi will deactivate this source."

"Yep." Preferably without supervision. Not that it mattered if the warlocks knew demonglass was once divine, not when they had more important issues to deal with.

I reached for the glass sheet, pressing my left palm to it. Celestial light filled its surface, cancelling out the darkness. The warlocks were damned lucky nothing had materialised on top of them, but Lythocrax had intentionally blown up the other source. Had he been trying to kill me, or create a portal? I refused to believe he'd die so easily. Part of him—that shrunken, weakened form—still existed in Purgatory, after all.

The glass gleamed, overflowing with celestial power. Nikolas moved to my side, his own reflection flickering in the glass. Our shadowy auras merged, and I broke the connection, wrapping my arms tight around him.

"I'm so glad you're alive," I murmured into his shoulder.

"Likewise." He hugged me back. "That bastard Lythocrax has been taunting me through the glass ever since I found it, telling me you'd die today. I had to resort to begging the celestial guild to allow me access to Purgatory, but they couldn't get in."

"Still locked out?" I loosened my hold on him, frowning. "Lythocrax—part of him—is still there, but… shit. I have a lot to tell you."

"Start with that," said Nikolas, indicating the glass.

"I cancelled out the demon magic," I said to him. "It wasn't my demon magic I needed to upgrade at all—but I don't know if Lythocrax is still hiding in any of the other pieces of glass in the city. His real body is still on Purgatory, as far as I know. What happened here?"

"I should be asking you the same question," said Nikolas. "The shadow demon left me back on Earth yesterday, and I had no way to contact you. I thought you were on Pandemonium when he attacked it."

My heart dropped like a stone. "What? Casthus attacked Pandemonium? Or Lythocrax?"

"Lythocrax." He moved towards the other warlocks, who'd gathered near the room's exit, out of range of the demonglass's brightness. He gave them a brief order, then returned to me. "Can you transport us to the warlocks' headquarters? I moved Javos's remaining demonglass there. Lythocrax never touched it, and we have it locked up so none of those angels can get through it."

"Sure." I took his hand and pressed my right palm to the glass.

In a flash, we landed in a small room filled with boxes. The rumble of voices came from outside.

"I gathered the other warlocks here," Nikolas said. "I sent teams to watch all five sources, once we tracked them down. How did you use your celestial power on the glass?"

"It was never hell's weapon," I told him. "Demonglass used to belong to heaven, but hell stole it, and pieces were left behind on the demon realms when they drove Lythocrax and the other Divine Agents out of Babylon."

His eyes went wide. "What?"

I quickly ran through what I'd learned from both Lythocrax and Casthus about how Babylon's conflict had really gone down.

"Obviously, Casthus knew Lythocrax by another name at the time, so he didn't know who I was talking about at first," I explained. "And he knew the Divine Agents were plotting against him, but not their identities. That's why he let me take the fallen."

"And he let you escape, too?"

"I guess he did," I said. "He got his fallen back, which is what he wanted. And he asked Lythocrax to spare Babylon when he declares war. But—Pandemonium. Did he really attack the palace? Is Zadok—?"

"He's in there." Nikolas jerked his head in the direction of the noise. "He conveniently forgot to tell me he set up a portal here to escape through if his new home came under attack."

"You let him come to Earth?"

"It was that or allow him to die at Lythocrax's hands, and despite all he's done to me, I wasn't about to allow him to die unnecessarily."

"He helped us save you," I said. "You know—wait a moment. That pentagram must still be in Casthus's castle. That's how he got through to Lythocrax's realm. I didn't know the fallen could be summoned, but they're partly demonic, after all. This is my fault. I should have known he'd see that trick coming. I mean, Zadok *is* his son."

"You couldn't have known he planned to trade you away to Lythocrax as bait," Nikolas said. "So you didn't upgrade your demon magic?"

"I did," I said. "But I'm not sure what good it'll do now. Got a demon name, too… which means I can't be summoned against my will, as long as nobody else knows the name."

"Good," he murmured. "I'm glad."

I leaned close to him. "It's Shadow," I whispered. "My name. But as I said—I've no clue what the Grade Four version of my power can do. It's an unknown entity."

"Take my power and see." He reached for my right hand, and my demon mark tingled in response. Shadows swept my palm, and I jumped, accidentally firing off demonic lightning in the process. It bounced off the floor, burning a hole in the carpet.

"Oops."

"Devi…" He pointed to my shoulder.

I twisted my head to the side. Shadows cloaked me from behind. "Hey, that's new."

Nikolas moved behind me. "It's also wings. Were you thinking of wings?"

"No, but I like them. They look kinda like yours." I twitched my shoulder. Shadowy black wings beat once, twice, carrying me up off the floor. "Whoa. Okay, I might need to practise."

"Do my eyes and ears deceive me, or is Devi back from the dead again?" The door opened, and Zadok stood in the entryway.

"Zadok," I said. "Believe it or not, I'm glad you weren't on Pandemonium when Lythocrax attacked. Let me guess —you had an exit plan."

"Several," he said. "Your friend and my other sibling have been quite agitated looking for you. I'm flattered that you were so concerned about me, too, Devi."

"Actually, I didn't know you were attacked until a minute ago, but—"

"Devi!" Rachel yelled. "I should have known we'd find you making out with Niko in a cupboard."

Fiona and Rachel both ran into the room and threw themselves at me with shrieks of delight.

"I knew you'd sneak back without being noticed, Devi," said Fiona, hugging me. "Uh. Wings? That's new."

I hugged her back, then Rachel. "Not quite sneaking. I think I freaked out the warlocks who saw me appear from the glass they were supposed to be watching for signs of Lythocrax."

"Glad you made it back, Devi," said Rachel. "I guess the war is off?"

"Not quite," I said. "I shut down four of Lythocrax's sources, but he blew the other one up, and I'm not sure if anything got out in the process."

"Damn, I bet he's pissed," said Rachel.

"You might say that," I said. "Part of him was still on Purgatory the last time I heard, but I guess someone's directing his army on Pandemonium, too. And Casthus swiped his original realm back and his fallen army along with it. So I might be second on his revenge list."

"Wait, Casthus did what?" said Rachel.

I told them, adding in a quick explanation of my new demonic upgrade and my affinity with demonglass. By the time I'd finished, they were all staring at me in shock. Even Zadok.

"I haven't had the pleasure of going to Lythocrax's

home realm," said Zadok. "It can only link to Pandemonium, correct?"

"And now Babylon, thanks to that pentagram of yours," I said.

He gave me a mock-wounded look. "How was I to know a fallen would count as a demon?"

"Aren't you the one who claims to always be prepared for every eventuality?" Nikolas enquired.

"I'm generally more prepared than you are," Zadok said. "You haven't even bothered to retrieve your warlocks from Babylon."

"I didn't need to," he said. "They had instructions to come here the instant Casthus left that realm, if he ever did."

"Enough posturing, demigods," said Rachel. "In case you've forgotten, there are two arch-demons with armies on worlds that don't belong to them, and a potential war coming."

Both Castor brothers scowled at one another. *At least they aren't trying to kill one another this time.*

Shouts came from outside the house, followed by a roar. With an alarmed look at me, Nikolas made for the door, the rest of us close behind him. We hurried through the hallway to an open door leading out into the back garden. Several winged warlocks had landed in a cleared space in the middle of the lawn, other warlocks gathering around on the grass.

"They're coming," said a female warlock with jet black wings. "Through the portal."

Shit. Lythocrax must have turned the source into a portal when he blew it up.

"They're attacking from the sky," added another. "Winged demons. Or angels."

Nikolas swore. More warlocks came out of the house behind us, but only a fraction had wings. "Anyone who can fly, come with me," he said. "Devi…"

"I can't fly," I pointed out.

"Looks like wings to me," said Rachel, poking my shoulder. I still wore Nikolas's shadowy magic. I twitched both wings, and my feet left the ground.

"Uh, I've never flown before."

Nikolas's own wings appeared, and he took flight, several warlocks tailing him. I hesitated, not having a clue what I was doing, but Rachel shapeshifted into a winged warlock and yanked me into the sky. I flapped my wings frantically, relieved when I stayed airborne. *I can do this. I'm a demon, and I can fly.*

Nikolas reached for my hand, pulling me to his side. We flew higher, until a thin mist rose to surround us, masking the buildings below. Damn, this felt amazing. No wonder Nikolas escaped into Babylon whenever he could. My worry that the wings would disappear melted away and I let go of Nikolas's hand, unable to resist doing a few loop-the-loops in the air. After years of defying gravity with my celestial power, flight didn't feel that strange at all.

We kept moving over the city, until Nikolas held out a hand, ordering us to stop. "There's someone else down there."

I squinted through the mist, seeing several winged shapes descending. "Are they demons, or…?"

Nikolas dropped several feet. "They're after the guild."

Shit. He was right—from above, the guild's academy was unmistakeable. And they weren't demons.

I descended, my heart hammering, and a sudden blast of air damn near knocked me out of the sky. A feathery shape with a familiar scarred face flashed by, descending swiftly. *Clover?*

Definitely Clover. She caught up to the winged figures above the guild, drawing them to an abrupt halt. I spotted a large number of people gathering in the guild's quadrangle, pointing up at the winged figures above.

I dropped to hover directly above them, and several hundred celestials gaped as they saw my wings. Some pulled out weapons.

"I'm not attacking you!" I dropped a few more feet until I was close enough to be heard. "Is Mrs Barrow here? The rebel angels are about to attack you from the sky." Did Clover's defences reach that high? I bloody well hoped so.

Sudden dampness touched the back of my neck, and I reached behind my head automatically. My hand came away red, and I tilted my head upright, seeing more moisture fall out of the sky. Not rain, but crimson droplets. Blood.

A moment later, Clover descended to hover above me, another angel's limp body in her hands. Above her, the group of angels appeared to have changed directions, flying away from the guild.

"Clover, you've been holding out on us," I said accusingly. "Did you drive them off?"

"For now," she said, looking downright sinister with a dead angel in her arms despite her own snowy wings.

"They're recently upgraded and drunk on power. When the real angels get here, they'll be sorry."

"Do—you mean the Divinities are coming?" *About damned time.*

"Tell them," she said, indicating the celestials below. "It's time they proved their worth. I will hold off the rebels."

"They'll listen to an angel," I said. "I look like a demon. They won't buy it."

And that was assuming the celestials hadn't already been claimed by Lythocrax... but that was impossible. He wouldn't have had time to recruit all of them when he was too fixated on saving his own skin.

"Anyone who saw what you did to those sources will know you for heaven's warrior," she said. "I felt their light come back at your touch, Devi."

"Not sure I wasn't too late." I indicated the retreating angels. "So—you got an upgrade, too?"

"Yes, I did," she said. "I have Lythocrax to thank for reminding me how to access my true form. And I must apologise for failing to come to the right conclusion. I thought upgrading your demon magic would help, but now I see that I was fooled as well as any. I did not remember the demonglass was once a weapon of heaven. Not until I felt your magic and saw heaven's light cancel out the darkness."

"Happens to the best of us," I told her. "All right, I'll tell the celestials that Harvey's back to make trouble again."

I descended, and hovered directly above the celestials. By now, Mrs Barrow had come to the front of the group, holding a pair of binoculars of all things. "Is that —Clover?"

"Yeah, it's her," I said. "The Divinities are coming here. Clover is on our side, but the other angels are rebels sent to wipe us all out."

"The demons have sent rebel angels against us?" asked Mrs Barrow, her face ashen as she lowered the binoculars.

"Lythocrax," I corrected. "His angels are working against heaven and hell alike. The warlocks and other preternaturals are already fighting. So if you want to join the battle, you have to be prepared to fight on hell's side."

"Don't be absurd," she said. "The demons are our enemy. We can't fight against the angels."

"They're not true angels," I said. "And the arch-demon who started this is definitely not a typical demon, either. He's a trickster who fooled even some angels into defecting. It's your divine mission to stop him."

"What are you, Devi?" she asked quietly, her gaze passing over my shadowy wings. "I've heard the rumours."

"I'm a celestial demon," I said. "The demon I was marked by fell. It could happen to any of you, and you don't have time to be petty. The portal is already open, and the armies are coming through. The warlocks are going to fight against them. You can come, or you can wait for the Divinities to show up. Your choice. But I'll be there."

Without waiting for an answer, I took flight. My wings beat, carrying me towards the portal, and the oncoming battle.

22

I caught up to Nikolas mid-flight. The portal was easy to spot from above, a mass of glowing light spread over the ruined warehouse, dark energies swirling above it.

"There's no way I can shut that thing down from here," I said to Nikolas.

I already knew what awaited on the other side. Flames rose from the portal as we flew directly into the swirling gulf, and Pandemonium's stone-coloured buildings replaced Haven City.

I expected to see Lythocrax fully manifested on the battlefield, but while armies of demons raged and fought in the street, there was not an arch-demon within sight. The portal swirled with light, but the city of Pandemonium was doing its damned best to put up a fight against the invaders. Stone-coloured demons shaped like houses reared up and snapped at the flying demons' heels or created huge fissures in the Earth that swallowed up anyone unlucky enough to get near. Lythocrax had seriously underestimated how pissed off Pandemonium's demons would be at having their home invaded again.

"He'll be in the palace," I said to Nikolas as we flew above the battle, occasionally blasting a demon with lightning. It was difficult to tell whose side anyone was on from here, but on the ground, it'd be all but impossible. "If he's planning to be reborn on this world, he'll do it there. His weakened form will have come here from Purgatory with the rest of his army."

He was using this world as a stepping stone to bring his army to Earth.

I turned back to the portal, my wings beating. I'd switched a similar portal off by transferring its power into the vampire king, whose demon mark had been Grade Three at the time. The overload of power had killed him. But maybe my Grade Four mark would be enough to contain this portal. It was worth a try.

A winged figure ascended, colliding with me in a crash that nearly knocked both of us into the portal. Fingers gouged at my neck, and Harvey's livid face swam above mine as I kicked out at him in mid-air.

"It's your fault," he screamed. "Devi, it's your fault I'm falling. You corrupted me."

I wrenched myself free of his grip, massaging my throat with one hand. His aura was no longer snowy white, and neither were his wings. Grey splotches had begun to intervene, along with bright red patches.

"Don't look at me," I said. "Guess the Divinities finally caught up with you."

"I *serve* the Divinities!" he screamed, blasting me with a bolt of energy. Immediately, my demon mark lit up, drawing his magic in. *Demon magic?* He was falling, all right. But I'd thought only the Divinities had the authority to push angels out of the heavens.

"Wait—did heaven finally take Purgatory back?" I said. "Is that why you left?"

"You ruined my life!" he screamed, his hands igniting. I dodged his attack, my wings beating. Fallen or not, he was still an angel—outclassing me on both my celestial and demon sides.

"Why the hell are you blaming *me* for the fact that you got duped?" I said. "I tried to tell you."

Celestial light blazed from my left hand, mingling with the remaining shadowy magic in my right. He hurled another attack, and I deflected it. My demon magic looked entirely like living shadows. I'd chosen my demon name well.

Shadowy magic turned to dark flames as it joined the divine fire in my left hand, forming a blade. I grabbed it, and slashed at Harvey in mid-air, dealing a vicious cut to his shoulder. Golden blood tinted with black flowed from the wound.

With a roar, he flew at me, his aura shimmering between dark and light. Nikolas blasted him with lightning, knocking him into the path of my blade. The rippling edge sank into the angel's neck. Harvey screamed, blood spurting.

"I doubt Lythocrax will bother reviving you this time, Harvey," I said, and sliced off his head.

The angel's body dropped out of the sky, and I held the blade upright, marvelling at its rippling shadowy surface.

"That's new," Nikolas said, flying up to me. "Is it from your demon magic?"

"Both," I said. *Light and dark are both divine.* Or both

demonic. Either worked. "Where in hell is Lythocrax hiding? I have to finish him off."

There was a blast of light from the palace. I wheeled to face that way, my wings beating frantically. A cold breeze swept in, and the palace trembled. Shards of demonglass hung suspended in the air, as though it'd imploded from the inside.

Then the light blasted outwards, fracturing along with the demonglass.

Glass flew wide. A roaring sounded in my ears. Air currents caught my wings, whirling me out of control, my limbs flailing. Screaming, horrible screaming, came from below.

My vision went white.

No. It can't end like this.

I beat my wings, fighting the roaring wind, and whiteness resolved into colour. The demonglass palace lay in shards, scattered, burned out. Within the ruin was a hunched figure, winged and slick with blood.

Lythocrax lifted his head and his gaze locked with mine. Terror rippled through me. His wings were ashy grey, his form humanoid and lava-coloured, and... bleeding. His own glass had cut him. *Serve him right.*

Nikolas flew to my side, also bleeding. Relief flooded me. He was alive, but the armies had stopped fighting, demons and angels alike speared with wounds from the shards of deadly demonglass. The portal remained open, a torrent of swirling light, but nobody paid it any attention. All eyes were on the wrecked palace, and the newly reborn arch-demon inside it.

Lythocrax's wings unfurled, his eyes stormy and wrathful. My mouth went dry.

"This is the last time you thwart me, Devi," he whispered. His voice seemed to echo from each and every shard of shattered demonglass. "This is for stealing my power, stealing my true name, and mocking me at every turn."

The shards of the palace's ruins rose into the air as he raised a hand, pointing directly at Nikolas and me. "I will kill him before you land."

Damn him. My sword had vanished, and even if it hadn't, I'd never reach him in time.

The demonglass ignited in mid-air, and a shadowy form appeared above Lythocrax, wings unfolding, a dark aura blotting out the sky.

Casthus flew down to land before Lythocrax. "You're disrupting all the infernal realms, you arrogant piece of demon slime. What did you do?"

"You," said Lythocrax. "You don't belong here. We made our arrangement."

"I don't remember conquering this realm being part of any arrangement, Remiel."

"I don't use that name any longer," said Lythocrax coldly.

I beat my wings, flying towards the arch-demons. "He also goes by—"

"Speak that name and die," he said, guessing I was about to call him by his true name.

Casthus laughed. "You're as insecure as you were as a divine one, Remiel."

"What do you want?" said Lythocrax. "This realm is mine. Soon, Earth will be, too."

"Actually, I think you'll find it's mine," said Casthus. "A huge fraction of your new so-called army is loyal to the shadows."

"That's Zadok, not you," I said, unable to help myself. Casthus wasn't on my side. Both of them would be happy to make Earth collateral damage, and they were too fucking strong for me to take out single-handed. Even with Lythocrax's demon name at my disposal.

Casthus briefly glanced my way. "I'd advise you to see to your own business, celestial. We'll finish this ourselves."

No. I have to kill him... I have to finish him off.

Nikolas touched my arm. "Let's leave them to their games," he murmured. "The other angels are still on Earth."

"The angels..." He was right. As Clover had told me, Earth was about to be visited by the Divinities. They alone could truly end the war.

23

The instant Nikolas and I flew close to the portal, its light swallowed us up. The whirling mass was vast enough to suck every other source into a blazing inferno. My wings beat frantically, and Nikolas took my hand, steadying both of us. We held onto one another as we flew out above Haven City.

Chaos reigned below, demons battling warlocks in the wrecked street where the demonglass had exploded. Zadok flew above the street, leading a group of bat demons. To my utter astonishment, Rachel and Fiona rode two of them—and Faye, too, who used her celestial blade to cut demons out of the air from the winged beast's back.

Zadok flew up to our level, clad in battle armour. "I suppose you're here to deal with the angels?"

"They're already here?" I asked. "The Divinities?"

"Not the divine ones," he said. "I believe they're your rogues."

Crap. Some of them must have survived. "Harvey's dead," I said to him. "I'll take care of the rest."

Nodding to Nikolas, I flew on, glancing up at the clouds in search of more winged shapes. In the streets below, the vampires had joined in the fight. I spotted Madame White, the vampires' leader, directing her army to tear into any demons which landed in one piece. She was even leading teams of the vamps who'd formerly been shunned by the high society vampires for getting infected with demon venom via the saphor demon eggs.

A dazzlingly bright low-hanging cloud drew my attention. *There they are.*

I flew toward the cloud, which resolved itself into a group of winged shapes. They weren't fighting, but watching the chaos below, as though it was simple entertainment to them.

That alone told me they belonged to the Divinities.

"Hey!" I shouted at the nearest angel. "Do you have contact with the Divinities? Because there's a massive clusterfuck happening here which they might want to look into."

The angel turned to me. He definitely wasn't one of the rebels. His aura and wings were snowy white, his hair was pale as snow, and his eyes gleamed with divine light. *Real* divine light.

Oh, boy. I probably shouldn't have shouted the word 'clusterfuck' at him. Wait, did they even speak English? My grasp of the heavenly language was rusty, to say the least, though it'd been part of the celestials' curriculum. None of us had ever reckoned on meeting the Divinities in the flesh. Least of all me.

"Are you Devina Lawson?" He spoke the heavenly tongue, and to my relief, I found I understood him.

"Uh. Yes." My celestial hand glowed, as though to remind me I was in the presence of one of heaven's foot soldiers. "Yes, I am. I need to speak to the Divinities. One of their own is making trouble in the netherworld."

I hadn't the faintest idea of the angelic word for 'Pandemonium', but 'the netherworld' spoke for itself.

"She's right," said Clover. In typical Clover fashion, she'd managed to conceal herself from view in plain sight among the other angels. "Is he there, Devi? Lythocrax?"

"He and Casthus are reminiscing about old times," I said to her. "I can kill him again, but he'll probably use his creation power to come back. The Divinities need to take care of him. It's long overdue." I gave the angels a pointed look, but aside from the one who'd spoken to me, the others seemed more interested in watching Earth than speaking to me.

"Yes, they do," Clover said. "However, the heavenly realms cannot send anyone directly into the demon realms. They haven't been able to since—"

"Babylon," I said, inspiration striking. "There's a pentagram there which can contain an arch-demon. Would I be able to take it into Purgatory and summon Lythocrax there? I take it that's where the Divinities are hanging out?"

Clover flew to the angel's side, who still watched me with narrowed eyes. They exchanged a few words, and the angel turned back to me.

"Bring the arch-demon before the Divinities, celestial," said the angel. "And justice will be served."

"You'd better keep your word."

I turned away from the angels and flew back the way I'd come, where Nikolas and his warlock allies continued to fight from the sky.

"Hey—Nikolas," I said, catching up to him.

"Devi." He disposed of another demon in a shower of lightning. "Those angels—are they heaven's?"

"You've got it. They'll handle Lythocrax, but I need to summon him to Purgatory myself. Do you think Casthus will have left the pentagram behind or taken it with him?"

"I'll take us to Babylon and we'll find out," he said, glancing over his shoulder at the still-glowing portal. "We still need to close that thing."

"When Lythocrax is gone, it won't matter."

As long as the angels kept their word.

Nikolas took my hand, and shadows folded around us in mid-air. Babylon appeared seconds later. From the sky, the moon looked even larger, while the castle appeared oddly small.

"He took his demons with him," Nikolas explained, keeping a firm grip on my hand as we descended together. My stomach swooped, and I wished we had more time to enjoy this. Flying with him, without limits… without the war… I wanted this. More than anything.

"Zadok said you took your warlock army back," I said breathlessly.

"They escaped the instant he left this realm." Nikolas flew on, his grip on my hand sure and strong. "I doubt Casthus knew or cared."

We dropped lower over the castle. "Did he leave the defences up?" I asked.

"He wouldn't have had reason to, unless he expected to come back."

The castle grew larger as we descended. "Maybe he did," I said. "But now he knows it was Lythocrax screwing with all of us all along. Pity we can't leave them to finish one another off."

"I think divine justice is more appropriate."

"Maybe you're right."

I spotted the pentagram lying in the space outside the castle where Casthus had once tried to make a bridge to link the demon realms. I landed beside it, finally letting go of Nikolas's hand.

"It's still tuned into Lythocrax's old realm, I guess," I said, moving closer to its gleaming edges. "He didn't need that world. He just wanted to piss him off—"

A snarling figure leapt from the pentagram, tackling me to the ground. My celestial hand ignited, and I gasped, breaking the fallen's grip with my other hand. "It's me!" I said. "Not him. He's gone."

"Devina." The fallen hunched back, his eyes wide and gleaming under the luminous moon.

"Casthus left you behind, huh," I said. "I'm going to the Divinities, but if you want to get back into heaven..." Recklessness seized me. "Get your people, move them to whatever source you just came through. I'm taking this pentagram straight to the Divinities."

The fallen stared at me. "Heaven?"

I nodded. "I'm taking this pentagram with me, but I'll need to use it for something else first. I'll give you the signal when it's time. If you bring your people through, you can get back to heaven."

I hope.

"I have lived my life to see the Divinities again, Devi. I will fetch my brethren."

He stepped through the pentagram and vanished.

"I hope I'm right," I murmured to Nikolas. "I'll have to open another portal if I want to carry this thing with me."

"I thought so," said Nikolas, "I'm going back to help Earth. I don't think the Divinities will want to do business with a warlock."

"For all I know, they don't want a celestial demon there either." I hugged him. "I want to fly with you again. When this is over."

"Done," he said, tracing his lips over my cheek. "I'll be waiting for you on Earth."

Nikolas disappeared into shadows, while I burned a pentagram onto the ground, picking up the handmade device. Then I stepped into the pentagram I'd created and spoke clearly: "I request entry to Purgatory. In the name of divine justice."

The handmade pentagram vibrated alarmingly as the light swallowed me up, and I toppled onto the ground of Purgatory.

The light didn't fade. If anything, it grew brighter. I scrambled upright, squinting at the sky. The red taint had gone, replaced with brightness.

Within, a winged being looked down on me.

My heart crept into my throat. Like an arch-demon, the Divinity defied description. The force before me was nature incarnate, wild and terrifying and blinding white. I blinked frantically, my mouth dry, my thoughts spinning.

Calm down, Devi. You've faced arch-demons, for the Divinities' sakes.

"State your name and business," said the winged beast, in the angelic tongue.

"I'm here to bring the arch-demon Lythocrax for a

trial." I put down the pentagram with shaking hands. "Or Remiel, as you might have known him."

"Remiel betrayed heaven," the Divinity rumbled.

"We could talk all day about the people he betrayed," I said. "But there are others in heaven who worked with him. Started him off on his criminal career, even. If I summon him, he can probably tell you who they are."

The Divinity continued to watch me, as though I was some fascinating insect. That's all I was to him, really. And I had no patience for it.

"Remiel killed a number of us," he said. "As punishment, he fell."

"He killed you—killed Divinities?"

Images entered my mind, stirred by the divine being's presence. I'd seen flashes of Lythocrax's memories, but now certainty seized me... he'd killed the angels. Including the one who'd sent him to mark me.

Maybe he'd killed the other Divine Agents before he'd even left heaven behind.

"He has creation magic," I said. "Will you take that from him? Because when he dies, he just comes back. He already did it once."

"That power should never have been his," said the Divinity. "Nor should our weapons exist in the hands of demons. Summon the traitor."

One did not disobey orders from angels. I turned to the pentagram, taking a steadying breath. "I summon Lythocrax, also known as Altheare and Remiel."

Light filled the pentagram instantly, as though the demonglass within reacted to the divine presence of the angel. In a flash, Lythocrax appeared, struggling, spitting curses. "Let me go immediately, Devina Lawson."

"Someone here wants to speak to you," I said.

Lythocrax writhed and fought the trap, looking up at the sky. His mouth dropped open, and the presence of the divine finally rendered him speechless.

"Remiel," said the Divinity. "Did you entice others to fall, too?"

Lythocrax twisted to face me, his face an ugly mask. "You will never make me submit, no matter how many alliances you make."

"It's not an alliance," I said. "Everyone hates you, Altheare."

I let shadowy magic spill from my hand into the trap. He hissed and ducked away, hands reaching for me, unable to touch me.

"Like that, Altheare?" I said. "You're trapped."

"You have made me suffer enough, Devina." He tilted his head to look up at the Divinity. "She has committed worse crimes than I ever will. She's worked with demons, cavorted with their kin—"

"Been to a warlock party on Babylon, blown up Pandemonium's tunnels, and cooperated with hell's best to make that trap you're stuck in." I rolled my eyes. "Personally, I think committing genocide and abandoning the fallen are worse than anything I've ever done, but what do I know?"

The Divinity descended in a beat of wings. *Ah.* Maybe I'd gone too far.

"You are responsible for the downfall of heaven," he said to Lythocrax.

"You brought that on yourself," said the arch-demon. "You ought to be thanking me. It was the other traitors I killed before I fell. Yes... I killed the Divine Agents. I am the last."

Downfall of heaven? Words I'd heard from Abyss as she died came back to me... *the heavens are splitting. He caused it.*

She must have known him as a Divinity, too. Maybe that's why he'd picked her as a target. They'd all known him. He'd betrayed heaven and hell alike.

"Finish him," I said to the Divinity. "Before he keeps you here all day."

I half expected him to tell me not to order him around, but he merely turned directly to Lythocrax. "Remiel, you are a traitor, and you will never be reborn again. I take the divine fire from you, forever."

Light erupted from the pentagram, painfully bright. Lythocrax screamed, struggling, wings beating, but he couldn't escape. Between one blink and the next, he was gone, leaving nothing but ashes.

The light faded. I released a slow breath. *It's done. He's gone.*

The Divinity looked at me as though expecting me to speak. "Uh. Thanks," I said. "He was... he killed..." So many. I'd wanted to take him apart with my bare hands, but I was so, unbelievably tired of being heaven's soldier. Let them clean up their own mess for a change. "Is heaven really breaking apart?"

"You are no divine one, mortal," said the Divinity, his voice soft and menacing. "I should strike you down, too."

"I hardly chose this. And I'm still a celestial." I raised my glowing palm.

"And a demon," he said. "A true demon."

"No," I said. "I never fell, because I never ascended high enough. I don't have a demon's weakness. And I don't want anything other than you people to leave Earth alone. You let the Divine Agents worm their way into the celestial guild when you should have seen them for what they were. You're not saying you were completely oblivious?"

"The challenge was yours, Devi. He marked you, and—"

"Is that what that 'champion of heaven' nonsense was about? I'm not your toy, Divinity. He marked me. That means I could have picked his side over yours."

"But you did not. You didn't pick a side at all."

"And I won't." I met his stare, even as my vision wavered. Scary bastard. Scary, selfish, unconcerned piece of crap. "I deserve compensation. You owe me. Leave Earth alone."

"Earth is no concern of ours," he said. "However…"

The pentagram glowed brighter, and a fallen appeared within it, caught between the pentagram's points.

"Uh… you were supposed to wait for my signal," I said.

The fallen looked up at the Divinity, and froze on the spot. So did I. Crap. Maybe he'd strike both of us down after all.

"What is that?" demanded the Divinity.

My tongue unstuck itself from the roof of my mouth. "Yours," I said. "Fallen, bring the others through. It's time."

"Mine?" repeated the Divinity, as the fallen vanished into the pentagram. "That monstrosity is not mine."

"They are," I told him, as several more fallen appeared. "They were abandoned on Babylon by heaven's soldiers. Casthus, the shadow arch-demon, plans to sacrifice them to create a bridge between the seven hells. I'm sure you don't want that to happen. They're immortal, like you. Half Divinity… half celestial?"

The nearest fallen nodded jerkily. "Yes, we were… we are."

"They cannot enter heaven," said the Divinity. The fallen continued to climb out of the pentagram, staring up at him.

"They are your responsibility," said a voice. Clover approached from behind us, casual as anything.

"Who are you?" asked the Divinity.

"You once knew me as Raviel," she said. "I was stripped of my divine memories when I was left behind on Babylon after the battle. As for who I am now… I am Earth's guardian angel."

I gaped at her. "That's a thing? How?"

"I'm not attached to heaven." She tilted her head towards me. "So I choose Earth. Granted, there's a lot to clean up on Purgatory, too, but I think the least I can do is take the fallen to the place where they belong."

"What… heaven?" She seemed to shine brighter than before, her aura shimmering almost as purely white as the Divinity's.

"Yes," she said. "I used Lythocrax's magic to be reborn, and I suppose the least I can do is use this new life to help protect Earth. Come with me." She beckoned to the fallen, and they moved towards her, slowly. The Divinity looked on with cold eyes, but didn't stop them.

I grinned at Clover. "Good luck up there."

Light bloomed, surrounding Clover and the fallen. As it brightened, the demon marks on their skin appeared to fade, and then they were gone.

Silence remained behind. The pentagram lay there, its

light fading. The fallen would never be Casthus's tools again. He'd be pissed off at me... or maybe he wouldn't care. I would never understand demons as long as I lived. Or angels, come to that.

I looked up at the Divinity. "I'm done here. Thanks for killing Lythocrax."

It was probably bad manners to run off on an angel, but I needed to close that portal before Earth became a demon realm after all.

Grabbing the handmade pentagram, I stepped back through the one I'd left open. Babylon's darkness replaced the light, its luminous moon blotted out by the two shadow demons standing nose to nose right in front of me.

Seven hells.

Casthus and Zadok both turned to me at the same time.

"What did you do?" Casthus demanded.

"I might ask you the same question," I said, staring between the two shadow demons. "What are you doing here? I thought you'd be conquering Pandemonium as we speak."

"That traitor and I have unfinished business," growled the shadow arch-demon. "I demand that you bring him back."

"Little difficult. The angels took him to pieces." I nodded to Zadok. "Don't let me interrupt your family argument."

"Am I to understand that you thought *I* was working with those rebel scumbags?" Zadok demanded of Casthus.

"You lived in their tower."

"Because your army forced me out of the castle you

saw fit to hand over to my brother," Zadok said. "Yet again, you blame me for his mistakes."

I spotted Nikolas standing a few feet away, and mouthed, *what the hell is going on?*

"I made an error of judgement," said Casthus. "I take it the rebels are taken care of, Devina, along with their leader?"

"Yeah…" I frowned. "Are you saying you thought Zadok worked with them?" In fairness, I'd suspected as much myself, once.

"You suspect everyone of wrongdoing, father," Zadok said. "Pandemonium isn't yours to take. You have your own world. An empire, in fact."

Not the fallen. Now probably wasn't the greatest time to tell him they were gone.

"Yes, I do," said Casthus. "I stayed here because I believed the Divine Agents would soon make a move, and I was right."

"Yes, and now they're all gone," I interjected. "You've no reason to stay here now. This realm belongs to Nikolas. And Pandemonium—did you just leave that portal open?"

"The traitor's armies are depleted," he said dismissively.

"The portal is burning out," said Nikolas. "But it does need to be closed."

I took a step back. "Can you refrain from killing one another while I go and deal with the mess the demons made on Earth?"

"I have nothing more to say to any of you," Casthus said. "This realm is a dead end, of little use to me. I'll see if I wish to expand my empire in the meantime."

And in a rush of shadows, he was gone.

"He could have left at any time he wanted to." I rolled my eyes after him. "Bloody Divinities."

Zadok flashed me a smirk. "He left me Pandemonium."

"Good luck with the refurbishing," I said. "Last I saw, your palace was in pieces. And you're to leave Nikolas and Babylon alone, clear?"

Nikolas himself took my arm. "We should deal with that portal."

"Yeah, we should. Come on, Zadok."

Shadows rose to surround us, and the next second, the three of us appeared in the ruins of the old celestial guild. No sounds of battle came from close by, but anything might be happening over by the portal. At least Lythocrax's armies were without a leader—and now Casthus had gone, too.

Nikolas took flight in a beat of wings. I called on my shadowy demon magic and did likewise, catching an approving look from Zadok. "You really do make a fine demon."

"Zadok," Nikolas said warningly.

"He's right. I made a terrible celestial, though." I flew higher, above the labyrinthine streets of the city I called home—the city I'd nearly died to defend. "Anyway, I thought you were going to tear one another to pieces just then."

"Believe it or not, some of us are capable of practising restraint," Nikolas said.

"Could have fooled me," I said. "Casthus won't come back and declare war when he finds out Clover took the fallen, would he?"

"She did?" asked Nikolas.

"I helped."

Zadok laughed. "He might not declare war, but I doubt he'll give you a royal welcome if you visit his empire."

He picked up speed, flying towards the portal, with Nikolas and I close behind him. Zadok flew through first, and I followed. The swirling light was undoubtedly smaller than before, less intense, and the armies had pulled back, away from the shattered remains of the palace. Nikolas hovered at my side, facing the whirling light above the portal. "Can you close it?"

"You bet." I held out both hands. My demon mark hummed, and so did my celestial mark, as the power died down, sucked into its depths.

The last of the portal's light disappeared. "It's over." I sagged against Nikolas, my wings nearly giving out in mid-air, but he held me upright, close to him. Relief crashed over me, making my eyes sting with tears. "Divinities. It's over."

"Yes, it is," he said. And hugged me.

24

"Here's your enhanced bloodstone, signed and delivered," I said to the vampire. "Please try not to use it all at once."

The vampire grinned and took the package from me, stepping off the doorstep of the warlocks' headquarters with a nod of gratitude.

Everyone had said it wasn't possible to help vampires walk in the daylight without side effects, but those people would underestimate an ex-celestial freelancer, a chameleon warlock, and demigod with entirely too much time on their hands. The other warlocks weren't best pleased with me selling to vampires through their new headquarters, but none dared argue with Nikolas's new rules.

I'd never thought I'd see Rachel and Zadok bond over explosives, but ever since she'd helped with the pentagram, Rachel had been making trips over to Pandemonium whenever possible. She'd claimed she wanted to take her mind off Javos and get to know the realm of her birth, but neither of those things explained why she kept taking Fiona with her, too. Still, the temporary blood-stones for day-walking vampires were just one of the many things we'd invented in the weeks since the battle.

"I have three more on standby," Zadok said from behind me.

"Not needed yet, but thanks," I said, closing the door and walking into the main lab. I'd had to move it here from Nikolas's house, because one more explosion would have wrecked the foundations.

Nikolas waited inside the lab, next to the table where I kept all my samples. "Didn't throw in any tricks that shouldn't be there, did you, Zadok?"

"I'd know if he had." I moved a few things around, clearing a space on the table. "Might need to replenish my stores of venom, but a trip to Pandemonium will take care of that."

"I can't believe you're voluntarily spending time with my brother to avoid the warlocks' council meeting tonight," said Nikolas. "The Wingless Warlock wants to meet you."

"I'm not on the guest list," I pointed out.

"That's never stopped you before."

"As long as he's wearing clothes this time." I'd seen entirely too much of that warlock all over DivinityWatch. At least it was better than seeing constant warnings about the oncoming apocalypse. "Does Fiona have an invite?"

"Yes, if she's done with her magic lessons."

"She will be," I said, pleased Fiona had taken to her new calling so well. The humans with demon magic hadn't developed any of Lythocrax's characteristics—and wouldn't, now he was dead—so the ones who wanted to train in magic had expressed an interest in a human tutor. Fiona was the obvious choice. Their presence had forced the guild to accept demon magic as on an even footing with their own, which was bound to sting a little, but I didn't much care for the celestial council's hurt feelings.

Rachel bounded in. "There's someone from the guild here to see you, Devi."

Speak of the devil… or close enough. "I'll be back in a second."

I walked back into the hallway to find the door open again. Several celestial novices had gathered on the doorstep, including Bad Haircut Sammy.

Behind them stood Clover, in human form, her wings tucked away. Her aura, though, betrayed her true nature—halo-white.

"Hi," I said. "What's the occasion?"

I'd been back to the guild a couple of times since the battle, but not often. I'd spent an awful lot of time avoiding funerals as a member, so they hadn't expected me to show up for the wake following the battle. The one huge regret I had was Lydia. She hadn't deserved what the fallen angel had done to her, and her body had never been recovered. Like everyone else, she'd just been trying to survive. As for the other fallen angels, Clover had seen to it that the survivors had been taken directly to heaven for punishment. They deserved nothing less.

"The new headquarters is finished," said Sandra, one of the novices. "We wanted to invite you…"

"To be an honorary guild member," finished one of the others.

I expected something like that. The guild's backup forces had arrived in town shortly after the battle, helping to replenish the celestials' depleted resources. I suspected Clover had had a hand in it, considering how few arguments they'd had and how quickly they'd constructed their new headquarters.

"Did you ask Faye?" I asked.

Guilty silence followed. Faye hadn't stuck around for long. She didn't feel comfortable living close to the guild, and too many people still thought her a criminal. With DivinityWatch's exploding popularity, she'd decided to go elsewhere to run her business in peace. I'd wished her well with it.

"She's more innocent than I am," I added. "My answer is no."

"No shit," said Sammy, who'd apparently tagged along for the sole purpose of being a dick. "She's no celestial."

"You're free to have that debate in your own time," I said, eyeing Clover. "Why did you come?"

"Just to make a friendly social call."

Angels. "Nice to see you all. Except you, Sammy. Goodbye."

I closed the door, shaking my head. "Really."

"I knew they'd want you back," said Rachel.

"So predictable," I said. "Casthus will be next, if he ever forgives me for stealing the fallen."

"I told him not to bother you," said Clover's voice from the other side of the door.

Yanking the door open, I frowned at her. "You have even more fun screwing with people as an angel, don't you?"

"Actually, I wished to speak with you alone. And your friend."

Fiona popped up at her side. "Hey, Devi."

"Where'd you come from?" I said.

"She kind of grabbed me when I was on the way here," Fiona admitted. "Anyway, she really does want to talk to us."

"All right. Be back in a minute." I closed the door before Zadok came out of the lab. He'd definitely try to eavesdrop if he could get away with it. He wasn't allowed to be on Earth unless one of us watched him, and took entirely too much pleasure in irritating the crap out of Nikolas.

"What is it?" I asked Clover, once we were far enough from the door not to be overheard.

"Nothing bad," Clover said. "The Divinities have asked me to watch the humans developing demon magic."

"It won't go bad, will it?" I asked quietly, with a sideways glance at Fiona.

"If they set foot on the demon realms, it's possible they might end up like you, Devi, and you too, Fiona."

"Oh," I said. "You mean, upgrading? Uh, I don't know if the humans want that."

"It's their choice," said Fiona. "But if they do, I said we might have to step in and help. I'm fine with that, but I wasn't sure if you were."

"You mean supervise?" I asked. "Of course I'm fine with it. If it's what the humans want." The most important thing was that they had a choice in the matter. "How's heaven, anyway, Clover? Has it changed?"

"Somewhat," she said. "Yet not at all."

"Cryptic, much?" I said. "I heard it's… falling apart. That's what Abyss said, anyway."

"The heavens have been falling apart for centuries," she said. "When they do, they'll split like the demon realms, and become many realms. I'm sure that'll cause a great deal of grief to the Divinities, but it's of no concern to Earth."

"As long as the Divine Agents didn't survive," I said.

"No," she said. "They did not."

Her aura brightened and her wings briefly appeared, before she vanished in a flash of light.

"I didn't think it was possible for her to get any more dramatic. I think being divine has gone to her head."

Fiona lowered her phone. "I nearly got a picture of her this time."

"Would she like you doing that?" I asked.

"I did ask her first," she said. "If anything, she enjoys the attention."

"Not as much as the Wingless Warlock," I said. "Who apparently wants to meet me at the warlocks' summit tonight, so…"

"You don't have to come," Nikolas said from behind me.

"Oh, I'll be there. Since I'm the unofficial celestial demon ambassador for Earth." I smiled at him, spotting Zadok and Rachel approaching. "Relax, nobody declared war."

"That makes a change," Nikolas said. "Can you all try not to make trouble while I take Devi with me for Babylon for a few minutes?"

"What, now?" I said.

"If it's not an issue."

"No, I just… why?"

"I'll explain on the other side."

Zadok put on his most charming smile. "I would never dream of making trouble, dear brother."

"You nearly started a riot in the Harpy's Nest the other day."

"If vampires touch me without permission, I can't be blamed if my magic reacts in self-defence."

I rolled my eyes. "Zadok, you turned the place into a shadowy ice rink."

"Frankly, I found it an improvement." He shrugged. "I'll forgive you for not inviting me with you to Babylon. I have a few more things I want to do on Earth."

"Like…?" I said warily.

"I'm taking him to the shopping centre," Rachel said, with a grin. "He's going to help me pick out some new shoes."

"I can hardly wait," Zadok said.

"You won't be able to wear that armour, though," Fiona added. "It's too conspicuous."

"Lucky we're around to give you fashion advice," Rachel said, beaming.

"What?" Zadok said in tones of disbelief. "I am *not* in need of—

In a flash of shadow, we were gone, reappearing on the darkened ground of Babylon.

Nikolas's hair gleamed dark red under the moonlight. "They'll be at it for a while."

"You think it's safe to leave them like that?" I asked.

"My brother has a lifetime of Earth experiences to catch up on. I'm not too worried." He slipped an arm around my waist and kissed me on the lips. "And I have some non-Earthly experiences I'd like to have with you."

"I'm assuming you mean in the non-apocalyptic sense." I kissed him back, wrapping my arms around him.

"You said you wanted to fly with me?" he asked.

"You bet."

My wings appeared at my command, and I took his hand as he left the ground. Babylon's wasteland spread below, bathed in starlight. Once, cities and towns had filled the space beneath us, the land had been fertile and filled with life, and heaven's angels had lived alongside hell's demons. Maybe not in harmony, but as close as possible.

Maybe one day, the same would be possible again.

For a moment, we flew, and I tilted my head back, enjoying the sensation of the wind in my hair. "You didn't just call me here to fly, right?"

"No." Nikolas changed direction, heading for the dark shape of the castle beneath the moon.

"Oh—you rebuilt it?"

He halted, wings beating, directly above the castle's sprawling form. "To my own design, yes. I thought you might want your own room here. And lab."

"Really?" I turned to look at him, his face lit under the starry sky. "You're not asking me to pick one world over the other?"

"No," he said. "You do seem to like those wings, though."

"Yes, I do." I gave a loop-the-loop on the spot, the wind deliciously cool on my face. "You never said if the council were nice enough to grant your request for a holiday. Is that what this is about?"

"Yes. Surprisingly, they didn't object to me taking a few weeks off," he said. "You pick the destination."

"Honestly?" I grinned at him. "Anywhere that isn't heaven or hell."

He grinned back. "Done."

We took flight again, soaring over Babylon. After everything I'd fought for, everything I'd sacrificed, I'd finally found my paradise.

ABOUT THE AUTHOR

Emma is the New York Times and USA Today Bestselling author of the Changeling Chronicles urban fantasy series.

Emma spent her childhood creating imaginary worlds to compensate for a disappointingly average reality, so it was probably inevitable that she ended up writing fantasy novels. When she's not immersed in her own fictional universes, Emma can be found with her head in a book or wandering around the world in search of adventure.

Find out more about Emma's books at
www.emmaladams.com.